Praise for the Legend of All Wolves series

"Wo...

VALE
Vale, Maria,
Wolf in the shadows /

...mes ...Wolf

"Pus... ...Wolf

"A b... ...ced exploration of werewolf concepts elevates this work above others in the genre."

—*Publishers Weekly*, Starred Review, for *A Wolf Apart*

"A wealth of sharply etched detail, snippets of pack history and lore, and a colorful supporting cast add another layer to this remarkable, strangely believable world."

—*Library Journal* for *A Wolf Apart*

"Vale's latest is lyrical and mesmerizing, the written embodiment of the wild depth where the Great North Pack resides… Prepare to be rendered speechless."

—*Kirkus Reviews*, Starred Review, for *Forever Wolf*

"Exquisite world building…[with] fascinating insights into pack life."
—*Booklist*, Starred Review, for *Forever Wolf*

"Adventurous readers will appreciate Vale's unique love story, including the unconventional but poignant happily ever after."

—*BookPage* for *Forever Wolf*

"Vale [gets] to the heart of her characters—their fears, their motivations—without sacrificing any of the grander picture… Her writing has never been better."

—*Kirkus Reviews*, Starred Review, for *Season of the Wolf*

Also by Maria Vale

WOLF
IN THE
SHADOWS

MARIA VALE

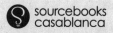

sourcebooks
casablanca

Published by Sourcebooks Casablanca, an imprint of Sourcebooks
P.O. Box 4410, Naperville, Illinois 60567-4410
(630) 961-3900
sourcebooks.com

Printed and bound in Canada.
MBP 10 9 8 7 6 5 4 3 2 1

To my mom, who walked her own path right to the end.

In our astronomy
the Great Wolf
lived in the sky.
It was the mother of all women
and howled her daughter's names
into the winds of night.

—"The Fallen" by Linda Hogan

Prologue

TWO DAYS AGO, I ATE MY FIANCÉ.

I let that rumble around in my head to see if it stirs anything up. Guilt or heartbreak or regret, or anything, really, aside from the nausea that is only now subsiding.

There is nothing. Well, not nothing. I do have one regret.

I would have liked to go back to Monsieur Trenet, the terribly posh and oily on-site event coordinator at the Windsor Grand Montreal who had helped me spend ever greater amounts of my uncle's money on personalized damascene linens with interlinked initials; on stippled mirrors cut to reflect the twinkling of hundreds of candles; on rows of ivy-encrusted chandeliers dripping with hothouse lilacs.

I would have liked to have seen his expression when I asked for my money back.

"*Malheureusement, j'ai mangé mon fiancé, alors… Puis-je récupérer mon acompte?*"

Unfortunately, I've eaten my fiancé, so…

Can I get my deposit back?

Chapter 1

Julia

THIS IS NOT MY NATIVE RANGE.

I hug the dyed mink-fur bucket bag that normally comes in indigo but because they know me at the little shop in Montreal's Mille carré doré, they put in a special order. Bright red, the color of sour cherries.

It was the color of Cass's favorite shoes, the bright-red rhinestone-studded, knock-me-down-and-fuck-me sandals I bought at the D&G also at the Mille Carré.

For the final touch, I'd taken the spool of thread that I'd used to help match the dye on my bag to the girl at La Belle Dame sans Merci, and we spent a good part of the morning picking over colors until we settled on a glossy sour-cherry red.

"It's called Irresistible," the girl said, shaking the bottle as she knelt before my freshly scrubbed feet.

La Belle Dame is just off the Boulevard de Maisonneuve.

In the Mille carré doré, the Golden Square Mile, because *that* is my native range.

Not this. Not sitting on a thin mattress barely supported by the sagging springs of a bunk bed deaccessioned from some military training camp and now jammed against the wall in a damp cabin in the middle of a mud-and-bug-and-blood-and-wolf-infested hellhole.

I would scream but I've done it already and no one heard me or no one cared.

When Cassius told me we were going to New York for the weekend, I went ahead and got tickets for *Hamilton*. I made reservations at Masa. I'd already picked out a black shantung suit—high-buttoned, fitted jacket, bracelet sleeves—because New York theaters can be so cold, but Cassius poked around my closet looking for "something…sexier." Eventually he pulled out this: a one-piece pantsuit with palazzo pants below, low-cut halter above. It is—was—beautiful. Made of a white silk that's heavy as chain mail, it flowed like water around my curves.

It did leave my back bare, but when the theater AC became too much for me, I would be able to shiver and rub my arms, and Cassius would roll his eyes and give me his jacket, the satin lining still warm from his body, to protect my nakedness, and I would feel cosseted.

Last minute, I took off the earrings and put on the four-strand collar of the palest blue pearls. It is my favorite. I like the way it sets off my throat.

Except the next day when Cassius met me at Saint-Hubert Airport, he came not with tickets but with a half-dozen rich old farts and a pimped-out van.

It turned out I'd been misled. Instead of flying with him to New York City, we were taking the pimped-out van and the half-dozen rich old men to some hunting retreat.

"You promised me, Cass."

"What I *promised* you," he said through clenched teeth so we wouldn't be overheard, "was a long weekend in New York. And we will be *in New York*."

"You know I thought you meant the City. And why do I have to sit in the back with the old farts?"

"Because I'm the only one who knows where we're going. And they're not old farts, Julia, they're *contacts*. Very useful contacts. This is a chance for me to get to know them, to prove myself so when August finally realizes that he won't live forever and needs to groom someone to take over, I—we—are in a position to inherit."

I felt used like I always do whenever Cassius talks about my uncle August. I mean, I guess I shouldn't blame him: there are only so many jobs for werewolves in Canada, and my uncle controls most of them. I just wish Cass would leave me out of it.

"Be charming. I know you know how to do that. Then when we're all done, I will take you to New York."

"*City*."

"Yes," he said. "New York *City*."

"I need to cancel my reservations. You know how hard they are to get, and I don't want to be put on a list of no-shows."

It didn't matter that I wasn't happy; I've spent a lifetime learning how to look like I am. I sat in the back and cooed and laughed and offered drinks while the old farts told me about the hunt my uncle had arranged for them. About how he'd stocked some ancient forest with game.

"Not game, Alfred. Predators are not *game*," interrupted Clement, a septuagenarian I knew through my mother and whose cock got hard when I was fifteen but now that I was thirty-two was energetically flaccid.

"Of course they are, Clement. Anything I can shoot is game. You could be."

I didn't know what the feud between these men was about but I knew it was my job to distract them.

I told them how I'd never killed anything and couldn't stand the sight of blood, then I lowered my head, bit my lip, and looked up at them through my lashes.

Every one of them—all but Clement—hurried to assure me that they would protect me from wolves. I smiled gratefully and shrugged diffidently and squashed any questions about what my uncle was up to.

Like I always had.

I was Irresistible all the way to a tent in the middle of mudville decked out like some vaguely rusticated wedding party with crystal that shone like Baccarat and chased silver dishes filled with food that I didn't touch, because as my mother always said, it's impossible to be charming when your mouth is full.

There was a lovely rich and meaty Bandol, though, and just as I was pouring another glass, the world turned upside down.

Two enormous wolves—one dark gray and one white— leapt on the tables and crunched on the hands of the old farts, the little bones making a *snick!* like celery sticks. These wolves stained the white damask tablecloths with blood, which I didn't care about, and with that lovely rich and meaty Bandol, which I did.

There were gunshots and a man I didn't know died, shot straight through the middle of his forehead. A puddled mess came out the back, staining the hem of my pants.

It matched my nail polish.

It was, I thought numbly, Irresistible.

It was the first death I've ever seen and I, of course, screamed. After that, I lost track of what happened. The old farts who hadn't even been able to protect themselves from wolves disappeared back into the van, and it was silent except for the humming of the generators.

Then a man loomed in front of us, cold as night, holding a gun.

I knew nothing about Tiberius, except that he was supposed to be dead and that while my uncle August was his father, his mother was not August's wife.

His mother was "a bitch." That's what *my* mother called her. I didn't think anything of it, figuring it was just my mother's general disdain for the hoi polloi until later I discovered that despite dressing like humans and talking like humans and going to school and work with humans, we were not, in fact, human.

The difference is that we Lukani don't give in to our bestial natures. The werewolves do. During the full moon, they are forced to trot around on all fours and bark and sniff and eat raw meats. Sometimes, I hear, they do it even when they're *not* forced to.

Tiberius, being Lukani like us, didn't have to but was

incomprehensibly angry about it. Shoving his gun into Cassius's face and yelling about the "Iron Moon, the three days out of thirty when the Pack must be wild. When *I* should be wild but *no*, because I have to fucking babysit *you*."

At first, I clung to the certainty that my uncle August would get us out of this mess, like he always did for every mess big or small, but then Constantine, his second-in-command, said that August is dead, which I can't believe because August is too powerful to just *die*. Even when Tiberius shot him through the neck, he didn't just *die*. Except Constantine insisted that he'd watched a werewolf kill him. No, that's not what he said. What he said was he watched while "*she* shoved a metal bar through his throat," as though a girl could kill August Leveraux.

Now, after three days, August still hasn't come, and all that's happened is I've gotten damper and colder and my feet hurt more and things—little birds and little animals—keep moving around and it reminds me of a horror movie about a cabin in the wood—in fact, I think that was the name?—that Cassius made me watch. He knew I hated horror movies, but he made me watch because one of the characters was named after me. Not Julia, which is my name, but Jules, which is what he calls me. That or "Baby."

They made us walk through the woods. My D&Gs slowly turning my feet from Irresistible to Irredeemable. As I sat staring at the mess of broken blisters plastered with drying mud, the most beautiful man I've ever seen knelt in front of me like in some perverted retelling of Cinderella.

Slim, graceful, eyes the bright silver of summer water

above high cheekbones, long sculpted nose. His upper lip is
a little short above a full lower lip. The long stubble would
look messy on anyone else, but on him, it was shadowing on
carved elegance.

"I forget how humans feel about socks," he said, looking
up under long, dark lashes. "Is it like sharing underwear?"

I don't know if I answered, but somehow, I ended up
wearing socks still warm from his skin and comfortable,
overlarge boots that are spotted and stained across the
saddle with toes worn to a shine.

Then he stood, tucking his hair behind his ear. I stared
at his long, pale, high-arched feet and Tiberius called him
Arthur like the king and I tried to think of something to say
to him that would show I was grateful but wouldn't piss off
Cassius.

I couldn't.

The next time I saw him, he was splayed out on damp
grass surrounded by hundreds of men and wolves. This time,
his entire body was bare. He was slim and perfectly propor-
tioned like a god, not one of the burly, chest-thumping,
thundering gods. More like Dionysus, though he had a
cock that was nothing like the discreet penises of classical
statuary, and when someone whispered to him, he tucked it
between his legs.

The bad feeling I had about whatever was about to happened got worse when a pale-gray wolf curled up next to
him, its head under his chin, its paw on his shoulder.

And ripped him open.

From shoulder to hip, it ripped him open.

Then they all just turned their backs and walked away, while gore bubbled up across the beautiful man's pale skin and watered the high grass. It was bright, I noticed, and sour-cherry red.

It was Irresistible.

At least there was someone screaming at the horror of it. It took me a minute to realize that the screams rattling around in my head were my own.

After that, it was all bad and blurred together until I ended up alone in this damp cabin on this thin mattress.

In the bathroom, on the wall above the enameled sink, was a tiny hand mirror hanging from a nail. Reflected in it is a woman I barely recognize.

With the damp corner of a towel, I dab away the taupe shadow that's run into dark puddles under my eyes and into tiny lines at the corners.

My pantsuit—the one that was once a beautiful white silk, heavy as chain mail that flowed like water around my curves—is now stiff and stained with mud and that delicious meaty Bandol and the blood of the man who died and the blood of the man who dared to help me.

Plugging up the sink, I run cold water. There is shampoo in the shower that has a picture of a dog. I try not to think about it as I pour long streams of it into the slowly collecting water.

Tears pour in long streams to join it.

When I was little, my father took me to the Botanical Garden in Montreal. I had seen a slug there, and being too young to know better, I'd thought someone had torn a snail out of its shell and left it naked and dying.

My father didn't know what I was crying about. He didn't try to find out. He just gathered me into his strong arms and held me tight and called me Princess and told me that I would never have to worry while he was there.

Then when my father died, August came. He didn't hug me, but when he saw how upset I was about the lobster tank, he raised two fingers in the air, and the entire restaurant was rearranged so I wouldn't have to see my dinner flailing as it was fished out of the water.

"You have nothing to worry about, Julia," he'd said. "I will take care of everything."

Now August is gone too.

I turn off the faucet and swish my pantsuit around, feeling just like I had imagined that slug had felt, naked and vulnerable.

Opening my mink bag, I pull out my lipstick and with a shaking hand trace the familiar bow and curve of my mouth.

I suck my lips in and let them go with a pop.

Once again, they are sour-cherry red.

Irresistible.

Chapter 2

Arthur

I can almost hear her again. The urgency in Gran Sigeburg's voice.

"If you are slighted?"
The fire will not burn.
"If you are angry?"
The fire will not burn.
"If you are in pain?"
The fire will not burn.

I was very little when I made that promise to her and to the whole of the Great North in return for my life.

Would you be proud of me, Gran Sigeburg?

Would you be proud?

———

A wolf's claws are not retractable. We are not like cats padding around with little switchblades tucked up inside. Our claws scrape across rocks and dirt and wood so that when Silver clawed me, it wasn't a clean razor slice. It was a ragged tear made with four dull screwdrivers.

The pain came in waves. Pain like pulsing whips of fire that broke nerves, followed by strangely comforting liquid warmth spreading across my chest, followed by a dull throb that emptied my body's blood and heat with every beat of my heart.

Coppery fumes surround me.

When I wake up, a wolf is howling. I know who it is though she doesn't sound like she did back when she was Varya, the Alpha Shielder of the Great North Pack's 12th Echelon. My echelon. Then she was stern and unyielding. Now she is tentative, questioning as she tries to understand who she has become.

One mountain stands alone to the west; taller than the rest, its pinnacle is scoured by winds leaving nothing but the thin, bent trees of the Krummholz, the crooked woods.

> *Winter-bearn, wind-woh,*
> *Se endeweard weorolde.*
> *Eal forsworen, forsacan*
> *Nefne*
> *Æcewulf.*
>
> *Winter-blasted, wind-twisted,*
> *The world's last sentinel.*
> *Forsworn, forsaken*
> *By all but the*
> *Forever wolf.*

August had timed the arrival of the hunters perfectly so they would come across us at the moment of our change when, neither wolves nor in skin, we are entirely vulnerable. We were all waiting for the pull of the Iron Moon on our wild when Varya told us that they were on their way.

Then the lone wolf she loved and had hidden from us howled to tell us that the hunters were already here and Varya did what she always had. She acted. The Iron Moon takes us as she finds us and makes us wilder. If she finds us in skin, she makes us wild. If she finds us wild, she will make us *æcewulfas*. Real wolves. Forever wolves.

The Alpha begged Varya not to change, knowing that if she did, she would never walk on two legs again. Never speak to her again. Varya did it anyway, then she and her white wolf clung to who they had been just long enough to save us all.

I touch the ragged edge of my skin. Varya had the same scars, the scars that were meant to brand a wolf who had broken the law. In the end—was it just a few days ago?—I told her that I would have the same marks she had. And that I would be proud to bear them.

Coyotes snuffle noisily at the edge of the Clearing, a reminder that if I don't get moving there will be no scars, no marks, no me.

I've never paid too much attention to coyotes before. They keep us alert when we are alive and eat us when we're dead, which is why we call them *wulfbyrgenna*, wolf tombs. They are usually only trouble for the very young, the very old, or the very injured.

I'm dizzy and tired and all I want to do is curl up in the grasses and sleep again, but I'm pretty sure if I do, I will be eaten.

I need to focus. Keep my mind from falling apart just long enough to get to the Innenlandes, the Inner Lands around the Great Hall. The Innenlandes are made safe by the constant comings and goings of wolves. Even the littlest pups run freely under the ferns and the fierce markings of the Pack.

At first, I try to pull myself up on my elbows, but contracting the muscles in my torso strains the few remaining fibers keeping my outsides together and my insides in. Lying back down, I pull my knees up, digging my heels into the soft, damp earth, then pushing myself backward like a naked, inverted inchworm through the grasses of the Clearing, focusing on reaching the dark, cool protection of the surrounding forests. Usually I—we—avoid the exposure of the Clearing except for certain rituals, most of which, now that I think of it, end with someone bleeding.

This was where we held the Slittung, the Slicing, when we killed drunken, exiled Ronan for kidnapping a pup. I took part. Every wolf did, so that we would all bear responsibility for the life we'd failed.

This is where each echelon, each age group, holds its Dæling, when wolves fight for position within the hierarchy and begin their lives as adult members of the Pack. This is where Lorcan fought and became Alpha of the 12th Echelon.

This is where I didn't fight and became the 12th's nidling.

There's an old saying that lone wolves at the bottom of the Pack are the only ones who always breed, their children being Frustration and Dissent. That is why they are given over to the echelon's Alphas, to be their servants, their *nidlings*. It is meant to be a life of endless submission, leaving the lone wolf too tired, I suppose, for either frustration or dissent.

I killed Victor because of dissent but it wasn't mine, it was his. He was our Deemer, our thinker about the law, and he spread dissent through the Pack, threatening the cohesion that is so crucial to our survival. Then he betrayed us to August Leveraux.

That is why I jammed a butter knife into his sternum.

Must be the blood loss, but suddenly that strikes me as the funniest thing I've ever heard: "I *jammed* a *butter* knife." I laugh until it hurts, which is immediately.

Silver is now the Deemer and she decided that *nidling* is one ancient tradition the Pack can do without, so now I will be the Omega. It suits me. I have always been attentive and now that is my duty. While it is up to the Alphas to manage fights, it is up to the Omega to look for silent divisions that are no less deadly.

The setting sun has gilded one side of the Clearing's grasses gold while the other is thrown into shadow and coyotes bark with bad intent. The sky is purple by the time I reach the woodlands and find a branch and a trunk and maneuver myself onto two feet, my weak right arm across my waist, trying to keep my intestines in. I stumble as my foot catches the thorn of one of the black locusts that have taken root.

What did I do with my boots?

That's right, I gave them to the female Shifter… What did Lorcan call her?

"Heo hy sifeðan."
She is the siftings.
She is what is left when everything of value has been removed.

I know why Lorcan said that. She seemed helpless as an injured pup but then I saw her. As my blood poured, she lashed out at Silver, fought Tiberius, and attacked the Alpha Rock as though she wanted to take on the Alpha herself.

Until the man in the black suit wrapped his arms around her and called her baby baby baby. Then the fire flared briefly hotter before it burned out entirely and left nothing but ash.

What's left when everything useful has been burned away.

There's a familiar noise. Paws changing directions, followed by a discomfited *rowp!* For a minute, I think this is it. It's dark now, and the coyotes are massing quietly in the trees.

Except the coyotes' warning is more of a *rarp*. *Rowp* is a sound made by wolves.

They are running in slow circles. I can tell by the way I lose their scent when they are downwind, only to find it again when they are upwind. The Alpha, Tiberius, Tara, Lorcan.

By law, they are not allowed to protect or comfort me. It's meant to teach the clawed wolf what the loss of Pack really means. Still, these wolves, some of the strongest of the Great North, run in circles, scaring off the coyotes. Wolves don't run in pointless circles. Humans run in pointless circles. I forgot what it's called.

Jogging, that's the word.

Finally, I reach the huge old cottonwood that blew down many moons ago and we never bothered to collect because it sparks and the smoke stings our noses. Beyond it is the safety of the Innenlandes. If I were wild, I would breeze over it. Now I sit on it and let myself fall backward. I give myself into it all: the deep striations of the bark rasping against my bare skin, the kaleidoscope of the stars above, the scent of black earth and wood rot below, and the warm and musky comfort of wolves.

Chapter 3

Julia

ANYONE WOULD RECOGNIZE ME AS A ST. AILBHE'S GIRL.
Anyone in Montreal at least. Even though it's been over a
dozen years since I last wore the plaid pleated skirt—rolled
up to midthigh whenever possible—or the bright-white shirt
with a Peter Pan collar that was stiff and smelled like bleach.

It's something about the polished skin, the makeup that
neither reveals nor covers. Hair, blown, layered, at a length
that cups the breasts if you have curls or runs over them like
a waterfall if you don't. The way of walking and standing and
sitting and talking that was burned into us.

"*Vous devez vous tenir bien droite, la tête haute,*" Mlle. Pivot,
the dancing mistress, would say.

You must hold yourself straight, your head high.

Except then she'd slap the back of my knees with her
cane. To remind me that in keeping my back straight, I had
to bend my knees as much as possible so that when our part-
ners from St. Hubert arrived, they could pretend to be taller
than I was.

One of the things I most loved about Cassius is that he
was tall enough for me to walk upright.

I bat another low-hanging branch away. It stings the hand that slapped Cassius. What was I thinking? He was so angry. I told him that I was confused and so frightened by the sight of blood. I licked my lips and told him how much I needed him. How I trusted him to take care of me. How I believed in him when he said he'd get me out of here.

Tomorrow, he'd said, four days in a row, not that I said anything, because saying anything would make him think I didn't believe in him and he would get angrier.

The roots of the trees are all tangled and humped together like heaving waves under my borrowed boots. Or not borrowed because the man who lent them to me is dead.

I started out this morning on my own because there is simply no way I am going to spend another night alone in that cabin. It is not a bright, cheery bungalow at the end of a broad path surrounded by climbing roses and meadow flowers like you see in puzzles. It's surrounded by a million dark trees and has exactly three dim lights that seemed to serve no purpose but to create creepy shadows.

And I, foolish girl that I am, had always believed that it was supposed to be warmer inside than it was outside, but that cabin was exactly as cold as the night air outside.

I tried to close one of the windows, but when I took off the screen and stretched my arm outside to pull the hinged window closed, moths flew in and hit my face and joined an army of thin green bugs flittering around the lights.

I dragged a mattress from a bunk and shoved it as far from the windows as I could, then lay down with two blankets over my head. I could still hear: the rattling screens, a moving of things among the leaves, the breaking of a branch, a bellow in the distance. Then there was a shriek right nearby, and that was when I promised myself that if I survived this night, I would not spend another one alone in the cabin in the woods.

Why did Cassius make me watch that stupid movie?

The next morning when I searched through the cabin, I found a spare pair of orange athletic pants that advertise HWS Lacrosse and an enormous bright-blue T-shirt with a charging bull that says "I Believe in Buffalo." There was also a water bottle that smelled funky, but I washed it with the PeltZ shampoo and I guess it smells all right.

I put it in my dyed mink bucket bag along with my brush, my bright sour-cherry-red lipstick, a travel size of the perfume Cass got me, my compact, several restaurant mints, and a phone charger but no phone because the damned wolves took my phone. Also that spool of thread I used to match nail polish to bag to shoes.

I took out my Dolces because I didn't have room for both them and the water bottle, but Cassius will understand why I left them behind.

I think. I hope.

Then I started on my great escape.

Which has none of the excitement of fictional escapes. I'd chosen to go north kind of at random, figuring that as long as I kept heading in one direction, I'd have to finally get out, and north would at least put me out somewhere closer to Canada. Problem is, the trees block out the sun so I have no way of knowing which way is which, but then

I remember something about moss growing on the north sides of trees.

I am inordinately proud to find myself in possession of this single piece of practical information.

God, it's tedious. Miles and miles of utterly identical landscape interrupted by the gross and creepy. When I find a rock shaped like an anvil that is dry and open to the sun, I rest and eat one of my restaurant mints. It's a formation that must be common to this area because I've seen more than one.

I stare at the mint in the plastic wrapper that says *COME AGAIN!* It's my last one and I don't know what I'll do if I don't find a way out of this hellhole soon. The only thing that could be worse than sleeping inside that cabin would be sleeping outside that cabin.

The diamonds along the sides of my rings scrape the skin of my middle finger and pinkie, so I play with them a lot. Using my thumb to move them around and make them more comfortable, though because the promise ring has emerald cuts all the way round, that's not really possible.

Maybe I shouldn't be wearing them, but I haven't seen a single person, and when I get out, it's all I have to convince any driver that a girl in a stained "I Believe in Buffalo" T-shirt can pay them back for a ride or the use of their phone.

Who should I call? There must be someone at August's compound who will know how to make things happen the way my uncle always could. Someone who will figure out where I am and who can gather up a force to come back here to rescue Cassius, though he'll be pissed if he finds out that I got out when he—

"I was sent to get you."

I freeze, blinking at the figure silhouetted against the sun. I knew it. I knew August couldn't be dead. I knew he would send his men to find me.

Except then I look more closely and realize that the tall, broad-shouldered figure with the long face, black hair, wide-set dark eyes, and a scarred cheek is a woman.

The remains of that stupid mint hit sour in my stomach.

"Who are you?" I ask, already dreading the answer.

"I am Inna Ardithsdottir, Delta Shielder of the 12th Echelon."

I try very hard not to cry.

"How did you find me?"

Inna frowns. "Were you trying not to be found?"

"*I was trying to escape. What do you think I was doing?*"

"Humans run around"—she circles her finger in the air— "when they are neither hunting nor catching, so I thought maybe you did too."

Numbed, I look down at my aching feet.

"It is called 'yogging,'" she adds.

"It's not called 'yogging.' It's called jogging and I was not jogging. I was *escaping*."

She leans down and picks up something that she holds out in her palm.

COME AGAIN! it says and smells like mint.

I look at the twin of the restaurant mint in my own hand and my anger burns away, replaced by dread. "Don't tell me." My voice sounds small in the vastness. "How far did I get?"

She frowns. "I cannot both tell you and *not* tell you at the same time."

"Just how far I did I make it?"

"It's hard to say exactly. The same way it's hard to measure the path of a possum with rabies." Suddenly, the werewolf angles her head to the side, her nostrils flaring twice. "We have to go."

My feet hurt and my legs hurt and I've got scrapes all over my hands and I'm sweaty and tired and I don't care if I've only made it as far as a rabid possum, it's too far to go back.

"I'm not going anywhere." Folding my arms over my bag, I no longer even try to look amenable. "If you want me to move, you're going to have to get me a Lyft."

Inna looks confused for a second, then shrugs her shoulders and kneels in front of me. Before I can say anything, she puts her hands under my arms and tosses me over her shoulder, catching me in the gut.

I clutch tightly to the handles of my bucket bag as she runs, her shoulder jammed into my sternum and knocking out every breath I might have used for screaming. The only thing that comes up is a bubble of mint-flavored bile.

Finally, she leans in and flips me forward. I tumble to the ground.

"What…the…hell…"

"You said you needed a lift."

I hate it here.

Leaving me curled around my knees, Inna lopes off and sniffs the base of a tree.

I hate it here.

I stop panting for a moment and listen. There's a sound

that's not a crack or a screech. It's more man-made. Like the *thunk* of a screen door.

I pull myself up to my hands and knees. Inna seems tied up in her tree sniffing and doesn't notice. In an isolated place like this, men will have guns. I hear the sound again and creep slowly toward it, keeping quiet and low among the ferns until I see an opening up ahead. Something built out of cut wood. I bolt for it; all I need is to reach the door and—

In front of the enormous high-peaked lodge, a huge man holds the door for wolves. As soon as they're in, the screen door closes with a solid *thunk*.

I stop, staring, and whimper.

Inna passes me. "Come, Shifter," she says, stroking a ball of loose fur to her cheek. "I don't want to miss the lentils."

All that effort. A whole day of walking and ten minutes of jostling, and I'm right back at werewolf HQ, my pride in my abilities crushed to nothing.

"Werewolf."

That gets a sour reaction from her.

"I am not a werewolf," she says irritably. "We are Pack. Or wolves."

"Well, *wolf*, tell me… Does moss grow on the north sides of trees?"

She looks at a huge tree with black bark and an over-skirt of velvety green filigree. She rubs her fingers across it as gently as if it were a baby's skin. "Sometimes. Sometimes not. Moss grows wherever it is damp enough and shady enough. Old woods don't act like new woods. The rules are different here."

For the first time since I was a child, I don't have to worry about banging into doorjambs or ceiling fixtures. I can straighten out my legs and my spine *at the same time*. I could even wear high heels here, if my feet ever heal.

It's all huge, from the big staircase leading up to the enormous trestle tables, to the wood trunks supporting the mezzanine that stride across the hall like giant's legs. Three of them are peeled wood; the fourth is covered by bark with deep furrows. A wolf rubs against it, first one side, then the other, and walks away, leaving tufts of fur.

The place is crawling with werewolves, none of whom are paying any attention to me. I want to protest, to ask someone *Do you know who I am?* but no one here cares.

Only a bird in the rafters notices me. It stares, its head cocked for a moment, and I wave. Then it dives down and flies back to its perch, a noodle hanging from its beak, reminding me how hungry I am.

Having eaten little except Bandol and mints since I left home, it's impossible for me to ignore the smell of basil and cumin and butter and eggs, so I pull out a metal seat from a big wooden table and sit down, my arms crossed in front of me.

When a woman walks by carrying two plates, I raise my hand, trying to get her attention.

A man's voice comes from behind me.

"You're at the wrong table," he says.

"Are there reservations?"

"You're supposed to sit with the 12th Echelon, right there."

"Thank you," I say with my best smile, not so big that my

cheeks look fat, not so small that I look smug, my mouth open a little. "Is there a menu? Or is it *à la française*?"

"Inna," the man yells, ignoring my most inviting smile. "Come get your Shifter."

Inna stomps toward me and I leap back in case she's thinking of throwing me over her shoulder again. Instead she grabs my wrist. "You made me get out of line," she says, dragging me toward a scrum of enormous men and women that in no way resembles a line. She shoves a big chipped plate into my hands and pushes me in the back with her elbow to get me moving.

"*And* you made me miss the lentils."

For the first time in my life, the thought of lentils makes my mouth water and each successive wave of lemon and thyme and roasted tomatoes and feta and hot bread and garlic makes my stomach rumble. By the time I can actually get a look through the broad backs to the crispy phyllo filled with spinach and cheese and asparagus and eggs shirred in something that must have turmeric, I am dizzy.

"Where are the mains?" I ask, carefully fitting a spoonful of bright green spaghetti with nuts onto my plate.

"The mains?"

"There are only sides here—salads, vegetables. I don't see any meat."

She points with her chin toward a door that gives onto a hallway. "If you want flesh, you'll have to get it yourself."

Down the hallway to the right is a door, and through that door, teenagers scurry carrying casseroles and bowls. "So I just go into the kitchen?"

"It's not in the kitchen. You think flesh comes from the kitchen? You have to hunt it. We are not carrion eaters. If you want flesh, you have to kill—"

"Me? I've never killed anything."

She takes a worn cloth napkin from a pile of them.

"We are all of us killers, Shifter. Some of us take responsibility for it. And *some of us*"—she looks at me pointedly, as though I'm too dense to understand—"pretend that we have no part in death that is done on our behalf. Utensils are there," she says, pointing to a stoneware container filled with mismatched forks and knives and spoons.

I'd argue with her but I can't over the big mouthful of pretzel bread.

When I turn around for cutlery, I meet Cassius's bright and angry eyes.

"Where have you been?"

I chew desperately, my mother's voice echoing through my head, telling me how impossible it is to be charming with your mouth full.

"I tried to get out," I say, swallowing again, my mouth crazily dry. His face has gone hard, and I realize that I've made a mistake and cast doubt on his promise and his ability to rescue me. I backtrack, telling him how I got lost and passed the same stone three times—silly me—and dropped mint wrappers but never noticed. Oh, get this—I didn't get more than a few yards away. I mention it because I know he'll find it funny.

I leave out the part about being carried by a werewolf.

"Didn't I say I'd take care of everything?" he says, his face loosening a little, though he still strokes his cheek—the one I slapped—so I'll remember what I did.

He eyes my plate. I try to figure out how to put this food back but there are too many enormous people in the way and I can't move against the tide.

"Shifter," Inna says sharply, looking not at me but at Cassius, "you are with the wrong echelon. You"—she tugs at my arm—"come."

Inna doesn't defer to Cassius at all, and I wait for the angry tone and the sharp questions that are like quicksand, deceptively calm on the surface and treacherous underneath.

It doesn't come. Instead, his attention shifts toward a man with a buttoned-down shirt and neat pants who looks like he knows his way around a boardroom. The man Cassius thought was the Alpha and turned out to be *an* Alpha but not *the* Alpha.

The Alpha is wearing a worn black T-shirt that for whatever reason shows a snarling wolf and says "This is my resting bitch face." In one hand, she holds a bowl of soup that was steaming when I first got in line but isn't anymore.

I follow Inna, and even though my stomach rumbles, I know I should've gotten salad. A salad would have taken the edge off. Always eat something before you go out, my mother said. No man wants to watch you eat.

Keeping my eye on Cassius's broad back, I curl my arm around the plate and twirl the green spaghetti on my fork until I see a shriveled inchworm in the pasta.

"Stop shrieking," Inna says. "It's not a worm, it's a fiddle-head fern."

Still, I push the plate away and slide my hands under my thighs. I watch enviously as Inna cuts a thick chunk of cheese.

"You know what the word for humans is in the Old Tongue?" Inna asks, though she doesn't look at me, only at the dark bread she is slathering with butter.

"What tongue?"

"Our tongue, the Old Tongue." She tops the buttered bread with cheese. "In the Old Tongue, the word for human is 'Westend,'" she says. "It means 'waster.'" She takes a big bite of cheese and butter and dark bread, and it distends her cheek as she chews. "We are not wasters. You take what you want, but you eat what you take. See her?" Inna nods toward a woman with a horsey face and a bright-yellow tank over biceps bigger than her breasts. She is trying to attract the attention of the blond man sitting at the head of the table. It's only when I see the tiny ponytail held back in the rubber band that I recognize him as the man I'd been foisted off on when the Alpha divided us all up.

What was his name? Logan?

"That is Tonia," she continues, not waiting for me to answer. "She is our Gamma. Excellent hunter. Took down a healthy grown moose by herself. She ate"—Inna now looks at me before continuing with special emphasis—"the liver and heart."

She finally swallows and takes another bite.

"So you're telling me that a wolf hunted a moose, killed a moose, and ate a moose? As stories go, that lacks a certain verve."

"*I am not trying to entertain you, Shifter.* I am telling you that a wolf ate *part* of a moose and let the rest go to waste."

Inna pours herself water from a stoneware jug the size of a Mini Cooper. "And when we discovered the remains of it four days later, she had to finish it. Maggots and carrion beetles and all. Our law requires that we eat what we kill."

I can taste green pasta rising in the back of my throat and swallow hard.

"That's just disgusting."

"Maybe. But that law is why you're still alive. We would have killed you, but you taste rancid." She tears another hunk of bread from the quarter loaf on the table and raises her chin to the worm-eating wolf. "It's not the maggots and the carrion beetles that are so bad, it's the loss of respect." The wolf in question narrows her eyes and stares back. Then Inna whispers, "I will challenge her, and before winter comes, I will be Gamma."

The little bird flitters from the rafters to the banister. When Inna turns her attention to using the crust to sponge up every bit of garlic and oil in her bowl, I tear off a large crumb and drop it discreetly to the floor, hoping the bird will see it and Inna won't.

The bird cocks its head to the side, one bright black eye focused on me. I pretend not to notice as it flies down and hops over, quickly scarfing up the crumb. Under the cover of the table, I drop the rest of the bread and the bird hops toward it.

Something jumps underneath the table. The little bird flutters around frantically, one wing held in a puppy's mouth. More puppies appear and start to chase the puppy still holding the flapping bird until Inna bends down and saves the bird from the puppy. Its wing flaps at an awkward angle from its body. Maybe she'll put it in a splint or take it to a vet or—

With a quick twist, Inna breaks its neck.

"That was not a good kill, Zvi," she says, dropping the limp body back among the puppies with their cocked heads and lolling tongues while I close my eyes and cover my ears, trying to block out the crunching of tiny bones.

I want to scream. I hate it here but I don't know how to get out and everyone who promised to take care of me is gone. Except for Cassius and he's angry with me, and then the one man who was nice to me is dead, and the little bird who could fly to freedom is dead and—

Something huge and heavy and furry scrabbles under the table and sits on my feet until I jerk my legs back from the enormous wolf that seems to be trying to hide among the forest of legs. I take my fingers out of my ears, hearing how silent it's gotten. The werewolves stare bleakly at their plates, shuffling their food around.

Even the Alpha sits for the first time, blowing at a spoonful of soup from a bowl that was cold twenty minutes ago.

The only real sound is the oblivious crunching of little bones.

Then the stairs outside creak. Slowly. One excruciating step at a time. It's like waiting for a mistimed jack-in-the-box to finally pop.

At another table, a man saws through a potato and keeps sawing until the woman next to him puts her hand on his.

I look to Cassius but he has his back to me.

"What—" I begin to whisper to Inna. She shakes her head and takes another piece of bread.

By the time whatever it is finally reaches the door, every nerve is strained.

It isn't loud, the screen door closing, but against the silence, it sounds like cannon fire.

Cassius tilts back on the legs of his chair, craning his head to search through the windows that lead onto the enclosed porch, a kind of mudroom where shoes are piled and clothes hung from hooks.

The man in the button-down shirt nods to a woman next to Cassius. She must have stepped on the base of the chair because it slams down, sending Cassius rocketing forward.

I turn away. He would not have wanted me to see.

Anyway, that is the moment that the door opens.

It's the beautiful man, Arthur, who should be dead. Looks it. All of his blood was left on the grass and his skin is the color of bone. His silver eyes float in dark-gray sockets like ice chips in Stoli.

He holds one arm close to his chest and shoves his shoulder against the heavy door, every muscle straining against wood and pain.

No one helps him.

Having finished eating her crust of bread, Inna has moved on to her cup, nervously turning it in perfect circles on the table. For some reason, every wolf is pretending not to see him, though clearly they do.

Maybe they feel guilty. I hope they feel guilty. The person who should feel the guiltiest of all, the young woman with the silver hair who yesterday morning tore away chunks of his chest, does look at him. Then she lowers her head.

He lowers his eyes in return.

Everything about his posture is tentative; he limps forward, trying to discover some way of walking, some way of standing, some way of being, that doesn't hurt.

When he makes it to the front table, he works with one hand. One hand setting the plate down. One hand serving food. One hand grabbing the edge of the table. One hand banging a heavy bowl that wobbles loudly in the silence.

Blood seeps through the material of his T-shirt.

"Isn't someone going to help?" I hiss at Inna.

"No," she says and swabs another crust around her already clean bowl.

Now I know why Cassius and my uncle call them dogs. They are nothing but animals.

The chair catches the back of my knees as I stand. Inna grabs at my wrist. She's a powerful woman—she did carry me here, after all—but I'm not as weak as I pretend to be. I wrench my hand free.

The man with the stupid ponytail stands and tells me to sit down. I ignore him. He puts his hands on my shoulders, turning me back to the table, and a string inside me pulled tight by these last few days of blood and fear and a lifetime of holding my temper and holding my tongue surges through my arms and he stumbles.

Standing close to Arthur, I hold my hand out for his plate.

"Leave me alone," he says.

Just like that, the lava cools to glass.

Chapter 4

Arthur

I COULD HAVE SLEPT FOREVER BUT THAT WOULD BE THE same as dying.

The last thing I ate was half a corn cake at the end of the Iron Moon. Even that went down resentfully, as though my gut knew claws would soon be scraping against its exterior walls and didn't want to deal with the corn cake inside.

When the floor tilts under my feet, I clutch at the edge of the serving table and unsettle a large bowl that wobbles like thunder.

I manage to hold on to the heavy wood, staring down at the dishes of food kaleidoscoping in front of me.

Gradually, I become aware of the Shifter female. She is next to me, her mouth forming around words that I can't quite make out. I think she's trying to help. I'm barely holding it together. Hasn't anyone explained to her that no one is allowed to help? I try to tell her but I may have done it wrong because she backs away from me, hunched.

The whispers start behind my back. A few words— *clawed...dead...butter knife...Victor*—so I know they are talking about me.

Not that I care. It's not like those weeks before the Iron Moon when Victor, our Deemer, our thinker about the law, whipped up dissent among some of the younger echelons by disparaging the Alpha for allowing the half-pack/half-Shifter Tiberius to stay. Then, to make matters worse, for allowing Thea Villalobos to live, even though she was *sum westend þe wat*. A human who knows.

Victor was so preoccupied with the Alphas of those echelons that he paid little attention to the lower-placed wolves and none whatsoever to the lowest-placed wolf of all.

"If you are slighted?"

The fire will not burn.

On the day before the Iron Moon when we discovered that he had betrayed the Great North Pack to August, no fire burned, but I killed him anyway.

I spoon the tomatoes and paneer and rice into a dish, because it is soft and near the edge of the table. The plate trembles in both hands but the 12th pretends not to notice me struggle to sit down.

Perhaps, I think, as I try to raise my fork, I will suggest to Silver that in the future she start the Clawing on the nondominant side. As it was, she dug her claws into my right shoulder and peeled away skin and muscle and fascia all the way down to my left hip. I switch the fork to my left hand.

Wolves are not much for small talk under the best of circumstances, and most say nothing, focusing instead on eating so they can head out and hang their clothes on a hook inside or a branch outside and run through the sweetgrass and balsam and splash into fast-running water until they come on something small and warm and crunchy for dessert.

It's the juveniles, sitting at a separate table under the watchful eye of their Human Behaviors teacher, who break the silence. Each year, Leonora takes her charges on field trips, trying to find which of the wolflings have what it takes to pass as human. The littlest ones in Introduction to Human Behaviors start with a trip to Pizza Barn. A few will graduate to Kitty's Cozy Café. Only a very few of the juveniles will make it through Advanced Human Behaviors and to some expensive place on Grand Isle.

Every year, those unlucky juveniles practice all sorts of skills including something called toasting. Every year, glasses break, and every year, the Pack laughs and shouts out *Wes hæl!—Be well!*—banging sturdy mugs together because Homelands has no use for fragile things.

"Omega?" Lorcan says, appearing suddenly beside me. He says the new title tentatively, rolling it around in his mouth, trying it out.

I turn my head toward him, moving my body as little as possible.

Things have changed for both of us. Lorcan sided with Victor, and while wolves do not have patience for regret, backing a traitor does require reassessing life choices.

"Omega," Lorcan says again, more firmly this time. "This is the Shifter. You will be responsible for her."

"I am thirty-two years old. I am perfectly able to handle myself," the Shifter retorts.

Lorcan pulls his Henley over his head and folds it

over the back of a chair. "She needed Inna to carry her to dinner."

"I didn't *need* her to. She—" The Shifter stops when Lorcan unzips his fly and slides out of his pants. He shakes them with a loud snap that seems to shock the Shifter because she slumps down, her head low over her plate, arms circled around the back of her head.

He retrieves his shirt and drapes both shirt and pants over his arm.

"Yes, Alpha." I know what Lorcan's doing. The 12th is the largest echelon and the one tasked with tending the Summer Gardens. When we are in skin, we are responsible for plowing and digging and kneeling down and stretching up, and Lorcan knows that plowing, digging, kneeling, and stretching will wreak havoc on the weak bonds barely holding my body together. Like the jogging wolves, he is protecting me while pretending not to.

I tap a finger against the back of my scalp. He smiles sadly and starts to walk away, pulling at the rubber band he so often forgets is holding back his hair. Varya used to be the one who reminded him, because if she didn't, he would change with a tuft of fur between his ears. It was vaguely comical and not a good look for an Alpha.

"Cassius," the Shifter says, her eyes turned to a male Shifter given over to the 9th's care. "I didn't mean to look… I didn't know he was going to do that." Her voice is nervous, breathy. "Please, Cass."

Then Elijah, the 9th's Alpha, yells for the male Shifter to follow the rest of the echelon. The female watches nervously until they are gone and sinks back into her seat, playing with the rings of glassy stones around one finger.

"What was that about?" she finally asks. "Who strips in the middle of the dining room?"

I try to think back to the few Human Behaviors classes I took before the Pack realized I would never be behaving or misbehaving with humans.

"Is this about Lorcan's genitals?"

The female opens and closes her mouth like a baby bird but doesn't answer. Then she starts talking loudly and jabbing her hand into her chest with each sentence. "*I was supposed to be in New York. New York City.* I had tickets for *Hamilton.* I had a reservation for Omakase Masa. I'd reserved Suite 5000 for the weekend."

I try to understand what she's saying but it's all gibberish and blood is seeping through my T-shirt and things are getting vague and slippery and I need to get back to the dormitory. Get some sleep. Maybe she'll make sense in the morning.

She screams.

Or maybe not.

Chapter 5

Julia

SOMEONE STOLE MY BAG.

"Shifter," Inna snaps, her hands clapped over her ears. "That is too loud."

I don't give a damn. *Someone. Stole. My. Bag.*

"That bag was specially made for me. I had it customized to match my *shoes*. Now that style is out of season and some fucker has stolen it and I'll *never* be able to get another one."

Inna looks at another woman who frowns and shakes her head.

"Does it smell like rodent?"

"No! It does not smell like rodent. It's *mink*."

The other woman grimaces. "Don't much like mink."

"Me either," Inna says. "Stringy in the summer. Bad mouth feel in the winter."

Oh my god, I hate it here.

Then I see a puppy race past the fireplace with a chunk of bright-red fur in its mouth. I run after it, clambering over the sofa, and when I get to the other side, I yank furiously, trying to pull the fur from its mouth, but it growls and pulls harder until Inna leans over the back of the sofa and grabs my wrist so tight that I swear my bone creaks.

"Shifter," Inna says, any lightness gone. "I don't know the human world well but here, in Homelands, if you hurt a pup, we will rip your head from your neck with our teeth and clean the floor with our tongues." She sticks her fingers between the puppy's jaws. "Soft mouth, John. Soft mouth. Here," she says, throwing the spitty piece of fur at me. "Enjoy your rodent."

Then she disappears, holding the puppy and cooing to it, nuzzling its face, leaving me to crawl around on all fours, trying to find the remnants of a bag that probably cost more than everything in this horrible place put together.

I finally find it. Under a table in the corner. I cradle it in my arms. The fur is ruined and it's only because of the satin lining that my few possessions are still here. I lay them out carefully—perfume, compact, lipstick, charger, thread— like relics of a great and bygone civilization.

I wish I'd brought my Dolces instead of this stupid water bottle. Then maybe like Dorothy in *The Wizard of Oz*, I could click my sparkling red heels together and wake up back in my apartment.

My hand shakes as I try to fit the clump of damp fur into the hole but it just falls out again and I clutch my bag close, sobbing into the tattered detritus of my life.

My father is dead, August is dead, Cassius is angry, and as I wipe my face with the back of my hand, I know that no one *cares* that I'm crying.

"Hello?" My voice echoes in the rafters because the hall is empty.

Even Arthur, who was *supposed* to be responsible for me, is gone.

On the wall separating the big hall from the mudroom in front is a handprint that was once red and is now brick-colored. It streaks across glass and wood before resting on the doorframe. A little bouquet of dark drops on the floor lead me to more blood smeared on the screen door. Shoving my feet into the boots, I head to the stairs. Much of the banister is marked by a rusty smear.

The moon is still bright enough and the trees around the hall spare enough to see the spot of pale gray at the forest edge, guttering like a candle in the wind.

"Thanks for waiting," I say, my voice stretched thin by sarcasm.

He doesn't answer or wait or anything, just moves slowly into the forest.

A shriek breaks above me. "What *is* that?" I ask, running to catch up with him.

"Barn owl," he says. His voice is dull but his silver eyes behind slitted lids are as bright as a new dime.

The shriek repeats and then dies out, and as soon as it does, a woman screams in the forest.

I grab hold of him. "And that? That's not an owl."

"Fox," he says.

"Do you know how to get out of here?"

He weebles forward unsteadily. For someone who's supposed to be taking care of me, he's doing a terrible job. He doesn't put his arm around me or ask me if I'm cold or tell me that everything's going to be all right. That he's there and everything will be all right.

The moon breaks through the trees and I see the blood turned black on his shirt and I pinch my hand for being angry with the one person in this place who has been nice to me and who...

Then something occurs to me:

Supposing they ripped him open because *he was nice to me?*

I lift his arm—

He sucks in a sharp breath and groans.

His *left* arm, then. I lift his *left* arm over my shoulder, and with my right wrapped around his waist and my hip pressed to his, I support him, he directs me, and together we soldier on like two drunk old men in a three-legged race.

Once we reach the cabin, I hit the light with my elbow and drag him the last few steps to the mattress in the middle of the room. I fall to my knees and he slides down with a soft moan. I cover him with a blanket, partly to keep him warm, partly so that I don't have to see the blood caking his front.

Again, several long pale-green-winged zombie bugs have managed to get in and gather around each bulb. The only difference between last night and this night is that I am not alone. I'm with someone, someone who needs me even more than I need him.

It's an odd feeling. Being needed.

In the dull light, with his dark hair tangled, his eyes like bruises in his bloodless face, his razored cheekbones, his full lips, Arthur is still the most beautiful man I have ever seen.

Last year, Cassius took me to Boston on a "work trip," which meant that I spent most of the time on my own. The second day was gray and cold, and though I'd meant to walk the old part of town, I ended up at the Boston Athenaeum instead, trying to keep warm while I waited for Cassius to pick me up.

"What are you looking at?" Cassius said when he came to retrieve me, adding dismissively once he'd read the label. "It's only a copy."

I knew it was a copy, but I made up something about wanting to do a posting about fakes for my Art_Tarts Instagram account. Cassius rolled his eyes and said he'd wait for me for a half hour at the pub across the street.

"But no more."

I didn't tell him that I'd already lost an hour with the St. Sebastian leaning against a denuded tree. He was carnal, ethereal, and indifferent to pain, and I didn't tell Cassius that the guard had yelled at me for standing too close as though he'd read my mind and knew I wanted to lick away the tiny trickle of blood that was all this sensuous man had to show for the three arrows.

Now I stare at a different beautiful man. This one is not indifferent to pain but he bears it. He is not of this world. Or maybe he is of *this* world, but he isn't of mine. Instead of a thin drop of blood oozing into the modest cloth slung across St. Sebastian's hairless pelvis, Arthur's body has been torn in half by a wolf's claw. He smells of flesh and metal.

And instead of St. Sebastian's vacant, heavenward stare, Arthur's silver-gray eyes watch me.

Gradually he becomes unfocused, hazy, and then he sighs. I press the back of my knuckle to his lower lip. It is as dry as onion skin.

Of course, he's thirsty.

I fill up the water bottle and try to hold that to his lips, but it comes out so fast and he starts to choke and then I have to turn him over while he coughs and wheezes.

I try cupping water in my hand but that just leaks out. Finally, I soak a clean towel and lean over him, gently squeezing the water in drip by drip.

The shallow lift and fall of his chest stops.

I reach under the blanket for his hand, my fingers twined in his.

Supposing he put his life on the line for me and then dies and leaves me alone?

"Please. Please, don't die. Please, please."

Then his throat works, he swallows, and I sob.

"Please," I say over and over again. *Please.*

Chapter 6

Arthur

TWO WINTERS AGO, I SAW IT. ABOVE THE JAGGED LACE OF dark pine, above even the distant outlines of the mountains, two eagles in the dark-gray sky were starting their courtship spiral, their talons locked.

They turned round and round and round, heads down, wings back, and I watched until they disappeared below the tree line. I didn't see what happened at the end, but I've always wondered—what happens to the ones who let go?

Do they fly off into the sky like shrapnel?

Their courtship failed, do they end up alone?

I am spiraling into the night but I hold on.

Plee, plee, plee.

It sounds like a phoebe singing.

Plee, plee, plee.

Water drops into my mouth and sings.

Plee, plee, plee.

Isn't it too dark for you, phoebe?

Plee, plee, plee.

Isn't it dark?

Plee, plee, plee.

Chapter 7

Julia

HE WAS AS COLD AND PALE AS A MARBLE EFFIGY ON A BED
that barely bent under his weight. I watched carefully for the
fluttering beats under the skin of his neck and the flickering
movement of his eyes under the translucent lavender of his lids.

Please, please, please.

Please, please, please.

"Phoebe," he whispered once.

"Not Phoebe," I told him. "Julia." He doesn't say anything
because despite whatever I try, I know he's dying. I lie down
against him, listening to the deep rattle in his chest, feeling
slight vibrations that mean he's still alive.

It's gray outside when a breaking branch wakes me.

I jump up and run to the window, and even though I
know it can't be Cassius, my mind desperately runs through
explanations for how I came to be sleeping curled around a
man in an isolated cabin in the middle of the woods. I wrap
my arms over the cold, tight tips of my breasts.

Problem is, I've never been good at lying to Cassius. I'm
not even particularly good at telling him the truth. He looks
at me with a hard, suspicious look, and then every word and

every thought cowers against the back wall of my skull and I know I look guilty. Sound guilty. Feel guilty.

Even when I would go out with the St. Ailbhe's girls—Jas, Adriana, Marie-Laure ("Mel")—he wouldn't ask, "Where are you going with the girls?" It was "What are you doing with the 'girls'?" a subtle, accusatory difference but one that made me apprehensive.

"Nothing. Going out to eat?"

"Hmmm. Hmm. How long will you be?"

"I'm…not sure?"

"An hour? Two? How long does it take to eat?"

And my thoughts and words scampered away and I'd try to figure out what he wanted me to say so he'd stop asking. Then I'd end up saying, "Sorry."

For what, I don't know.

Sorry?

Afterward, he never asked me simply if I'd had fun. He'd asked where I'd gone with "the girls" and what I'd eaten and what "the girls" had talked about and had we talked about him, and I did my best to make us seem silly and inconsequential. Tried to make it seem like they didn't really matter, not in the way he did.

Of course, next time I wanted to see them, he would bring up the silliness and the inconsequence again and wonder what I was doing wasting my time.

Until bit by bit, I stopped seeing them.

I wish I hadn't now. Then maybe there'd be someone left to worry about me. Someone who would wonder why they hadn't heard from me.

It's like that Zen thing: If a tree falls in the forest and no one is around to hear it, does it make a sound?

If a girl leaves and no one notices she's gone, did she ever really exist?

I don't think I even told Jas that I'd gotten engaged. I know I didn't: I would have remembered her oohing and aahing over twelve carats of internally flawless clarity.

I look down at the rings of my wedding suite, this proof of Cassius's undying love.

Who might miss me?

Not my mother. She'd sent me off to St. Ailbhe's almost as soon as Aurelian showed up. Needed to make room for husband number two. I had made a perfunctory call to her, telling her that Cassius and I were driving down to New York.

"From Montreal? Why not just take a plane?"

"Because Cassius has something to drop off for Uncle August," I'd told her, knowing that a single mention of Uncle August would put an end to any further conversation.

How long would it be before she tried my cell, and what would she do when I didn't answer? Her default had always been to call August with anything troubling or expensive, and I know in my heart that my mother will fret about August's absence long before she worries about mine.

Would Mr. Luddy wonder where I was? Not likely. Henri Sallman would have. He covered Quebec for the *Star* and gave me my first job out of McGill, not because of who I was related to—I certainly didn't tell him—but because I knew the city.

Cassius didn't like the job, the hours, or the pay, and he hated Henri.

Then one day he announced he'd found a job that paid better, had better hours and better benefits at the prestigious Galerie Jerome. Mr. Jerome Luddy obviously did know who I was related to. He was always so quick to tell me how indispensable I was, but even quicker to give me time off whenever I asked. I'm sure the second he heard that August was dead, the only thing that he felt was relief.

A bird flits up into the eaves of the cabin, carrying a mouthful of pale-gray fluff.

The only people likely to notice my absence are the followers of my Art_Tarts Instagram account where I combine the best of Montreal's contemporary art scene with must-try makeup.

I crane my head, following the little bird into the depths of the eaves at the little home of twigs and dry leaves lined with wolf fur.

Something squeaks and I look over my shoulder to a bed empty except for the chaos of bloodstained sheets.

The faucet squeaks again and water splashes to the floor of the shower stall. Arthur hadn't closed the door so I can see him, fully clothed, one hand propped against the wall, while a thin spray of water soaks into his T-shirt.

He lifts his head to the shower and lets it drain into his mouth.

"Do you need help?" I ask from the door.

He shakes his head and turns the squeaking knob a little more. I know how long it takes for the water to warm up and how cold it must be. A blood-flecked stream swirls around the drain.

He pulls on the hem of his damp shirt and grimaces.

"Whatever your problem is with me, you need me as much as I need you. The only way we're going to get out is together."

He splashes a handful of water onto his face.

"Out of the shower?"

"*Not out of the shower.* Out of *here.* This…this place. I have money. Once we get to Montreal, I will make arrangements to send you anywhere. Toronto, New York, LA, wherever."

He pulls at his sleeve, shifting his elbow closer in. "Why would I want to leave Homelands?" he asks, and pulling one arm in, he manages to peel off his shirt, exposing an expanse of ruined skin and opened flesh that makes him look like someone only just barely failed to turn him inside out.

The water runs over him and more rust-red flakes swirl around the drain.

"Have you *seen* what they did to you?" I ask.

He turns off the water and steps toward the sink. He takes a look at the wreckage of his chest and dabs with the wet T-shirt at the dried blood around the gouges.

"Hmm," he says. And begins to soap up the T-shirt, alternately squeezing and scrubbing with one hand.

"I know it's got to be hard for you to focus, but can you stop messing with that shirt for a minute." I point to his chest. "I need to know… Did they do this to you because of me?"

"Because of you?"

"Because you were nice to me. Because you gave me boots?"

"What are you talking about?" he says, letting the soapy

water out of the sink. "Why would they claw me over a pair of boots?"

"*That's what I'm asking you.*"

He frowns and shakes his head. "They clawed me," he says, filling the sink again with clear water, "because I killed a wolf. Not just any wolf but Victor, our Deemer, our thinker about the law."

"So it didn't have anything to do with me?"

"Not really. Not directly, anyway. You came with the hunters but it was August who sent them, and Victor was the one who betrayed the Great North to them. Victor imagined that when August's hunters took their trophies and the strongest wolves were dead, he would be the Alpha of whatever was left.

"If we'd had time, the Pack would have found him guilty and he would have died, but the Iron Moon was coming and we didn't have time. I did what I did so the Pack could face the danger in front of them without worrying about a traitor behind them, but I still broke the law and had to be punished." He shrugs and grimaces. "Usually the penalty is death, but Silver, the new Deemer, decided that because Victor had betrayed us, he did not deserve the law's protections. So she clawed me instead."

He wrings out the T-shirt and hangs it over the towel bar.

"They should be treating you like a hero. Instead they ignore you even though you clearly need help."

"The ignoring is part of the punishment. A Clawing is not just the act of being clawed. It is meant to remind a wolf who has committed a great crime what the loss of Pack means.

What it means to be vulnerable and alone. The Pack cannot tolerate weakness, but by ignoring me, as you put it, they pretend that I am not. Weak."

He hooks his thumbs over the bloodstained waistband of his sweats, and they slither down his legs to the floor in a breath of damp and rust. A thin path of dark hair leads down, down, down... I spin around quickly, thwacking into a towel hook on the door.

"*Owwww.*" I press my hand to my forehead. "Don't *do* that."

"What did I do?"

"That." I motion with my free hand to what I presume is the unseen area of his pelvis.

"Ahh. I thought it was just Lorcan, but you have a generalized aversion to genitals."

"I don't have any *aversion.* I've seen a zillion of them."

"A zillion? How many is a zillion?"

"*It's not a real number.*" I could just scream. I'm going to have a bruise right above my temple, and my concealer is in my suitcase in the back of a pimped-out van with a bunch of old farts. "It's just a thing you say. The point is I only want to see them when I want to see them."

"That is a tautology. Of course you want to see them when you want to see them. You cannot expect wolves to accommodate your eccentricities, but I will do what I can."

"It's not an eccentricity, it's... Never mind. Can I turn around?"

"Yes."

Oh god.

And this time when I spin back, I crack my knee into the doorframe.

"I thought you said I could turn around." I gingerly touch my knee. That is going to swell.

"I did and you could."

"I thought you meant you were decent. Will you just cover up?"

After some shuffling, Arthur says, "Done."

I suppose, technically, he's done what I asked. That tiny towel is draped around his hips, like the fig leaf added to statues by more prudish eras, but it certainly doesn't make anything better, that damp cloth slung low.

But it's too late to make anything better. The image is already seared in my brain.

Arthur's body, torn in half by a serrated red riband from his right shoulder to his left hip. Newly freed blood rolls down his chest, curving at each rib across the ridged plateau of his belly, and seeps into the towel slung low around his pelvis and the thick, soft cock that is just barely hidden.

I try to remind myself who I am. I am Otho Martel's daughter. I am August Leveraux's niece. I am Cassius Despres's fiancée.

How can that not be enough?

Arthur bends his head to the side and looks into my eyes, and I feel like it isn't enough and that it never has been.

Chapter 8

Arthur

I HAVE NEVER HEARD SADNESS SUNG IN SKIN BEFORE. IT is racked and hiccuping and painfully private, not at all like the hollow ache launched into the sky by wolves until it is joined by the whole pack so that one wolf's pain will be shared among all of us.

So that no wolf will be *ansangere*, a singer alone.

Once I pull on clean sweats, I sit on the mattress where the Shifter collapsed, the pillow clutched to her chest, singing her song of sadness. I clear my throat and join the Shifter in her song. Try at least.

"What do you think you're doing?" she asks.

"No one should sing the song of sadness alone," I answer, "but I've never done it in skin."

She looks at me for a moment and starts singing her song louder. Her face turns red and she rubs roughly at her eyes with her forearm. Her lids are swollen and her lashes are spiked and her cheeks are wet with a vitreous hemorrhage.

I hold her head in my hands, checking her eyes, though I cannot see what injury caused the hemorrhage. When I lick her face, it is salty.

"*Stop it*," she says and pushes me away.

"Your eyes are leaking. I—"

"My eyes are not *leaking*. I'm *crying*. See?" She jabs her finger into her cheek. "These are tears. Are you telling me you don't cry?"

I shake my head.

"Yeah, well, that must be nice," she says, burying her face in her hands. "Never being sad."

"I didn't say we weren't sad. Just because we don't have tears doesn't mean we are not sad. We have had centuries of sadness and we have"—I hesitate and then plunge ahead with the hyperbole she taught me—"a zillion words for sadness."

She smiles weakly.

"*Inwitsorh, geomorfrod, dreorigmod, dreorigferþ, morgenseoc, siþgeomor, wintercearig*—"

"Why do you need so many?" she says and props her head on her arms. Her nose is pink and shiny.

"Because there are many different types of sadness. Sadness of the mind, of the soul. Sadness caused by malice or distance or age. Sadness caused by love."

The Gray calls from the heights of Westdæl.

"*Winegeomor*. The sadness of the loss of friends."

And every wild member of the Great North responds.

"I thought you said something about the Pack 'not tolerating weakness,'" she says with a sniffle.

"Being sad is not weakness. It is being strong enough to recognize how fleeting and fragile life is. There is no stronger wolf than our Alpha but she sang the song of sadness for two nights when her mate was killed. It was not weakness for her to mourn a life that is lost just as it is not weakness for you to mourn a life that is over."

The Shifter topples over and curls in on herself like the pea leaves at night. I sit beside her, accompanying her song in the low, stilted howl of shallow lungs. She buries her face into my hip and her hand on my knee. I wait until her hiccuping breaths lengthen and her hand drops away.

———————

"Are you ready, Shifter?" I ask.

"Not quite," she calls from the bathroom.

I stroke the bit of fur gnawed from the red rodent bag. I rub my cheek against it, smelling the scent of our pups, then I set it back on the Shifter's bag. She has lined up the things she brought from her home on the sink in the bathroom. A green tube that makes her lips smell like swamp candleberry and look like blood. A purple bottle etched in flowers and the word GUILT. It is sweet and strong and makes my nose itch. A handkerchief. A brush. A shallow gold box with a mirror and a powder that dances in the sunlight when I blow on it.

"Don't waste that," she says, taking the box from my hand.

She dabs at it with a little pad and then dabs the little pad on her face.

"I was thinking," she says, turning her head from side to side as she looks in the bathroom mirror, "seeing as how you've licked my face and all, maybe you could stop calling me Shifter."

"What should I call you?"

"Julia," she says, closing the gold mirror with a sharp snick. She watches it twist over and over between two fingers. "Not Jules, though, okay? Not Jules."

"I understand. Julia is your name and that is what I will call you."

She nods and puts down the gold box, picking up the green tube instead.

"How about you?" she asks. "I've heard you called Arthur and Omega. Which do you prefer?"

"Omega is my position in the hierarchy. As you are not part of the hierarchy, it is meaningless to you. So Arthur is better."

She stops, the red wax poised at her lower lip.

"Can I ask you a question?" I don't understand why she asks me if she can ask me something, but before I can puzzle it out, she just goes ahead and asks.

"If the Alpha is the boss, what is the Omega?"

"The Alpha is not the boss. The Alpha is a position built on strength and the willingness to sacrifice."

"You're strong. You certainly sacrificed. Why aren't you the Alpha?"

"Position in a pack is determined by challenges. By fighting." I lean back against the doorjamb. "I can't fight."

She sucks her lips together, then separates them with a pop. With a twist, the red wax swirls back into its green tube.

"Can't or won't?" she asks, treading dangerously close to something I don't even discuss with wolves.

I'm certainly not going to discuss it with her.

Luckily, at that moment, she sprays a mist from the purple

bottle with the flowers and the word GUILT onto her wrists and into the air, and I start to sneeze. I wrap my arms around my chest, trying to keep my skin from opening up again.

"You should have told me you're allergic to lilac," she calls to me near the window.

"I'm not allergic to lilac, but I think I may be allergic to Guilt."

She laughs, not like last night when she giggled nervously with Cassius. This is different: strong enough and loud enough to pulse in her throat.

"Can I be honest?" she asks, soaping up her wrists.

"Why do you ask permission to ask questions? To be honest?"

"I'm not asking *permission*. It's just something people say. It's part of making conversation."

"I didn't think conversation required so much work."

"It usually doesn't. Except when you have to explain absolutely everything, and now I don't remember what I was saying."

"You were asking permission to be honest."

She looks at her hands. "Now it sounds like I'm making some big confession when all I was going to say is that while I like lilac, I've never liked this. I wear it because Cassius had it flown in from Paris. Not this little one, they gave that to him for free, but the big one. Anyway, I don't want him to think I'm not grateful."

She turns on the faucet and soaps up her wrist.

"Do I have your permission to be honest, Julia?"

"No…yes," she says, rinsing her hands. "You don't have to ask. Really."

"I think you hide a lot."

"Me? No." She raises her hands in the air on either side of her. "This is all there is."

I watch her arms drop and her mouth tighten. She gives her nose one last pat with the powder from the shallow gold box.

Unlike most wolves, though, I know something about pushing things down deep. About repressing.

I take her the long way toward the Great Hall.

"Watch the wall." I push at the vine-and-fern-covered ridge with my foot. "It's not stable." Two ancient bricks tumble loose, releasing the scent of moss.

A few paces later, glass crunches beneath my feet, muted by the decades of leaf litter.

"Where are we?"

Birds fly from what was once a peaked roof. "This used to be a farm; now it's a place for swallows and mice." I step carefully around the mossy bricks that once formed a chimney. "We have a picture of the farm. This used to be the front door. There used to be carved-wood columns on either side with lilacs on either side of those. They'd been cut and trained to look like little round trees. Over time, all the things that didn't belong crumbled—the roof, the walls, the door, the columns—everything except for one lilac that was strong enough to survive and now it does belong."

One of the winds that begins on Westdæl's summit races down the mountain's slope and hits a cottonwood hidden in the forest, loosing a thousand downy seeds that float gently like snowflakes in the sun.

A leggy branch of the lilac that looks nothing like a lolli-pop bobs up and down, releasing the fragrance of its short-lived flowers, and the plea of the phoebe dwindles overhead.

Plee.

Plee.

Plee.

Chapter 9

Julia

I'VE SPENT MY LIFE IN THE CARE OF STRONG MEN. My father called me "princess" and said I had nothing to worry about as long as he was there. August called me "girl" and said I had nothing to worry about as long as he was there. Cassius called me "Jules" and said I had nothing to worry about as long as he was there.

"What is it?"

"Gnocchi," Arthur says, pointing to the bowl with pale dumplings in a creamy tomato sauce. "Use the ladle to stir in the butter. There's Parmesan somewhere…"

Arthur is nothing like them. He helps me navigate this strange world but doesn't treat me like a glass figurine, fragile and in need of a constant polish of compliments.

I don't actually miss it as much as I thought I would.

I stir in the butter and ladle it into a bowl, top it with Parmesan, then thoughtlessly add a salad of grilled vegetables with feta and red onions as well as a plank-sized slice of olive rosemary bread that I bite into immediately. A drop of salty olive oil escapes, but since I'm balancing the plate in one hand and my plank of bread in the other, I wipe it against my wrist.

"Jules?"

Fuck.

Cassius calls me "Jules" because, he says, I am sparkling and expensive.

I freeze, the only sparkling the butter glistening on the top of my creamy tomato gnocchi and the olive oil shining on my mouth and wrist.

"Is that all yours?" Cassius asks, looking at my cheeks distended by half-chewed bread.

I begin to choke and Arthur eyes me curiously.

"This?" I mumble, holding up the gnocchi while trying desperately not to spit crumbs. "It's his. He needed help?" I glare at Arthur, hoping he understands my tacit plea.

But I don't think Arthur would understand a tacit plea if it hit him with the terminal velocity of a meteorite. "That's yours," he says, lifting his plate. "I've got mine right here." I watch him head toward the table with the rest of the 12th, and when my head is turned, Cassius presses his cock against my ass.

My overfull bowl of gnocchi sloshes.

"Missed me?" Cassius whispers. "Missed *this*?" I can feel the sly grin in his voice.

"Every night." I say, still searching for someplace to put the bowl and the bread.

"But not during the day?" The tone is jesting, but I know better than to treat it that way.

"Of course, during the day too. Always. You know that. Every second." I drop my voice, trying to be as seductive as it's possible to be with tomato sauce running down my fingers. "I can't wait to get out of here."

Somehow that was the wrong thing to say, because Cassius pulls abruptly away, his face angry.

Shit.

"I am working on it," he hisses. "You have no idea what's involved."

"I'm sorry, Cass. Of course, I don't." My hands full, I push my hip against him.

"Move it, Shifter."

Cassius rolls back his shoulders, his eyes narrowed, his lip curled and a kind of conspiratorial look that I know means "watch this." But this time when Cassius wheels around, it's not a man, it's a woman who rolls her own shoulders and lowers her head and from the depth of her chest lets go with a snarl that makes me step back.

A banging rings through the floorboards and everyone swivels to look at the Alpha squatting next to a dark-gray wolf. The pommel of her dagger is still vibrating on the floor, and while her head is next to the wolf's muzzle, I feel the weight of her eyes on us.

By the time I turn around, Cassius is sitting, his head over his food, a foul look on his face.

Somehow, I know I'm going to pay for that. I don't know exactly what I did, but I'm going to pay for it.

I sit next to Arthur, my gnocchi cold.

"Thanks, by the way, for your help with Cassius."

He looks at Cassius with the expression of someone walking into the middle of a movie he hadn't bought tickets for.

"I did not help."

"It was sarcasm." I pour water on a cloth napkin. "You do understand sarcasm, don't you?"

"Not really. I didn't get that far in Human Behaviors."

"It's… It's not worth explaining is what it is." I wipe the tomato sauce from my hand. I glance toward Cassius again and shudder, wrapping my arms in front of my chest.

"Why does your bedfellow make you so small?" Arthur asks.

"What?"

"Your bedfellow. Why does he make you so small?"

"He's not my *bedfellow*, he's my fiancé. And he doesn't make me *small*. He watches out for me. Loves me."

Arthur watches Cassius intently though I wish he wouldn't.

"Whenever he looks at you or talks to you, you become"—Arthur drops his chin to his chest—"small." He curls his arms around himself. "Even your voice becomes quiet and careful and everything is a question and you say sorry for I don't know what and—"

"*That's not true.*"

I unwrap my arms and flip my hand so he can see my almost complete wedding suite. The promise ring, the framing ring, and the fucking twelve-carat engagement ring with internally flawless clarity. "See this?" I wiggle my ring finger. "Cassius gave these to me as symbols of his promise to care for me forever. And when we get out of this hellhole, we will get married and we will be together. Forever."

I stab my fork into the bowl of gnocchi and chew stubbornly, tasting just how long and cold and rubbery forever with Cassius will be.

Chapter 10

Arthur

A DULL SEAX IS THE SIGN OF A WOLF WHO IS COMING apart. The pack will eye them uneasily and wolves lower down in the hierarchy will challenge them and win.

My seax is not dull. The honed blade cuts easily into my thumbnail. The point slides into the gray weathered wood of the stump in front of the dormitory.

With two hands, I hold a large, well-used T-shirt against the dagger's edge and saw gently through the hem. After that, the blade moves through the fabric like water, turning it into a long strip that I loop over my shoulder so it won't drag on the ground.

Wiping my blade on the sleeves that are left, I put it back in its sheath and start to unbutton my shirt.

"What are you doing?" Julia asks, taking a bite from one of the large bright apples we get from Offland. She doesn't seem to mind that they taste like cardboard.

"I'm going to work in the Summer Gardens."

Tying a knot into one end, I tuck that into my waistband. Then I start the laborious process of winding my makeshift bandage around my chest so it will reinforce the ruined cage of my skin during the hoeing and spreading and staking and bending and stretching.

"They're making you *work*?"

"No one's *making* me work. I work because that's my responsibility."

"I thought I was your responsibility. That's what the guy with the ponytail said."

I wave my hand dismissively. "Lorcan didn't do that to take care of you. He did that to take care of me when I was first injured. Now I don't need that care, and you never did."

"That's not true. You're *still* injured. You're bandaging yourself as we speak." She jabs her hand toward me. "And I do need care. I don't even know how to get to *breakfast*. If you're working, what am I supposed to do?"

"I don't know the answer to that. That is something for you to decide." I go back to wrapping my torso but the fabric's gotten twisted. Grinding my teeth, I set about the painful process of undoing what I'd done until my weakened right arm drops and I close my eyes, waiting for the throbbing to go away.

"Let go?" Julia lifts the fabric, her cool fingers pushing the knotted end deeper under my waistband. Then she reaches around, unspooling the skein and smoothing it against me.

Her hand is gentle as she touches my naked skin. This is the one touch that pack crave enough to put aside their wild, even if only for a little while.

With a sudden thickening ache, I understand why.

I try not to. I try to focus on something else. I try to read the history written in the rings of the gray stump. The drought that stunted it. The high temperature that made it blossom. The lightning that scarred it. The proximity with another life that thinned it, attenuated it, made it more vulnerable until eventually it became unstable and fell.

"Lift your arms," she says, standing closer, her hands passing around me in cycles. Forward, around, touch, draw back.

A touch, a stroke, a caress, a scrape.

Pain. Pleasure.

Then the last turn is made and the last end is tucked and she stops, behind me still and waiting. Her breath like liquid warmth licks against my neck before draining down my spine and unleashing throes worse than the pain of being torn open by wolves.

At least with that, I knew the pain would eventually fade.

When her arms tighten, I feel first the sweep of hard points against my shoulder blades, then a crush of softness, then her hands flitting over the bandage until they sweep thoughtlessly against the crown of my cock.

I grab my shirt and stumble forward, my fingers moving without thinking along the placket, as I try to button everything up again.

The 12th pretends not to notice that I can't raise my right arm higher than my chest or how many blows it takes for me to drive a metal spike into the ground to make a hole for the wood from last year's trellis.

No matter how hard I work, I can't keep my mind from

wandering to Julia. I don't understand what she was doing. I have no experience of humans—or of any females for that matter. None of our own would take the risk.

Unable to reach the top where the two poles intersect, I lay them down and lash them slowly on the ground.

She has a bedfellow. If she were pack and I wasn't what I am, I would have to fight Cassius for *cunnan-riht*, for fucking rights.

What does she think she's doing?

The back door bounces closed. Julia followed me wordlessly all the way to the Great Hall, then slipped inside. She must have gone to the kitchen and the library because she sits on the low steps, a muffin in one hand and a book open on her lap. My ears strain for the whispered sweep of pages as though something in them will help me understand.

The pages stay still. Her head is down, but her eyes are not on the words.

I hit hard on the metal spike, and the reverberations course up my arm and into my shoulder. The hammer slips out of my nerveless grip with a dull thud.

The 12th continues to work, using hoes and rakes to ready the land that meanders among the ancient fruit trees, the survivors of an orchard planted by the bankrupt industrialist who sold this land and the Great Camp on it to an earlier Alpha.

"He still bleeds, you know," Julia snaps at Editha, standing near her, sharpening the blade of the scythe. "When he does too much, he still bleeds. Why doesn't someone help him?"

Without stopping the arced strokes of wetted stone

against metal, Editha asks, "And are you not 'someone,' Shifter?"

This time the silence is longer and wolves don't pretend they aren't watching.

Julia brushes muffin crumbs from the book before snapping it shut. Then she goes inside.

Lorcan stretches out his back and motions toward the screen door with his head.

"*Sifeðan*," he says with disgust and Editha nods.

Picking up the hammer, I start again. Lorcan is wrong about her. He only knows how hard it is to prove yourself against the expectation of strength. He doesn't know how much harder it is to prove yourself against the expectation of weakness.

I do.

I have seen Julia make herself small. I have felt her fire burn and then watched her bank it and I know how hard it is to bank the embers in your soul without extinguishing yourself completely.

The door closes again, not with a crash but with a controlled bump. At the top of the stairs, Julia stands bookless, smoothing back her hair with one hand, then the other before taking a rubber band from between her teeth and threading it around. She takes the steps in one stride and grabs a maul from the garden tools neatly arrayed against the wall. Marching toward me, she hoists it in the air, bringing it down on a metal stake with a sharp thud.

Lorcan watches a couple more blows and, with nothing more but a raised eyebrow, returns to the broccoli.

Julia and I build the frames that will hold the twine that will support the peas that will feed the wolves until the sun sinks and the 12th edges toward the tree line, leaving clothes hanging from the branches like so many tent caterpillars.

I start to collect the tools.

It takes longer for the largest wolves, so those who are already wild race to the tops of boulders and fallen trees before springing on packmates who yelp and snap and wrestle. There is a half-hearted howl from Ulrich that no one answers, because it's not a question, just a peevish "Aren't you ready yet?"

When he is finally done, Lorcan scrabbles to his paws and shakes himself off, shooting me one last look along his flank before disappearing.

"Are they gone?" Julia whispers, sitting next to me as I clean the tools.

Turning my head, I scan the woods for the sounds of paws leaping to the ground and growls muffled in muzzles, for the smell of moldering leaf litter and warm fur.

"Yes." I pick out the wire brush from the bucket and clean the rake.

"I'm sorry. About this morning," she says quietly. "I–I don't know why I did it."

Then I scrub the trowel with a linseed-oil-dampened cloth.

"Maybe it's because I'm not used to being ignored? I don't know." She stares at the trowel in my hand and emphasizes the word *ignored* as though I'm doing it even now. "I am Otho Martel's daughter, August Leveraux's niece, Cassius Despres's fiancée, so I'm kind of used to being noticed."

With each name, she had raised her hand in the air, though at the end, her hand falls back.

"That's a lot of people to belong to."

"Are you being funny?"

Was I? I don't know. It was a lot of possessive nouns.

"I don't *belong* to them. I'm just saying I am used to being somebody and now I'm not."

"But you are somebody." I wipe down the blade of the hoe, making sure it's dry. "You're Julia."

She snorts. "I hate to tell you this but Julia? Just Julia is no one."

The ax has a spot of incipient rust that needs to be scrubbed with steel wool.

"So is that what you were doing this morning…trying to get attention?"

"No…yes…maybe at first. I wanted someone to pay attention to me. I wanted to feel like I mattered to…to someone. Anyone." She bends over, her chest against her thighs. She looks toward me, the fall of her hair hiding her face. "Except as I was doing it, I realized that I didn't want to matter to some random one. I wanted to matter to *you*." She pushes her hair back behind her ear. "I don't know what I would have done if you hadn't walked away."

I try to focus on the small tasks that I know and understand. Wolves are so much simpler. Receptive wolves fuck— sometimes fight and then fuck—but there's none of this yes but not yes. This mattering but not mattering. I don't understand this other thing, this human thing. Then again, I'm not sure she understands either.

"Did you think about it—about me—after?" she asks, not looking at me but at the leaf litter at her feet.

"I was confused," I admit. "Wolves have bedfellows, so I don't understand how financiers are supposed to work."

"Not financiers." She straightens up, a smile on her lips and an acorn cap on her thumb. "Fiancées." She bends her thumb toward me. "I am Cassius's fiancée," the hatted thumb says in a disapproving voice.

"Fiancées, then." I dry the pruning shears carefully, checking to see if they need to be oiled. "Bedfellows have to fight if they want to fuck outside the coupling."

"So guys fight over who gets a woman?"

"Females fight for a male just as often, and whoever is being fought over must be receptive. We've done it for centuries; it's the way the Pack has ensured that strong wolves mate with strong wolves to breed still stronger wolves."

I grip the ax and hoe in one hand, the trident and pruners in another.

She flips away the acorn cap and picks up the trowel and the maul and follows me toward the shed.

"So supposing I wasn't Cassius's fiancée. Supposing I was his...his bedfellow," she asks. "Would you want to fight for me?"

"Why do you ask? Is this more about mattering? Because in Homelands, the only way to matter is to be strong, be useful, and be willing to sacrifice."

"No. It's about you. The man who was nice to me when no one else was. The man who cried with me so I would not cry alone." She goes silent for a moment, though I don't think she's finished speaking.

"The most beautiful man I've ever seen."

Now, she's finished.

"I am not a man, Julia, and I am not nice either. I helped you when you couldn't walk because a Clawing requires the whole Pack to witness."

In the shed, even the garden twine has its place.

"Arthur? You didn't answer."

"About what?"

"When I asked whether you would want to fight for me."

I close the door and slide the shaved wood slat that holds it closed into place. "Those are very different things, Julia. I might want to.

"But I never would."

———

As soon as we open the back door to the Great Hall, Julia's hand shoots out, stopping me.

"I don't want to see him right now," she whispers, flattening herself against the wall opposite the medical station. Looking down the length of the long hall, I see "him," Cassius, leaning back in his chair, craning his head toward the front door.

I nod to the kitchen and we slip in, dodging around kitchen wolves busy bringing things out and putting things away. It feels like being a pup again, steering clear of the adults' legs while stealing food.

In the end, we have a towel filled with odds and ends. Olives. Bread. Pears. A container of fresh cheese with walnuts. We wait until more wolves carrying more dishes block the hall to slip back out the back way.

Julia giggles when we reach the tree line, then puts her finger to her lips and says, "*Shhhh*," even though I wasn't the one who laughed.

Near the broken farmhouse, we spread the cloth over a stone and lean against it with our sandwiches of grain bread and homemade cheese and walnuts with Offland pears.

"So here's a question," she says, licking pear juice from her wrist. "What do werewolves do for fun around here?"

"You mean wolves or pack, not werewolves."

"Fine. Yes, what do wolves do for fun."

"Mostly, we run. Hunt. Eat."

She holds up the pear core. "What should I do with this?"

"Throw it. Something will eat it, or if it's strong enough, it will grow."

She throws it, then wipes her hand on the towel. "Are there as many words for fun in the old language as there are for sadness?"

I think for a bit under the lilac-scented breezes while swallows fly overhead. "Not really. There's taking joy in the land. Joy in being among one's own. Joy in eating."

"Not quite sure you understand what 'fun' is."

I shrug. "Well, what would you do for fun if you were home?"

She stretches out her legs. "After work, I'd probably hit the treadmill for a while, then go out to dinner with friends."

I wipe my fingers on the towel.

"In other words, run and eat."

"You know"—she wraps the knife in the towel—"sometimes I almost suspect you might, just might, have a sense of humor."

Julia looks distractedly at the moon touched leaves that ripple against the sky like waves in summer water.

"You miss it?" I ask. "The fun Offland."

She sighs and stands, brushing off crumbs. "Not really. I missed it long before I came here. When Cassius and I got serious, I dropped a lot of things." She twirls around, slipping past me. "I used to dance. I liked dancing."

Now she throws her head back, her step wolf-sure and wolf-light under the waning moon.

"You move like a samara."

"A samara?" she asks.

Kneeling gingerly, I run my hand across the ground. They're always here, except now when I'm looking for one. Finally I find it and struggle up, the samara high in my left hand. "They dance to escape the shadows. Or that's what wolves say."

When I let it go, it swirls in a gust, landing in front of her foot.

"We call them whirligigs," she says, picking it up, "though samara's a prettier name."

Then she tosses it and watches the dry maple seed twirl gracefully away, landing on some bit of earth that may be hospitable or may not. With a mischievous smile, she scoops up my hand, placing it on her hip. She puts one hand on my shoulder and takes my free hand with her other.

"What are you doing?"

"Dancing. Don't worry, this isn't hard. All you have to do is pay attention, do what I do. And *try* not to step on my feet."

She's right, it isn't hard. Or the movements aren't hard in any case. Following her is like hunting. It's being aware of the tilt of her head, the flex of her muscle under my hand, the movement of eyes. All the little signals that let wolves move together, fluidly, silently, fatally.

I use all of that to move with Julia, until her steps become smaller and smaller and the space between us is so tight that not even a samara could fit between us.

And then even that disappears and Julia's hand leaves mine, slipping instead around my lower back, and we are hand to back, hand to shoulder, breast to chest, hips to hips. Her eyes unfocused, Julia sways, each movement a flint striking at the tinder of my body. A cloud rolls away from the moon, its brightness reflecting in the curve of her eye as she turns, catching the glinting of the stones on her finger resting on top of my shoulder.

She pulls her hand away. Head bowed, shoulders hunched, she twists her rings around and around and around as though there is something she can do to make them comfortable.

Chapter 11

Julia

ULTIMATELY, THE GOAL OF ALL THE DANCING GIRLS OF Mlle. Pivot's Upper Sixth class at St. Ailbhe's was to see who among us would make one of the spots at the cotillion known simply as Le Bal des. In theory, those spots were reserved for girls of pedigree and artistic or athletic distinction.

Aside from my years with Mlle. Pivot, I had no athletic or artistic distinction. I had something better than pedigree though. I had an uncle who with one whispered word made even pedigreed people afraid.

The dancing girls of St. Ailbhe's seethed when I received the pale-ivory envelope of impossibly thick paper and impossibly neat calligraphy. They whispered to the boys in their circle, their eyes on me. The boys would inspect me with a dark furtive look in their eyes, but as I was already over six feet tall, most of them agreed that I was too gauche, too nouveau. Too big.

My mother must have said something to Aurelian who must have mentioned it to August who sent Cassius. He was, my mother said when she called to tell me he would be my escort, "like us."

The night of Le Bal des, I wore a dress of fitted white silk, soft and heavy as chain mail, the hem hooked around my finger. The other hand was curved around Cassius's bicep, thick and impossibly strong under his vicuña tux.

Reveling in the flash of the Bal's official photographers, we walked slowly down the thickly carpeted staircase, one step at a time, a tulle shawl clinging to my shoulders.

It was, I think, quite the entrance.

Older than I am by five years, Cassius was old for the Bal, but somehow that too was arranged. So while the other girls were escorted by gangly, boyish *frotteurs* who used the dance as an excuse for rubbing their groins while the chaperones pretended not to notice, I danced with Cassius, whose hand was so wide, it felt like he covered my whole back, his pinkie just brushing the curve of my ass. He was so much larger than the others and carried himself like the ultimate Alpha male. A man who knew dangerous things. A man who, armed with nothing but his boss's dictate and two dancing lessons, took charge of me and my four years under Mlle. Pivot.

"Just follow me," he said. Then he pushed me and shoved me around like bread dough that had been proofed too long. I was compliant because I loved what I saw in the mirrored wall: I was beautiful, he was strong, and the pedigreed girls around us were jealous, which was the main thing.

Last night, there was no dress, no mirror, no girls, no music. Nothing but a wolf whose body flowed against mine like water. Somehow, he managed to keep a slim crevasse between us for desire to drain into. To fill up. To drown in.

When was the triple time burned into my brain by Mlle.

Pivot replaced by a swaying as subtle as wind dying in the branches? When did my hand creep to his neck? When did my fingers stretch up to the base of his skull, exerting the tiniest bit of pressure to pull him in?

When did the moon break through the clouds and make my twelve-carat diamond with internally flawless clarity glare down like a malevolent eye?

━━━━━━━━━

He's dangerous, Arthur is. I feel him standing in the way of my escape from this place. I try to stay away from him and remember who I am. I am Cassius's fiancée, and when we get out of here, I will be Cassius's wife. I will be by his side when he takes over my uncle's domain.

Maybe.

That's in the future though. Right now, I am working with wolves digging a trough for kitchen scraps. It's the hottest day we've had: the sun blasted the earth until it couldn't take any more and blasted it back. I'd sort of hoped that all the sweat and compost would kill any desire for my beautiful wolf.

It didn't.

In the afternoon, when the trough is dug, filled, and covered, Lorcan sprays it with water so the worms can get to work and turn it into black earth.

Ulrich calls to his Alpha, his arms spread wide. Putting his thumb to the nozzle, Lorcan sprays his Epsilon and I can almost hear the sizzle as water hits hot skin. Lorcan aims the hose into the sky and lets the mist fall down until we all sparkle with tiny diamonds.

All hell breaks loose and Inna grabs the hose from her Alpha and sprays it directly at him. He shakes his face in it, his mouth snapping at the water before wrestling the hose back and spraying her, except she holds up the palm of her hand and deflects it to Kyle. Gwenn yanks the tubing a few feet back and Inna stumbles, losing the nozzle, which squirts water everywhere. Reinholt lunges for it and slips on damp ground. Editha yells for me to grab it *quick* before Reinholt gets it again, and I launch myself toward it. Landing on the ground and laughing, I hold the hose aloft while the fountain burbles onto me and the air is bright with the mineral smell of water mixed with the muskiness of wolves.

"What do you think you're doing?"

My laughter dies. It was my mother and the matrons who said that laughter was loud and attracted attention and St. Ailbhe's girls were not loud and did not attract attention. It was Cassius who said it made my cheeks look fat and gave me crow's-feet.

"Jules?"

I pretend not to hear because I'm afraid to turn around. My shirt is wet and muddy and my hair is sticking to my face and my nipples are tight and hard from the cold water.

"*Jules.*"

I step away from the scrum of huge hot, wet bodies who have gone silent and rub my hand over my face, trying to smooth away the incipient crow's-feet, the fat cheeks, and the wild hair.

Then I wrap my arms around my waist and turn to face him, unable to swallow.

"It was hot and I was digging and…and I fell?" I wave my hand toward the trench that had taken so long to dig and fill and cover and felt like a real accomplishment, but now he looks at it with one raised eyebrow, reminding me that it's just dirt.

The faucet knob near the back door squeaks as Ulrich turns it off.

"I'm sorry, Cass," I say like I always do. When I walk toward him, I am aware of how hot my feet are. How heavy my legs. How much effort it takes to shape my mouth into my best smile, the one where the corners of my lips lift slightly and my mouth is open.

Like a fucking invitation, Cassius used to say.

Lorcan murmurs something in the wolfish language and George runs into the Great Hall. Then Lorcan slips between us, like he is trying to block Cassius from me.

"Get out of here," he says to Cassius. "*Now*."

"Why? So that you can have her? I don't think so." Then he cranes his head. "Or have you already let him?"

I open my mouth but nothing comes out.

Lorcan looks over his shoulder and bellows, "*ELIJAH SORENSSON!*" at the top of his lungs.

Other men and women and wolves have started gathering at the corner of the Great Hall, rubbernecking. If they're hoping for a fight, they'll get one. Cassius does not tolerate disrespect. Footsteps pound down the hallway and the screen door slams behind the Alpha.

Her eyes skim quickly over Cassius and me and Lorcan and finally settle behind me, her lips tight.

"Leave," she says to the rubberneckers and wolves at the edge of the gardens. "*Gefædlic, wulfas*," she says without looking at them. "*Quietly.*"

Elijah Sorensson, the man Cassius had thought was the Alpha fights through the tangle of pack trying to get away.

"Elijah, get him out of here," the Alpha whispers. "Get them all out."

"I told you—" Elijah snaps at Cassius.

"You don't tell me *anything*," Cassius answers, but when Elijah grabs his arm, Cassius stumbles away.

"The first thing I'm going to do when I get out of here is—"

"Kill me?" Elijah says with one raised eyebrow. "So you've said."

I keep the yearning, anxious smile plastered to my face until Cassius turns the corner. Until his footsteps fade and then the sound of his angry voice. All the wolves except the 12th have disappeared. But even with Cassius gone, they are standing utterly stiff and still. How is it that they don't understand that the tension is broken and things can go back to the way they were?

"*Ic eom þin weard,*" the Alpha says behind me. "I am your Alpha. *Me behede, wulf.* Heed only me."

I turn my head to see who she's talking to. It's just Arthur. He's standing utterly still, his head down, his face hidden under his hair.

The Alpha bends low, like she's trying to see something. She holds her hands behind her back, not touching him, which seems odd because wolves are very…tactile. They're always touching each other. Their personal space starts where their skin ends. They read lying against one another. They eat with one leg thrown over another's thigh.

They bite each other, lick each other.

"Lorcan," the Alpha says quietly without taking her eyes from Arthur. "Get them out."

Lorcan strikes the air behind him with the flat of his hand, and the wolves of the 12th Echelon turn instantaneously, bumping into one another as they rush for the trees.

"*Mynaþ*, Arthur," the Alpha says in a voice that is half command, half lullaby. "*Mynaþ, þæt ge beoþ.* Remember who you are."

I don't understand what's going on. Arthur is the one who translates, who helps me make sense of things, but he's gone silent.

"Arthur?"

Slowly, he lifts his head, his chin cocked slightly to the side, and I see his eyes. They've changed. The silver has thinned to a whispered rim around empty black.

The Alpha sees too.

"*Rinnaþ*," she whispers.

"Run," Lorcan growls.

And though I don't understand why, I run.

———

I have run six miles on a treadmill without breaking a sweat. This run, the run back to the cabin, is nowhere near that long but something about jumping over logs and slipping on rocks and tripping over vines and being dragged up by an angry Alpha has left me winded. Plus, I think I've strained my ankle. As soon as we get to the cabin, I collapse on the chair.

"I've got to get back," Lorcan says. I grab his wrist. He tries to pull away but I breathe in deeper and dig in tighter until his fingers start to turn purple.

"What," I choke out through the stitch in my side that feels like a stab wound, "is wrong with Arthur?"

He stretches his hand, his tendons moving under my fingers.

"Let go of my wrist," he says. "I'm losing feeling."

"Something happened and *you* need to tell me what it is."

"I am the Alpha of the 12th Echelon of the Great North. I don't have to tell you—"

He screeches when I push the plunger on the little purple bottle because, as I know from experience, Guilt stings the eyes.

"I've had a lifetime of domineering types and I am sick of it." I shake the bottle and point it at him again. "So why don't you just tell me what happened to Arthur?"

"Do that again," he says, looking warily at the bottle in my hand, "and I *will* bite you." He rubs his eyes on his sleeve. "You have no idea what you're dealing with. You need to leave him alone."

"You were the one who put us together and now you want me to ignore the only man who's been nice to me here."

"He's not a man—"

"I know: Wolf. Pack. Whatever."

"Not quite." He stretches his tongue, as though he's trying to clean his eyes, until he remembers that it isn't long enough. "Werewolf."

"Inna said you weren't… Now you *are* werewolves?"

"Only Arthur." He looks through the window at the lowering sun. "I really don't have time, but you need to understand that you are playing with something dangerous."

"I am not *playing* with anything," I snap.

"Then listen to me. Arthur was born with something we call the Baelþræcu, the madness…?" He hesitates, his hand reaching for a translation. "No, the *violence* of fire. Like fire, it has no logic, feels no pain, and doesn't recognize the difference between friend and enemy. It is simply destruction. There was a time—centuries ago—when human warlords and kings valued those wolves. They called them Ulfheðnir or Berserkers, and used that madness to terrify their enemies. Packs knew better. We called them *werewulfas*—manwolves—because like men they would slaughter their own.

"Then something happened in the human world, and warlords and kings wouldn't take them anymore. So the Packs killed them out of self-defense, and whatever it was that made them became very rare.

"We hadn't had one for generations. Only Gran Sigeburg recognized what he was. She was the one who said that he was still small enough. She said to wait and watch until we knew whether he was able to control what he is, and he has. Even during the Clawing, the Alpha trusted him to control it."

Alpha, Arthur had said, while wolves stood at the ready, one at each arm, Lorcan at his ankles, *I can do this myself*.

And the Alpha waved them away while Arthur stared at the mountains and did nothing.

"What will she do now?"

He heads for the door. "It depends on whether he can hear his Alpha," he says.

"And if he can't?" I ask, following him, as he lopes across the grass.

"*Answer me*. What happens if he can't?"

He stands with his back to me, staring into the wooded tangle.

"Then we have no choice but to do to him what packs have done for centuries." He takes a single step, before stopping again. "Shifter, *if* Arthur lives, your bedfellow will not be allowed near the 12th again."

"Yes, fine," I answer, numbly. "Will you come back? Will you tell me? I need to know that Arthur is…"

Safe.

Alive.

He looks at me quizzically; a second later, he is nothing but the flash of red among trees, and then he is nothing at all.

I don't care if I don't see Cassius again, but I need to know that Arthur was able to hear his Alpha. Heard her, like I know in my soul that he heard me. When I called his name and he looked up with those black eyes rimmed in silver like the night sky when the new moon has passed.

At home, I'd kill time by cleaning out a closet. Bag up stuff I no longer wanted for some charity I couldn't name, but pack don't have a lot of stuff, and they don't have places to store the stuff they don't have. There are only two drawers. I fold the odds and ends of hand-me-down clothes I've been wearing. Then look in the other at the book of crossword puzzles with no pencil, an old water-stained directory that says *NYS Government Information Locator Service*, and a thing that I thought was a gnawed piece of wood but now realize is a gnawed hoof.

There is a shirt that Arthur bundled in the corner, and I shake it out to fold it.

It smells like blood and woodsmoke.

I collapse onto the mattress with the shirt pressed to my nose. I don't know how much time passes. I only know that his shirt is still pressed to my mouth and I am still breathing him in when the Alpha howls as she does every evening. I never really paid attention, but I do now, trying to figure out if this Evening Song, as Arthur calls it, contains even a hint of a song of sadness.

I can't tell.

Running to the edge of the dark woods, I scream Arthur's name. There is no answer and I take a step toward the forest, then another, looking back nervously at the weak light through the windows. Two more steps and I'll lose even that. The place is a maze, and I'll never find my way—

Back.

Stumbling into the cabin, I rummage through the things I'd carried with me: perfume, lipstick, a wrapper that once held a restaurant mint, phone charger because the Pack took my phone, not that I'd know what number to call to find out whether a werewolf heard his Alpha.

Finally, a thousand yards of thread the color of tart cherries and blood. The color of the string Ariadne gave Theseus to lead him back through the Minotaur's maze. I think triumphantly to my art history degree. Useless, Aurelian had said. Useless, Cassius had echoed.

Leaving on all the lights to serve as a beacon, I head as deep as I dare into the woods before picking at the spool with my fingernails. When I finally find the end, I tie it to a branch, then stick another very thin, very straight branch through the middle of the cardboard tube so it will unspool easily as I walk.

Now, I start out toward what I hope is the Great Hall and Summer Gardens to find someone, anyone, who can tell me what happened to Arthur. I walk past things I recognize, like the boulder that looks like the squashed face of a grumpy old man and the tree standing above a swale. So much earth has fallen away from its knotted roots that it looks like it's balancing on point.

A bush with thorns grabs at my shirt. Beyond this is a copse of pale birches surrounded by ground cover that smells like root beer if you walk through it.

Something is crumpled against a tree, looking as pale as birch bark.

"Arthur?"

There's a sound like a whimper and I run toward it, toward Arthur sitting with the palms of his hands pressed hard against his eyes, his fingers spread wide, cradling his head.

I squat in front of him, my hand on his leg.

"We need to get you out of here. Can you move?"

His head falls to one side, which I take to mean "no." I look around to see if there is someone who might be able to help.

A squirrel runs along the length of a branch before leaping across this aerial bridge to another branch of another tree.

"Is there anything I can do?" I ask, though I can't imagine what that anything might be.

He is silent for a long while, though he does finally say, "Talk."

"Talk? About what?"

He peeks out from under his palms, and for a second, I see his eyes. See that they are not as black as they were before.

"You," he answers. "Talk about you."

Me? Why me?

"Your voice," he says as though I'd actually spoken. "Brings me back." Beneath the hands clamped over his eyes, he grimaces.

I sit next to him, hip-high in leaves that smell like root beer.

Jas would have been able to do this. She could talk about anything. We were close in the way of young women bound by experimenting with nascent sexuality, but I was jealous of her too. She was—is—bright and effervescent and told stories that made the table laugh. I said something about her once to my mother, not because she was a confidante but because she was the only person I knew who wasn't at St. Ailbhe's and so wasn't smitten by Jas.

My mother waved me away. "Let me tell you a secret," she

said. "Men don't want a woman who will shine brighter than they do. They want a woman who knows how to listen. How to laugh and make it sound like they mean it. They want a woman who knows how to pay attention to them."

It was good advice and I've followed it for so long that now I can't think of what to say.

"Lorcan says you're dangerous. That I should leave you alone."

"*Pfft,*" he says, which I think means something like *Look at me. Do I* seem *dangerous?*

"Someone called me dangerous once. The fencing instructor in my Upper School." It's a story. Jas would have told it well. Would have made everyone roar with laughter. I just didn't find it quite so funny.

"Fencing?" Arthur whispers, his head still cradled into his hands.

"Sword fighting."

"Unh," he says.

"We used to have this old Russian fencing instructor at my school. He had hairs coming from the tip of his nose and from the insides of his ears and he smelled like buckwheat and onions and no one wanted to take fencing. Then he retired and was replaced by a young French instructor who smelled like cedar and wine."

"Liked him?" he asks.

"I wouldn't say I *liked* him but I went to an all-girls school." I leave out the part about how someone had smuggled in a copy of *The Delta of Venus* over the long holidays and how that single copy was passed from bed to bed to bed. How it had become water-spotted and dog-eared. How if Anaïs Nin was not clutched in our gloved hands, she was certainly clutched in our souls and between our legs.

"Anyway, we all tried out that year."

M. Van Osten would make a few thrusts and parries before saying something to one of the matrons armed with a clipboard. I remember my inner Anaïs Nin seethed as I was pushed in front of M. Van Osten disguised in a secondhand jacket, plastron, vest, breeches, and too-tight shoes damp with the sweat of girls who had gone before. Hidden under a mask that smelled of rust and Clearasil, how would M. Van Osten see me? Know me? Know that I was beautiful?

Clearly, he didn't, because he did the same thing with me that he did with every other girl before. He slapped me in the torso with his rubbery saber, and I exploded with the fury and lust that had been brewing inside me. I stabbed and sliced and blocked his every attempt to hit me until what seemed like hours later, M. Van Osten held up his hand and, for the first time, took off his mask.

He combed his fingers back through his sweaty hair and raised his eyebrows. "You"—he bent toward the matron who whispered something back—"Mlle. Martel, are a dangerous fighter. You could be a great swordswoman."

I remember almost none of the men who called me pretty, beautiful, lovely, a babe, hot, blah, blah, blah, but I do remember M. Van Osten, who called me a fighter. And dangerous.

"Did you?" Arthur asks, using one finger to thrust and parry in the air.

"Fencing? No." I shrug, and when I do, my arm slides against his. "I took ballroom dancing instead."

Exactly *why* is the reason I don't find it funny. But that's not for Arthur to know.

I lean into his shoulder.

"Glad you looked for me," he says with effort.

There's something about the way he says it—*Glad* you *looked*—and I lean closer.

"Glad I found you."

The moon rolls across the sky and some bird sings *whew-hoo-WHEEW* against a background of relentless chirruping.

Arthur lets one hand fall, covering his eyes with the other. Then he leans his head toward me, letting his face rest against mine. We sit that way for a long time, my werewolf and me. I like it. I like it more than all the other spitty fumblings and squeezings I'd thought I'd wanted before, and I hold my body utterly still as though this moment were a wild thing that I'm afraid to scare off.

My back aches and my arm hurts and my coccyx—the less said about my coccyx, the better. Eventually, though, he pulls away and I feel the loss like the ache of a phantom limb.

"Are you ready?" I ask.

"Slowly," he says, struggling up. "The world is swirling and the sky is too bright."

I look up at the night sky and the stars and the clouds covering the waning moon and say nothing.

With his lids squeezed closed, he asks if I can find my way back. I extract the spool of thread that I'd put in my pocket when I'd found him. It looks exactly the same as when I set out—still a thousand yards of bloodred string—only now one end is frayed.

I shove the spool back in my pocket.

Yes, I say to myself and mean it. *Yes, I can.*

And I do.

Chapter 12

Arthur

MY HEAD HAS NOT RECOVERED. EVEN THE DUSKY LAVENder of early morning stabs like an awl straight through my lids and into my brain. I try to remember how long it took to recover last time but that was decades ago and there were, as Tristan said, extenuating circumstances.

Julia moves quietly around the cabin until I swing my legs over the side of the bed and lean on my palms.

She watches me, combing her hair, each stroke rough against my ears.

"We need to talk about yesterday," she says.

That's sort of what I was expecting her to say, though right now my mouth feels like dry rot and my tongue like sandpaper. I push myself up, careful not to hit my head on the bar of the top bunk because it would, without a doubt, split it right open like a bruised pumpkin.

In the bathroom, I drink glass after glass of water, brush my teeth, my tongue, my gums before lurching back to the mattress Julia dragged to the middle of the room. I collapse there because I can't make it any farther and it is safely away from the dangers of top bunks.

Draping my arms around my bent legs, I prop my forehead on my knees, my eyes closed. Julia moves the single chair across the room and sits in front of me.

"Lorcan called you a werewolf," she says quietly. "He said they call you that—they call you manwolf—because you kill your own."

I lick the front of my teeth.

"That makes it sound intentional. It's not. And I've never killed anyone during the..." My voice trails off.

"During the violence of fire?"

Hmm. Lorcan has been surprisingly open with the Shifter. I've always assumed that the rest of the Pack knew, but thinking that they might be discussing my condition among themselves makes me feel flayed open, exposed.

"Yes. No. Never during the Baelþræcu."

"That wasn't what happened when you killed the lawyer?"

"Our Deemer? No, I knew exactly what I was doing. I killed Victor not because I'm a werewolf. I killed him because he was a traitor."

She taps her brush on her thigh, a nervous gesture, and looks out the window. I close my eyes again both because of the light and because I don't want to see the wariness in her that I sometimes see in wolves, as though they are trying to figure out if even now it wouldn't be better for everyone if I was put down.

"How often does it happen?" she asks.

"Once. It's only happened once before. A long time ago."

I feel the movement of air against my hand as she stands. The floor creaks as she walks to the desk, followed by the hollow knock of wood against wood as she lays down the brush. The floor creaks again.

She sits closer this time, her shin touching my leg.

"What happened the other time?"

"I don't really remember."

"Please," she says. "Whatever you do remember. There's something I need to understand."

I wish *I* understood. It is, after all, the event that cut my life in two, but gathering those thoughts has been like re-creating a tree after the leaves and branches have been scattered by a gale.

"It was my Year of First Shoes."

"First Shoes?"

"We let pups stay wild for a long time, but eventually every wolfling has to learn how to be in skin. The year that happens is called the Year of First Shoes."

"Because it's the first time you wear shoes?" she asks.

"Shoes are the least of it. When we are in skin, we have to sit still and in chairs and eat with forks. We have to use words we don't know with tongues that are short and thick in our mouths. And when we're in skin, we can't mark each other, comfort each other, puddle together on the floor."

"Ahh," she says, as though some part of her understands what a loss that all is.

"That year, we made our first trip Offland. It was a dollar store. I think Leonora took us there because there was only so much damage we could cause." I would laugh but I'm afraid of shaking my brain. "It was so confusing. The lights were bright; they cast no shadows and didn't move with time. The sound came from nowhere and everywhere. And the smells were all wrong. They didn't tell us if something was good to eat or poisonous or anything we needed to know. Then Inna reached into a cage and picked up a circle of gold, and when she opened it, her face stared back. That's when the screaming started and a man with no eyes tried to take her. Tried to take Inna. Then…"

The chair scrapes as she gets up. I wait for the sound of her step across the floor. For her hand on the door and the creak of the stairs outside.

"Then what?" she asks, because she's still here.

"I don't know, Julia. I've tried, but all I remember is a brightness that bleached out everything. A static that drowned out every sound. My skin burned, and it hurt so much that I couldn't feel anything. And the rest is gone."

The mattress curves under her, and it's so unexpected that I fall into her orbit for a second before righting myself again. She slides her hand to my knee.

"Like now?"

"No, this was not as bad. I heard the voice I needed to hear."

Everything is still loud, bright, and intense. Even the absentminded sweep of her thumb on my jeans sounds like a torrential rain over Home Pond and feels like fire on birch bark.

"Why now?"

"What?" I try to focus again.

"If it hasn't happened for so long, why did it happen now?"

Shaking my head, I move her hand away. I know why and the Alpha does too. That's enough. It won't happen again.

"The Alpha says she is going to keep Cassius away from the 12th. She'll let you change echelons if you want."

Julia stares through the windows, twirling the rings on her finger as she so often does. Then the mattress rises and she stands, and through lids half-closed against the morning light, I watch her walk, not to the door and away but to the sink. After a silent pause, precious metal and precious stone plink on old porcelain.

Chapter 13

Julia

I DROP MY RINGS INTO THE ROUND INDENTATION OF THE old speckled-blue porcelain toothbrush holder.

A month after Cassius proposed, I'd asked a jeweler in the Mille Carré if there was anything that could be done to stop my engagement ring from slipping.

No, he said with a noxious grin. It's the cross girls with twelve-carat rocks have to bear.

I didn't ask him about my promise ring—a circlet of emerald-cut diamonds—that irritated the skin between my fingers no matter what I did. I just kept twisting them, like someday, somehow, I would screw them on properly and be comfortable wearing them.

They were never comfortable, less so in the past weeks when they caught on garden twine and roots, when they felt tighter, a constant reminder that I'd gained weight, or when they scraped my skin as I swatted at blackflies, the miserable clouds that descend upon us biting open our skin before lapping up blood.

They come out in the morning and evening and during cloudy days, which means we are to work the Summer Gardens at night.

It's ridiculous, I say: How can we be expected to see at night? Arthur listens and nods, then asks for a twist tie, and when I pluck one from the bucket of tools and drop it into his hand, he smiles and my complaints fade with a sigh. I pick up a garden rake and dig at weeds that are little more than shadows limned with dull pewter moonlight, my fingers feeling into night earth still exhaling the day's heat with an almost audible relief.

When the rest of the echelon goes hunting, we sit with a bowl of walnuts and a pitcher of iced rose hip tea.

"Is that the Milky Way?" I ask. I've never seen it before. Back home, the light leaks from streetlamps, shop windows, curtained apartments, headlights, taillights, the glare on a puddle, and it's rare to see even a star. Let alone this thing that looks like a white rimmed fissure in the fabric of space.

He frowns. "The Milky Way? Why do you call it the Milky Way?"

"It's not just me. Everyone does. On account of it looking like spilled milk?"

Arthur reaches into a bowl. Something cracks in his clenched fist. He tosses his head back, hand cupped to his mouth.

"What do *you* call it?" I ask.

"We call it the *Weardes Widlast*. *Weard* is the Watcher, the Guardian. It's what the Alpha is called in the Old Tongue. So *Weardes Widlast* is the Watcher's Path."

He throws the shells into the woods.

"Why the Watcher's Path?"

He takes two more walnuts.

"We have a lot of stories about the first Pack, the wolves of Ironwood and their battles with the gods. Of course, in the end, the gods killed them and the whole pack ends up in the Unwild, the land of death. It was white and clean and featureless; it looked like nothing, sounded like nothing, smelled like nothing, felt like nothing.

"As soon as the wolves of Ironwood arrived in the Unwild Eormenburh, the first Alpha, put her nose down, looking for a sign, any sign. She didn't find it but she kept looking, not because she knew there was something better but because she knew there was nothing worse than hopelessness. She wandered for a long time, comforting her wolves when they needed it, fighting them when they needed that instead, until finally after so many eons of nothing, they came to something: the Endemearc, the Last Lands, where it is always autumn and the trees are gold and the prey is fat and wolves' fur is thick and the pups have survived denning.

"So now, in death, every wolf follows the Watcher's Path and leaves fresh marks in the Unwild for packmates who are yet to come. That's the story at least." He holds out the bowl of walnuts. "Do you want some?"

"Are Alphas always women?" I ask, taking a walnut and turning it around, looking for a way in.

"They are never women, but when a new way must be found, they are often female."

He leans his head back and drops another handful of nuts into his mouth. I watch transfixed by the column of his throat, by the sound of inhaled breath, by the tightness of the tendons, by the stretched skin, by the throbbing pulse.

A wolf howls in the distance and he stills, eyes closed.

"I don't suppose there's a nutcracker?" I ask when it ends. His eyes open and he looks at me, his brow furrowed as though he is trying to remember where he is and who I am.

He holds out his hand, two walnuts nestled into the hollow, then he squeezes them between thumb and palm. The shells crack. He shakes out the meat and pops it into his mouth.

I put the walnuts into my palm but when I squeeze, nothing happens.

"You want the seams together like this," he says, holding out his own hand. "Then..." I watch him squeeze again, and the shell shatters with a muted shot.

In my mother's house in Montreal, there's a drawer in the pantry. Inside the drawer is a leather box lined in white silk. There are two nutcrackers and four little diggers for digging out the meat of nuts my mother never had in the house because she didn't like the mess.

There is a pop under the pressure of my thumb and I open my hand, surprised that something so simple would work.

"I can't do this anymore," he says.

I choke on the walnut, because that's *my* line. The one I used to rid myself of the nameless men who were nothing but chew toys for a werewolf princess.

Is he trying to get rid of me?

"I can't stay in skin any longer," he says once I stop coughing. "Tomorrow I am going to change. I want you to be there just in case."

"In case of what, exactly?"

"In case my skin doesn't hold during the change. I think it will but if it doesn't, I need someone to deal with the coyotes."

He presses his fingertips against his belly with a dreamy expression.

"So let me make sure I've got this straight: you want *me* to watch you turn into a wolf, because if your entrails fall out, somebody needs to fight off coyotes?"

"I really don't think it will happen."

I stare down at my feet.

"Look, here's what I'm known for: I'm known for my Instagram account, a facility with Adobe Suite, ballroom dancing, and an ability to hold convincing cocktail conversation about art while looking smashing in festive attire. Now what about that CV makes you think that I am the right person to fight with coyotes over your intestines?"

He tosses more walnut shells into the trees. "Do you know what the Pack called you when you first came?"

I shake my head. I barely remember anything from those first days.

"They called you *Sifeðan*, the siftings. It's what's left when everything useful has been removed. But I've watched you. I've seen what you are, and it's not what you pretend to be. A bitch who is willing to take on the Alpha for a wolf she doesn't know is certainly dangerous enough to take on a couple of coyotes for one she does."

He hands the bowl to me. "Walnuts?"

This is the second time someone has called me dangerous. I can only hope it turns out better than the first go-round.

I pull the blanket up over my shoulders, remembering the days that followed M. Van Osten's prediction, when it became clear that *could* be dangerous did not mean *would* be.

One by one, the girls of my cadre got permission from parents and began looking through catalogs of fencing whites. My mother was silent when I begged her to give permission. She said she would call back that night, but she didn't. I didn't hear anything until the matron ran down the hall to fetch me late the next evening.

Usually hard and disapproving, the matron stood in front of my door wringing her hands, which was how I knew that my mother wasn't on the phone.

"No," August said on this first and only time he ever called me. The communal phone was in a three-sided wood-and-glass box with a ledge for writing notes and a chair that was too low to reach the ledge while sitting.

"The instructor said I was a fighter. That I could be a dangerous swordswoman. It would be like self-defense," I said, using the same argument that had worked for Jas and Mel. "Don't you want me to know how to defend myself?"

"*No*," he said again.

"Why?" I whined. "Everyone else—"

"I promised your father that I would protect you, and I will." There was a noise on the other end of the line. "Close the door behind you," August snapped, and a second later, the lock caught with a bright snick. "Did it never occur to you to wonder why your father—a man in his prime who died of a heart attack—would need a closed casket funeral?"

My father was supposed to be a distributor for an import-export company. I didn't know what that meant and didn't ask, not that I would have gotten anything but the tightened lips that were the sign I'd stumbled onto a taboo subject. I did know, though, that none of my friends had panic rooms stocked with two cots, gas masks, water and a twenty-to-one ratio of weapons to snack bars.

"No, but what does that have to do with my taking fencing?" I asked, painfully naive about the man I was haranguing.

There is a power in silence that lasts too long. As each second dragged on, I felt that power, felt it squeezing whatever rebelliousness I had borrowed from one encouraging word and a damn sight too much Anaïs Nin.

"Uncle August?" I asked, falling back on my wheedling voice, the one that sounded like tears trembling in the corners of eyes.

"Your father did not die of a heart attack. Your father died slowly, cut to pieces bit by bit while still alive. The reason the casket was closed was because there was only so much we could retrieve from the drainpipe in the steam room at the Racquet Club that my wife, his sister, *your aunt*, had taken over for what she called a 'private event.'

"Drusilla has reason to be angry with me and she felt betrayed by your father. Your mother has survived by being exquisitely inconsequential. And that, Julia Martel, is what you will strive to be as well—exquisitely inconsequential. Drusilla dismisses you as a little princess. If she ever thinks that you are anything more, if she ever thinks you are a threat, I will be digging *you* out of the plumbing."

With that, whatever spunk I'd ever had leaked away, like gobs of my father's flesh into the drain at the Racquet Club.

"By the way," August said, "your mother has signed you up for ballroom dancing."

Chapter 14

Arthur

FOR THE MOST PART, WOLVES DON'T WEAR BUTTONS. When the need to be wild takes us, we have little patience for pushing tiny plastic circles through tiny cloth slits; it leads to irreparable wardrobe malfunctions. Sometimes, though, buttons are unavoidable, like for lawyers or for those wolves whose seams are weak and can't quite lift their right arms over their heads without ripping them open.

Julia has never changed. At least that's what she says. I think she may have seen it once, though, and is skittish, which I understand. Even wolves don't like watching other wolves when they are midway, neither one thing nor the other. Without any understanding of what it means to break out of the husk that insulates us from the world, it must be hard to see the point of becoming something so grotesque and so vulnerable.

"Nothing," I tell her as we walk to the edge of the woods. "I can't see, hear, smell, speak, or move. So don't bother to say anything to me because I won't be able to hear and I certainly can't respond."

There's a bush near a covert of pines. In another month,

we will scrape up our hands picking blackberries to be made into jam, but for now there are no berries, just molted fur trapped among the brambles, little wisps of gray and brown and black that smell like pack and make my hands tremble as I fumble with the buttons, desperate for my own wild.

"Wait," Julia says. Using my sternum as an anchor, she begins to undo me. Fingers pressing and tugging, one button at a time.

I inhale all the familiar scents—fur, blackberry leaves, damp earth—and one that isn't.

I lean in closer.

"Artemisia."

"What?"

"I've been trying to think what it is. What you smell like. It's artemisia."

"Better than Guilt," she says, her fingers cool against my skin. "Is it some kind of flower?"

"No. A grass really. It's bitter green and dangerous. Addictive." I suck in another deep breath.

A corner of her mouth rises in a half smile. "Lift your chin."

She models what she wants me to do, lifting her chin, exposing her neck, like a wolf does when they want to say, *See me. I am vulnerable*, waiting in that silent moment for the gentle grip of fangs, the equally wordless answer that means *Trust me. I will not hurt you.*

Not that I've ever done it. What wolf would trust me?

The last button is the one below the notch of my collar-bone. It takes longer than it should but then it's done and

Julia's hands linger over my naked skin as she slides the shirt down my arms, trapping my hands behind my back.

The shirt falls from my suddenly lifeless fingers and we both bend down to get it.

"I'll take it," she says, holding it to her face. When she breathes in, her lids flutter down over her eyes. Her eyes are like autumn: the last green of summer past and the gray of winter to come, sliced through with shards of gold.

Julia of the Autumn Eyes.

I hook my thumbs under my waistband and then stop.

I only want to see them when I want to.

Clutching the sweats bunched awkwardly on my heavy cock, I turn away and sit down on the soft bed of pine needles, then I lie down on my side, my back toward her, my body gripped by the familiar desire to be wild and a new desire, an unfamiliar one, that feels even wilder.

"Hold on a sec," Julia says. A branch snaps, she grunts, and it snaps again. I feel her come closer, and when I look over my shoulder, she is kneeling on the ground, a long sturdy beech branch held in one hand.

"Ready when you are," she says.

"I'll get you in the morning," I answer.

"You do that."

Every wolf's trigger is different. Mine comes with clenching my shoulder blades together, forcing me to open my chest. It is, if I understand this very human concept rightly, ironic.

I suck back the grunt of pain until the familiar feeling begins with a tingling in my feet, the dulling of my fingertips, the itching in my sinuses that I can't scratch.

Gradually sound dissolves in a wave of static; floaters coalesce, covering my eyes in an opaque gray film; my nose is already useless, my muscles stagnant.

I still feel though. The damp prickle of the pine needles beneath me, the warm breeze over me.

And Julia's touch.

She grazes the curve of my shoulder and waits. Then her hand moves more boldly, slow as honey down the length of my chest. She doesn't avoid my clawing, but she's gentle there, pressing her fingers as though trying to hold the edges together. Not so gentle with my left nipple, the one that is still whole. She pushes on it, sending a shock that would have made me cry out if I'd been able. Then she draws her hand along the outer edge of my hip, where it dips before rising to bone.

What is she doing? Does she think I can't feel? What did I tell her? That I can't hear, that I can't see, that I can't smell, that I can't speak, that I can't *do* anything.

I didn't tell her, but I should have, that the Moon in her infinite wisdom leaves us with the ability to feel. To feel the small pain of wounds tearing open and the excruciating ache of Julia's hand on my still-furless skin. My complete helplessness, my inability to respond in any way, makes it so much worse. I can't do anything as she touches my ass before continuing firm and insistent to the inside of my thigh.

Then her hair tickles my waist, her breasts press against my ribs, and her palm strokes lightly down the length of my erection before her fingers curve around one by one and I feel her inhale, then exhale, the warm breath swirling across my crown. My muscles, despite being half-formed and wholly confused, push by some carnal instinct into the excruciating tightness of her hand.

Her hand, her breasts, her breath, and her touch disappear and I am left alone in the burning cold.

When I finally manage to stumble up on four legs, Julia is sitting at a distance, her back toward me, her head and eyes down. I can't stop her from shrinking in on herself around Cassius, but I can't stand it around me.

At first, I chuff at her hair, but she doesn't look up. I bop her chin with my nose, but she only turns her head to the side, exposing the sharp line of her jaw and, when I nip it, a tiny smear of red drips down and autumn eyes meet mine.

I rub her cheek with my muzzle and twirl away like a samara toward the trees that embrace me, the wolves who surround me, the streams that clean me, the blood that feeds me.

Chapter 15

Julia

I'VE BEEN TRYING TO REMEMBER EXACTLY WHAT HE SAID.

It's not like I haven't touched Arthur before: held him as he bled, brushed fingers while passing gardening twine, leaned my head on his shoulder. They were small touches, more...companionable than anything. Then I sat next to him lying naked, smooth skin tight over long, hard muscles; puckered wounds over ribs; soft lips over opened mouth; velvet skin over long, thick, hard cock, and I didn't want the small touches.

As I stretched out my hand, I told myself that it was safe. There were no witnesses: Even Arthur couldn't know. Hadn't he told me how cut off from the world he was when he changed?

Except when I wrapped my hand around his erection, breathing in the smoky scent, his hips jerked forward into my fist as though he were pulled by a string. Panicked, I let go and he fell back down, that string cut.

So what exactly did he say? I replay it in my mind over and over, and now I realize I can't remember him saying that he couldn't feel.

I can't see, can't hear, can't smell, can't speak, can't do anything.

Shit.

Why did I do it? Why do I find myself drawn to him? He's nothing like the men I've been attracted to all my life. Big men. Aggressive, bellicose. The kind of men who owned any room they walked into. The kind of men humans would call Alphas.

Arthur is beautiful and strong and he sees me. Listens to me, even when I'm not speaking.

And then I feel him up like some sleazy barfly taking advantage of a girl he's roofied, because I am a coward, still clinging to the idea that someday I will tuck myself under Cassius's protective arm and replace this strange, harsh place with the comfort and convenience of the Mille Carré.

After an eternity of waiting for the ravening coyotes who never come, the grunts and groans and twangs behind me stop. I hear him get to his feet. Four of them. I close my eyes, praying that he'll just run away, but he doesn't. He stops in front of me, breathing against my hair.

I screw my eyes tighter and lower my chin further and this time when he taps my chin with his nose, I bend my head, trying to get away. When I feel teeth, though, that's when I open my eyes to a huge wolf with fur the color of dark ice over deep water and eyes like polished silver. He is gray and gray and more gray and, even in this form, beautiful.

He nuzzles against my cheek, and I let myself be nuzzled by the felted softness of fur that smells like cured tobacco, by the sharp hardness of teeth and the wet nose that breathes me in.

Then he licks his nose, shakes himself roughly, and slips away between the trees. The cloud of fur he had shaken loose hadn't had time to fall when he is gone.

I take my stick and head back to the cabin.

━━━━━━━━━━━

It was during the summer after my first year at St. Ailbhe's that I learned I wasn't human.

My mother sent Yolanda to fetch me.

"What for?"

"She doesn't tell me," Yolanda said. "She only says you have to come to the study."

Why my mother called it "the study," I have no idea. It's not like there was a desk or a book or anything else that might be involved in studying. There was only an enormous television and a huge, stupidly deep U-shaped sofa that required me to sit on the very edge to keep my feet on the floor. My mother didn't like anyone putting their feet on the upholstery as it was white.

I suppose she called it a "study" because "TV room" didn't sound quite so posh.

The only thing that could make "the study" less appealing was the presence of Aurelian, my mother's still newish husband, and my uncle August. "Here she is," my mother said, taking the remote control out of the little shelf under the coffee table where it hid. "I'll leave it to you boys to handle this."

"Handle what?" I asked, my hand on her arm as she tried to escape.

"You're of an age," she said, pulling her arm away, "to learn certain things."

"Is this about sex? Because you shipped me off to an all-girls boarding school, so there's nothing about sex that I don't—"

"Don't be crude," my mother snapped and opened the door, calling down the hall for a cedar sour.

"Make that two," Aurelian said and followed her.

Neither of them spared a backward glance for me or August, who pushed a button on the remote, waking up the sleeping screen. Something about it made me nervous. There were no ovaries or testes or howling babies pulled bloody out of screaming mothers. Instead it was a blur of green leaves with one word in rough red letters: "Highlights!" it said.

"Usually fathers have this talk with their children." He reached for his own drink, and though it was nearly twenty years ago, I still remember the smell of tonic and rye with elaborately curled lemon zest.

He drank slowly, watching me over the edge of the glass.

"Have you ever wondered why you never go to a doctor?"

"Dr. Pelletier sends in my medical forms to St. Ailbhe's?"

"But you've never seen him. Been examined. By anyone."

"No?"

"And you've never wondered why?"

"Because I've never been sick?" The memory of the nausea as I said it is as fresh as that tonic and rye.

He pointed to a damp circle on the marble. "There are no coasters?"

I didn't know anything about coasters. All I knew was

that there was something coming that I was not going to like, and coasters didn't figure into it at all.

I shrugged.

He frowned and wiped at the circle with his thumb.

"You've never been to Dr. Pelletier, partly because there is no Felix Pelletier but mostly because you are not human." He leaned into the corner of the sofa. A drop of condensation rolled down the glass and trembled, stuttering at the bottom.

"I need a coaster."

This time, I didn't shrug. This time, I stumbled immediately for the door, because in a secret part of myself, something about his ridiculous assertion rang true.

You are not human.

I ran for the kitchen and the kitchen staff who I knew in that same secret place were. Human.

"Coasters," I snapped as things that I'd swept under the carpet of my consciousness started to make grim sense.

Yolanda nodded to the new woman with black and gray hair and the nervous disposition of someone with dubious immigration status. She must have come while I was at school.

You are not human.

It wasn't just our secretiveness about the "import-export" business. There was something else we were hiding. Something that lived deep in our bones, that we didn't dare let out.

The woman hustled to a drawer filled with coasters. *Why do we have so many?* My mind was frozen by indecision because all I could think was if I found the right coaster,

August would put his tonic and rye on it and say something dismissive about how I had misheard or it was a joke or something.

Cork? Too plain. Rubber? Too industrial. Woven? Too folksy. The one with the moon phases? No, not that one. I didn't know why but definitely not that one.

"Pick one," I told the woman who lived in my mother's house but whose name I didn't know. I needed someone else to be responsible.

Her trembling hands fluttered over the silver before landing on a porcelain Morisco tile from some museum shop.

You are not human.

I returned to the study. August sat head back, eyes closed. He breathed in deeply.

"Don't be afraid, Julia. I promised your father I would always take care of you, and I always will. Now," he said, flinching when the porcelain hit the marble with a loud clatter.

Then he put his glass on it and the condensation caused it to slip slightly. It was the wrong choice, but it wasn't mine. I wondered then if I should tell him it was the choice of the woman with the black and gray hair with dubious immigration status?

"Sit," August said, and I perched at the very end of that stupid sofa, so my feet would touch the floor. "Have you ever felt a place on your body that you wanted to itch. Something that needed release?"

I stopped for a moment, looking up to him with what I realized then was an awkward grin on my face. This was, after all, just a sex talk. I remember my body softening with a combination of relief and embarrassment.

"It's not sex, girl. Scratch that itch all you want. It's not like you're going to catch anything." He wiped his damp hand on our sofa. My mother would have yelled at anyone else, but August could do whatever he wanted.

"But I'm old enough… I could get pregnant."

August stopped and stared at me for a moment before scratching the side of his mouth and laughing with his lungs but not with his mouth or eyes.

"Sabina really hasn't told you anything, has she? Humans can't knock you up. Find one of our own, get pregnant, and I will set you up like a fucking goddess." He settled himself into the corner of the sofa. "The itch I'm talking about is something else. Some*where* else. It's different for everyone so I don't know where yours is, but I can tell by your expression that you do."

He picked up the remote control from the sofa arm. "Don't go near it. Don't scratch it, don't touch it, don't stretch it, because if you do, this is what will happen." He hit Play, and the CD whirred, followed by an explosion. I couldn't tell what was happening, because the camera seemed to be mounted near the head of someone running low to the ground. Leaves slapped at the lens and the only sound was panting until, with another explosion, the camera jolted and flopped over, staring unblinking into the tree-laced sky. It jiggled back and forth, then a man's face came into focus. He waved a wolf's tail at the lens and reached for the camera.

August watched with half an eye as more hunters shot

more wolves. Big wolves, small wolves, gray wolves, black wolves, red wolves. In fall, winter, and spring. In fall, they held up their big furred bodies, guns slung around their backs. In spring, they shot into a den. The dying screams brought the adults running, knowing that they would die too.

I tried to look away, but every time I did, he barked at me. "You can look away from everything else," he said, "but not this. I need to be sure you understand what is at stake, and I don't have time to argue the point." He shook his glass until the ice that had stuck together at the bottom broke apart again.

Arguing would require a voice, and I didn't have one.

"We are Lukani, what you would call werewolves. We can change into wolves. There is no magic about it. It's simply a long and tedious process during which you are both completely helpless and"—he looked at my black velvet capris and white silk shirt and fresh blowout—"grotesquely ugly."

The thing is, there was always some game with August. Some ploy. I had to be careful. He was trying to catch me out with this ridiculous story. Make me look like a fool. So there was something about us. A genetic disease maybe.

Lupus? I thought to myself, drawing on my first-year Latin.

"If your mother had told you when she should have, this would not have fallen to me. No doubt she would have been gentler or at least less direct, but you'd be just as confused as you are now. Sabina!" he yelled, his voice louder, it seemed to me, than was humanly possible.

My mother came in. She'd changed into one of the

countless pairs of Venetian slippers that she wore whenever she was trying not to disturb anyone.

"We could use a snack, I think."

"Of course, August," she said, visibly relieved. "Anything."

August stared at the corner of the room, stroking his beard. "You had that black pepper ice cream. Do you remember? That would do."

My mother's mouth fluttered open, then closed with a snap. "I'll...I'll tell the girl to get started on that right away. It may be a minute."

"No problem," August said graciously. "But, Sabina, come back when you've told her."

As my mother whispered away on her silent feet, the painful focus of August's eyes returned to me. "Were you here last time? When they had the black pepper ice cream?"

I shook my head.

"At school, no doubt. It was very good. I don't often have seconds, but I had seconds of that."

I nodded then, speechless, because for some unaccountable reason, I'd started to hiccup.

"Do you like it at St. Ailbhe's?"

I shrugged. "'S'okay [hic]."

Finally my mother came back, saving me.

"Sabina. This"—he raised the now empty glass—"was delicious. I'm afraid I have one more favor to ask you."

"Yes, August?" It was half question, half statement, but fully dreading.

"Your daughter is having difficulty comprehending what I've told her. I really don't have time to do a whole presentation. So in order to cut to the chase, as they say, why don't you show her?"

"Me?"

"Yes, of course you. You made quite a hash of things. As it is, I've spent as much time on this as I can. You don't mind if I use your computer, do you?"

My mother nodded dumbly, staring at her hands.

"I presume Aurelian knows the password."

She nodded again and August loomed over her, taking her hands in his. At first, I thought he was trying to comfort her until I saw him work off her big diamond engagement ring and the diamond-studded wedding band. She watched him drop them both in the hand-turned bowl. How many times had she yelled *That's not a bowl, that's art* when some new member of the household staff had added potpourri or, god forbid, an apple?

She didn't say anything to August.

"I assume you don't want to lose those."

Like a sleepwalker, my mother took off her cashmere sweater, not noticing when it slithered to the floor.

"Close the door, Julia."

As my mother continued to her silk chemise and the embroidered gray wool skirt, August easily slid the heavy marble coffee table across the carpet.

I remember how uncomfortable she looked in nothing but her matching bra and panties. Like me, she was—is— broad of beam. Her shoulders wide, her chest barreled. It's not a good look on her, and she knew it.

"Get on with it, Sabina. I could not care less about the

treasures you think you're hiding. And don't worry, I'll leave as soon as I'm sure you've started."

With a whimper, my mother stripped away even that last inch of camouflage. I'd never seen her without makeup, let alone in underwear. Let alone naked.

She lay down on the carpet, on the track left by the weight of the marble coffee table. She looked at me once, pleading, but for what, I don't know. She twisted her torso far to the right.

"Now, you see, that's her trigger," August started. He kept talking but what he said, I don't know, because I was focused on the way the arch of my mother's foot had started to extend. The way her calf muscle tightened, bringing her heel up to an impossible height. It didn't happen quickly, but it did happen. Minute by minute, her rib cage pushed forward, her hips shrank. Her skin grayed and her teeth extended, no longer disguised by lips.

"Julia." A voice knocked at my faded consciousness. "*Julia.*" I turned toward August standing at the door. "I'm glad we had this chat. I'll make sure no one disturbs you two."

As soon as he was gone, I looked around the room, desperate for some safe harbor. Not the screen that dominated the room with a frozen image of a dead wolf.

Not at my mother writhing on the floor.

Leaning against the sofa back, I stared at the corner, petting the softness of cashmere and hearing the small sounds, tiny twanging and whimpers, coming from the floor until all that was left in the place where my mother had been was a wolf with powdered fur and carmine lipstick on its teeth, its baleful eyes focused on me.

I stumbled back to my bedroom.

My mother had decorated my room in ecru with purple accents as befitting a girl I hadn't been for years. It wasn't the bright, tacky purple of violets or orchids, but the more subdued heathered purple of lavender or asters. My mother had gotten me stuffed animals in the same hue. A rabbit. A calf. A pony. A lamb. Nothing, I suddenly realized, with sharp teeth. No lions or bears. Only things that might be eaten.

Someone knocked tentatively on the door.

"Miss?" came a voice.

"Coming." I picked up my mother's sweater and walked silently past Yolanda, holding an untouched frozen container of black pepper ice cream toward me.

She peered with a confused and weary expression into my room and at the cottony stuffed animal entrails scattering down the hall in my wake.

August had long gone when I next saw my mother, dressed in an elaborate embroidered kimono, with black slippers. My mother rarely wore her hair back because she felt it made her look older. She did now; she pulled it back so tight that it made her eyebrows arch up. She had colored her lips with a thick layer of her signature carmine red.

As soon as she saw me coming toward her, she knew.

She knew that what I saw was the carmine red smeared across the length of the frilled black gash that had replaced her lips. That I had seen the whiskers piercing her powdered cheek. She knew that I would never see her any other way.

I rarely saw her at all after that. We would talk on

the phone whenever I needed her to sign something, but her voice was cold and resentful and her answers monosyllabic.

She got an email account so she wouldn't have to do even that.

———————

In the night, the wolves howl. The thing about the wolves is that they never howl alone or at least not for long. Listening to them here with Arthur beside me, I never paid much attention. They were the other, the thing that was happening outside. Lying here alone, I am very aware that they are all together, Arthur too, and that only *I* am the other.

Skritch.

Skritch.

Shibble, shibble, shibble.

Skritch.

Something has started running around inside, and however long I wait for it to stop, it doesn't.

Skritch.

Skritch.

Shibble, shibble, shibble.

Skritch.

I grab Arthur's dagger from under his pillow where he put it and turn on the light.

Nothing but silence.

A few minutes later, I turn the light off again.

Skritch.

Skritch.

Shibble, shibble, shibble.

Skritch.

I pull the pillow over my head and finally fall asleep.

It's still pitch-black when claws scrape at the lever outside and the door creaks open. Paws tap softly on the hard floor.

Plack.

Plack.

Plack.

Silence.

PlackplackscratchplackplackplackSCREEEEEEEECH.

Crunch, Crunch. Gulp.

Plack

Plack

Plack

Arthur collapses beside my bed with a soft whoosh. I pretend to turn in my sleep, letting my hand drape on his fur. He nuzzles it with his head and sighs.

He smells like blood.

The sky is turning purple when he changes back. I don't watch, but I hear the occasional pop and a sound like sinew stretching on the floor beside me. He stands slowly. His shadow teeters slightly before he gets his balance and heads for the bathroom. He turns the light on, and in that moment, his eyes catch mine. He doesn't hide anything: not the hair tangled with flat, ferny pine; not the dirt ground into his toes and fingers; not the dark, bright-red blood smeared from his reopened clawing; not the older blood at the corner of his mouth.

The door closes, the shower starts, and gruesome girl that I have become, I touch myself.

Chapter 16

Arthur

"We have to talk," I say, pulling my lips back and checking my teeth for fur and tendon and other stringy leftovers that might be stuck there.

"I know," Julia says, finally alighting outside the doorframe after several minutes of nervously flitting around the cabin. "I didn't…" She stops, and when she starts again, it's in double time. "When you said what you said, I thought you couldn't feel. Not that it should make a difference one way or another but that's why. And I'm so sorry."

I look from her worried reflection in the mirror to the unopened tube of toothpaste in my hand.

"What are you talking about?"

"Well, I'm… What are *you* talking about?"

"The Iron Moon. We have to talk about the Iron Moon."

"The Iron Moon?"

"Yes, it's coming soon. We have to be wild. *You* will have to be wild."

"Oh," she says. "Okay. Yeah, the Iron Moon."

She seems relieved, like she has dodged a bullet.

"Were you worried about touching my penis?" I ask,

squeezing a dollop of pale beige toothpaste onto my toothbrush.

"*Oh my god.*" She snaps her eyes shut, her skin flushing. "Do you *have* to be like this?"

"Hmm, you mean like someone who says 'penis'?"

"*Yes!*"

"Would you rather I say 'cock'?"

"I'd *rather* not talk about it at all." She turns abruptly on her heel, and I finish brushing my teeth.

Julia is making her bed. It is a daily ritual of elaborately folded corners and carefully flattened sheets that she performs every day, and though the end result is the same, some days the pillows are plumped, some days they are pummeled. Some days the sheets are smoothed, and some days they are slapped.

This is a day of slapping and pummeling.

I kneel on the floor opposite her, tucking the bottom quarter of the sheet before folding the corner under and the side down on top of it, the way she has always done.

"The matrons taught me how to make my bed," she says as she watches me. "Who taught you?"

"You did."

She shakes out the top blanket. I grab the other end and fold it.

"Julia, I have very little experience of humans and none at all of fucking, but—"

"Wait… Are you telling me you're a virgin?" She walks the folded blanket in.

"I'm not sure what that means. 'Virgin.'"

I take her end and she takes the fold hanging below.

"What do you call someone who hasn't...you know?"

"Fucked?"

"Yes, all right...'fucked.'"

I think about it. Unlike the word *fun*, which we definitely don't have, we do have a word for this. "We would call him *hagosteald*, one standing at the edge."

Like this. Like Julia and I are, standing in front of each other, hands touching, an old wool blanket bundled between us.

The flush of blood that had colored her face drains, leaving her pale. She takes the blanket from me and clutches it to her chest.

"We should make your bed," she says, pivoting toward the bottom bunk where I had folded up the sheets and blankets.

"I don't need it anymore. I'll be sleeping wild from now on."

"So you'll just leave me alone?"

"Hmm."

"Every night?"

"Unless you change too."

"I told you already. I've never changed. And that's the way I'd like to keep it."

She places the old wool blanket neatly at the foot of her mattress, making sure the moth hole in the corner is hidden.

"That's what I was trying to tell you. The Alpha will not allow anyone to be in skin during the Iron Moon."

She looks down at her hands.

"No." She tucks her hands under her arms, hiding her

thumbs and prehensile fingers as though we might forget about them if they're hidden.

"You have no choice. The Great North is not going to have someone calling 911 or Animal Control during the three days when we are without words or thumbs."

The scent of sun-warmed grass and pine sweeps through the window on the *doowhitadoowhitadoowhitadoo* of a warbler.

"Supposing I promise not to? Call Animal Control or whatever?"

"If Shifters were in our position, would they take that promise?"

She opens her mouth but then snaps it shut.

"I do *not* sniff butts," she says, finally.

"Then it's going to be an awkward few days."

―――――――

It's been an awkward few days.

I've stayed wild longer, changing just in time to shower and walk Julia to the Great Hall. Today, I'd been preoccupied with chasing a duck who'd made the mistake of wandering too far from water and too far from clear land. By the time I returned, Julia was slowly making her own way. I run on ahead to the training bathroom on the second floor where the older wolflings learn how to clean themselves with sinks and showers rather than with tongues and teeth.

There is a drain in the middle of a floor tiled with slip-resistant flooring, since little wolves have enough trouble standing on two feet without the additional treachery of water and soap.

Low chairs are arranged around the enormous open shower stall equipped with large unbreakable pump bottles that say

SHAMPOO
(for the top of the head)

SOAP
(for everyplace else)

The moment I step into the shower, First Shoes and juveniles pull up the chairs and gather around. Initially, there is a lot of staring at my clawing, even from pups who have joined me in the stall just beyond the spray of the shower. The older wolves watch my technique, mimicking the way I tug out the burrs clinging to my hair and the mud caked between my toes, making me wonder if there is a test.

"Arthur?"

"Yes, Aella?"

"Leonora says you only gets one squeezes for each body parts."

"No, *you* only get one squeeze for each body part. My body parts are larger, so I get more squeezes."

"Arthur. Why is shampoo for the top of the head and soap is for everywhere else?"

"I don't know. That is more advanced than I ever got."

"Ardur? Do you got a whole squeeze for de peens?" says

Edmund, who like many First Shoes has become hyperaware of genitals. Judging by what follows, this has been the topic of heated conversation already and Leonora appears to have said that one does not get an extra squeeze for the penis, but Edmund is trying to get a second opinion, and a fight breaks out and teeth are used and the pups cower behind me in the stall to avoid the blood and slippage, and next time, I will wash in the Bathhouse.

By the time I've pulled on the clean clothes I'd retrieved from the basement and head back downstairs, Julia is sitting on the sofa facing the cold fireplace, a newspaper in front of her.

She doesn't seem to notice me as I perch on the arm, staring at the bricks of the firebox. The old one had blackened over a century of use, but then it had been destroyed in the fire set by August's men. Now we have a new one, its bricks barely touched by the gray shadow of ash, and August's niece sits in front of—

"I want you to teach me," she says without putting down the paper.

"Teach you what?"

"I want you to teach me how to be wild."

Chapter 17

Julia

HAVE YOU EVER FELT A PLACE ON YOUR BODY THAT YOU wanted to itch? Something that needed release?

Can't he just get out of my head? I'm trying to figure out how to make this thing do whatever it's supposed to, and all I can hear is August's voice.

Don't let your curiosity get the better of you, girl. That is an itch you must never scratch.

Now I'm freaked out. Supposing August's fuckery is so deeply embedded in my brain that I can't get it up anymore? Then what am I? I'm not a human. I'm not a wolf. Just a Shifter with a kind of lupine erectile dysfunction.

I didn't want to change outside naked because, well, *bugs*, so instead I'm lying down on a mattress in the cabin with a blue-and-green-plaid blanket loosely wrapped around me while Arthur sits on the floor, stroking the inside of my wrist with his thumb.

"It takes time to figure out," he says as though I'd actually said something rather than just panicked inside the privacy of my mind.

It's easier to switch my focus away from August when

Arthur puts his hand on my hip and gently murmurs *Twist*. On my belly. *Stretch*. On my lower back. *Tighten*.

Finally, I raise my pelvis into the air, and there is a dull twang like a rubber band at my core that unwinds through my entire body. I feel it everywhere, from the roof of my mouth to the tips of my toes, and now I'm afraid and want it to stop.

"Wait, I'm not ready, I…" I grab on to Arthur's hand, holding it against my skin. "Don't leave me!" I wail, my tongue already loose against my teeth. "Don lee me. Don loo. Don…" The roof of my mouth disappears.

Don't look.

I'd seen what had become of my careful, elegant mother when her nose blackened and mouth narrowed and stretched forward as though it would never stop.

He leans in and presses his cool lips to my forehead before moving to the side, his thumb still stroking the thin skin of my wrist while his beautiful face dissolves into a swarm of tiny squiggling pixels that no amount of blinking will clear.

"I'm here, Julia," he murmurs. "And I promise it will all be worthwhile in the end.

"It will all be worth it in the end."

He keeps up his gentle reassurances until I can no longer hear over the dull static roar. I try to open my jaws, try to pop my ears, but I can't and I'm left with nothing except the warmth of his hand and the soft stroking of his thumb.

Clinging to his touch, I enter a dark place where my body is buffeted by invisible forces that bend me to some will no longer my own, remaking me from inside and out. His hand holds me while my bones contort, muscles churn, organs shift. My skin itches, my tendons throb, the only pain from the tearing of a shallow scrape I'd gotten from the blackberry bush. What must Arthur have gone through, I wonder, and how—*how?*—can it possibly be worthwhile in the end?

Eventually the itching and twanging and rebuilding sub-side and I feel warm, too warm. Arthur's hand is still there. I can feel the pressure of it but not the intimacy of skin against skin because there is a layer of hair between us.

Not hair.

Fur.

Something brushes against my back, and I turn my head to see who it is: but it's not a who. It's a breeze coming from the window moving against me, a physical thing that strokes my hair.

Not hair, I remind myself again.

Fur.

The breeze brings with it not only the touch on my back but a terrifying confusion of smells and sights and sounds all jumbled together like a broken mosaic.

Arthur caresses my cheek—muzzle?—and whispers my name over and over.

"Let's take it slowly," he says. "We are always so aware of what we lose when we put on skin. I've never really thought of how overwhelming it must be to be wild for the first time."

I raise my face to his, but my nose is so long I hit Arthur in the eye.

Bop.

He will change too, soon, and we will run Homelands. That's what he tells me.

Run?

I don't think he understands who I am. I am the girl who made a statement senior year by walking the hundred-yard dash in high heels and a pencil skirt. I look down at my feet.

There are no high heels now, only broad, ungainly paws with dark claws and gray fur that follow me when I try to back away from them.

Arthur is well into his change when from somewhere in the distance, a sound rolls across the hills. It's a wolf's howl no different from the dozens I've heard since first coming to Homelands, when they reminded me of the babbled screams of drunks on the street after closing time.

Now, I hear it for what it is: it is a question that wraps around my heart, envelopes my soul.

"Are you?" it asks.

Are you wild?

Are you with me?

Are you?

And before the last yearning vibration of the question ends, scattered wolves answer.

We are.

We are.

We are.

I lean into my ungainly, bestial front paws and call out a broken, quiet *growlp*.

I am.

Given how long it took me to stand upright, there's no way I will ever run.

Arthur doesn't try to help; he just walks patiently beside me. When I fall down the three short steps that lead from the cabin, he doesn't coddle me or fret over me or make ill-considered jokes about my clumsiness.

He waits while I take my first tentative step on the cold evening earth of Homelands. When I take my second and trip over my back feet—paws!—he circles slowly around me, over and over as I watch the pattern of steps. The bright moon is high in the sky by the time we make it to the tree line.

Is it possible I have lived only half a life?

There is so much more to this world than I ever imagined, and I discover it in dribs and drabs as I stagger and trip.

Musky amber and resin.

[Stumble.]

Green and newly raw.

[Stumble.]

Torn earth.

[Stumble.]

Gnawed wood.

[Stumble.]

Iron.

All of this vast tangle prickles at my consciousness, but I can't make sense of it until I find the end of one thread that leads me through the maze. It starts with a tree and a deer. I pick out her trail—How do I know it's female?—from the tangle and head toward rubbed bark where she is followed by a coyote—How do I know he came after?—then I start to move faster.

When I was very young, I made a zoetrope out of an oatmeal carton on a dowel. I'd carefully carved out narrow windows and affixed a printed strip with disappointingly static birds inside. It was only when I twirled the dowel between my sticky palms that the birds inside flew.

It's the same here. As I move faster, the story of my deer flies. Rubbed bark, a sickly-sweet smell. My deer is not well. Coyote markings. Churned mud.

Blood.

I race ahead to find out what happened next until Arthur leaps at me, snarling, his teeth around my jaw, his body an implacable boundary. I growl back because I have finally found this story and I need to see it through to the end, but Arthur stands firm, his chest against mine, his teeth clamped tight.

Finally, I pay attention. I'd been so fixated on the ground below that I hadn't seen the river of stars formed by a break in the trees. I stop pushing and Arthur lets go, though he stands close; I know he will bite me again. This time, I move slowly to the river of dark in front of me, a chasm carved by a stream that no longer runs this way and so it no longer sounds or smells like water. At the bottom among a jumble of smooth rocks is the deer's carcass.

Coyotes look up from their meal, eyes glinting bright in the moonlight. One, bigger than the rest, moves away, trying to decide whether to let her little pack eat or make them flee.

I step away from the edge. Let them eat. I know now how the story ends.

When I lean my head against Arthur, he chuffs out a breath and I feel it move down in ripples across the fur at my shoulder.

He turns and heads down the edge of the gorge, his head curved back, watching me along his flank. I give myself a shake vigorous enough to unsettle my footing and fill the air with bits of fur and forest and follow him to a safer crossing.

Arthur and I have no words, and yet in this moment, I feel known by him in a way that I never felt with Cassius in the thirteen years since Uncle August first sent him to accompany me to Le Bal des.

Arthur is aware of me. And I am aware of him, aware of the white framing of his eyes that shows me where he's looking. Aware of the twitch of his ear that tells me where he's listening. Aware of the warmth of his body near mine. Aware of what is said and what is unspoken.

What neither of us will say.

———————

Wolves cooped up during blackfly season become increasingly anxious and unrestrained.

A fight breaks out between two wolves of the 13th who crash into the table. It ends the way most of these do: their Alpha drags them apart and bangs them around. When they submit, she comforts them.

A moment later, a pup yelps, followed by the skittering of

tiny claws, and the Alpha immediately leaps over the table. One hand holding a crumbling scone, the other wrapped around Cassius's collar. She throws him toward Elijah who drags him away, his feet pounding on the floor, his hands clawing at the fabric stretched tight around his neck.

Since Arthur's brush with madness, I haven't seen Cassius. Not beyond the occasional glimpse before Elijah hurries him out the door or Lorcan holds the 12th back. On those occasions, I cower in the back to avoid his judgmental eyes.

Hunh. That's interesting. The Alpha stays low, sitting on the floor with Constantine next to her.

I met Constantine only once. Once before the wolves, I mean. It was the day of my father's funeral. My mother and I stood stunned at the side of the raised oval holding the metal casket surrounded by red velvet ropes and murmured our thanks to the long line of mourners, very few of whom we recognized but all of whom seemed anxious that August had noted their presence.

My uncle himself spent the day shadowed by a tall, silent man who was always the exact same distance behind him, more like an accessory worn on August's right shoulder than like a man. So I was shocked when he stepped away from August, over the velvet rope and onto the viewing platform. My mother's lips tightened, but she did nothing. Constantine—because that's who it was—eventually moved away, leaving the imprint of his palm on the shiny bronze. Then he came toward us, and my mother, with not an ounce of subtlety, dragged me away.

"Death walks in that man's footsteps," she whispered and pushed a paper cone of water into my hand.

Unimportant and unseen, I watched him after that. Curious about why my mother found him so worrisome. I think it was his eyes. They were the color of moss and seemed to look everywhere and nowhere at the same time. There was a blankness about them. I couldn't tell whether there was something inside him that was tightly shuttered or whether there was simply nothing at all.

But when he talked to the Alpha, those same eyes looked nowhere except at her, and when she walked away, his shuttered eyes followed her, pleading.

A moment later, Arthur stiffens beside me, his eyes sliding over my shoulder. I steel myself for seeing Cassius. I'm wearing neither his rings nor the expression he likes best. Even worse, I'm not sure I remember how.

But these footsteps are different, almost silent, less like a bull, more like an adder.

Constantine holds something toward me. I look at it, confused at first, thinking it's a sugar packet, but it isn't; it's a folded piece of paper emblazoned with handwriting I know too well. I turn away, sliding my hands under my thighs, hoping that Constantine understands the subtle message that I don't want it.

Arthur is less subtle.

"It's for you," he says.

All around the table and under it too, pups and wolves and men and women stare at me, curious to see what I will do.

So I oblige them. I take the note from Constantine, and

glaring into his eyes, I dare him not to notice what I'm doing. Then I rip it into a thousand tiny pieces that drift to the floor.

"And yes," I snap to the 12th, because someone is going to say it, "I know I have to sweep that up."

Arthur smiles and laughs and I laugh too. A loud laugh. Full of teeth. That makes my cheeks look fat.

Chapter 18

Arthur

SOMETIMES SUMMER STORMS ROLL DOWN QUICKLY, UNAN-nounced. Not this one. This one holds Homelands in a shimmering vise of damp and heat.

As soon as we get back to the cabin, Julia bends under the shower, letting the water run over her head, while I brush my teeth.

She giggles to herself and I can't help but smile. She's been laughing at the most improbable things ever since she tore up that little piece of paper. It was as though something that had been trapped inside was suddenly released.

As a wolf, she is curious, attuned, and brave, and maybe that wolf simply can't bear to turn over, her belly exposed, like a possum playing dead, to a fool like Cassius.

When I put away my toothbrush, I knock over her little stack of rings. They have become dulled by a film of soap and toothpaste, these things that once confined her finger, marking her as belonging to someone else. What I want to do is destroy them like she did that piece of paper. Instead, I draw on a long experience of control and pile them one on top of another, into an empty column.

Julia flings back her hair, drenching me with water.

"Hey," she says, bumping her hip into mine. "You're hogging the mirror." She rubs down her hair with a stiff towel.

I move to the side, giving her room at the sink. A single drop of water trembles along the vulnerable place where her pulse throbs before following the trace of her collarbone to the graceful notch.

My eyes follow its slide down to the deep V of her T-shirt. Her nipples are knotted under the thin cotton.

I see Julia's eyes in the mirror and know I've been caught out.

She bends her head to mine, I feel the weight of her, and when she moves, I feel the softness of her cheek. One more tiny adjustment and I feel the corner of her mouth.

"Why," she asks, her tongue darting out to catch a drop of water, "is it called a man at the edge?"

Her darting tongue touches my skin. She sees what she's doing to me. She has to.

Gran Sigeburg was the one who took my training in hand after the incident at the dollar store. She was the one who warned me about the thing inside me.

The fire will not burn.

I had been so intent on one fire that I had never imagined there might be another, one that burns with even greater intensity and that I haven't been trained to control.

"I don't know," I choke out. "Probably it came from a time when there were many packs and dispersers who found themselves at the boundaries of new territories, looking for mates."

Right now it feels like something different. Like after a lifetime of restraint, I feel myself teetering at the edge of a precipice, and I know if I fall, there is no climbing out.

Scraping my fingers through my hair, I turn to hang up the towel. She's there, with her autumn eyes. Summer's end, winter's beginning. The transition from life to death.

"You've got to stop," I whisper as she moves closer.

She stops but doesn't move back. "Why? In case you didn't notice, I'm done with Cassius."

"It's not about him."

Now she moves away, two lines between her brows. I miss the warmth of her body buffeting mine.

"Are you saying you don't feel anything?"

She knows I do. She can feel it now as her hip brushes against my straining cock. I move away, turning on the sink faucet. "It's because I know what the consequences are."

"And what consequences would that be? I can't catch diseases. I doubt you can either."

Bending over the sink, I soak my face in water that will never be cold enough.

She reaches across me, her belly against my hip, her breasts at my back, and turns the faucet off.

"What consequences, Arthur?"

I stay bent over, clutching the sides of the sink.

"You could get pregnant."

There's a long pause and then she laughs, hard and joyless, not like before.

"Let me tell you something, werewolf. When I was fourteen, August gave me what I thought was going to be a sex talk, you know, what it meant to be 'young and a woman.' It turned out to be a talk about what it meant to be 'young and inhuman,' which was way harder. As long as I didn't change, August didn't care anything about sex. 'Scratch that itch as much as you want' is what he said. Then he told me I couldn't catch anything and wouldn't get pregnant." She stands up and grates the towel roughly over her exposed skin, like it would scrape something away.

"So I did it. I scratched that fucking itch. I developed a taste for men who were powerful, who might have the... I don't know, the *potency*, to prove August wrong."

Finally, the promised thunder rolls in from the north. Cool breeze and petrichor blow through the window.

"They didn't and he wasn't."

She pokes at the tower of rings, grimacing when they fall.

"Do you know why your uncle was obsessed with the Great North?"

"Money, I guess? Something to do with Tiberius? Nobody ever told me anything. Not that I asked."

"I don't know what he thought at the beginning but his *obsession* started when Silver became pregnant. It's very hard for us to get pregnant too, not impossible but hard. Something about getting the chromosomes to match up at exactly the right stage at the right time. It can take years. *Does* take years. But August had barely touched Mala when she became pregnant with Tiberius. Then the same thing happened with Tiberius and Silver. No one believed it was a coincidence. Least of all your uncle."

The muscles over her clenched jaws fluttered.

"Since Shifters had stopped reproducing, he wanted our females—"

"*I don't want to hear it*," she hisses.

"As breeding stock."

"I said, 'I don't want to hear it.'" She starts toward the door.

"Not hearing something, Julia, doesn't make it untrue."

Almost as though it was waiting for the door to slam behind her, the storm opens up, releasing the full, splashing force of summer rain.

I close the windows a little to keep the mattresses from getting soaked, then grab a dry towel and head to the porch, leaning against the wall, watching her back as she stands facing the forest. I know she heard the door close and the planks creak but she doesn't move when the heavy drops start to fall. She doesn't move even when it drenches her. She stands like a statue, her rain-blackened hair plastered to her skin while water sluices from fists clutched at her sides.

She stays even when lightning hits a white pine with a deafening crack and the smell of electricity and burned resin.

Only when the worst of it passes toward Home Pond does she turn around, her eyes hollow, a drop trembling from her top lip. Pushing myself away from the wall, I hold out the towel. She's shivering and she doesn't seem to be able to unclench her fists, so I wrap the towel around her shoulders and pull her stiff and cold and wet against me.

"When August told me we weren't human, I already knew. Somewhere inside me, I knew. I knew this too. Or not *this*, but I knew what they were capable of. August, my father. Cassius. But I never asked because once they told me, I would have to do something, which would be so hard. Or do nothing, which would be even harder." Her hands finally soften their grip and her arms bend around me and I rock with her the way we did that one time when there was no space between us.

"I was a coward but I don't want to be a coward anymore."

"I don't want to be a coward either."

She chortles a little. "Sorry, buddy, there's no room in the coward caravan for a guy who doesn't make a noise as he's shredded by a wolf."

"I did make a noise, only you were louder."

Then I bring her hand to my chest, flattening it against my beating heart, and wait until I'm sure she feels how fast it is.

"You can feel it, can't you? How afraid I am?" She nods against my cheek. "It's like I'm standing at the edge of a precipice and I know if I take another step, I am going to fall too hard and too far to ever get out again."

She pulls her hand away and presses her ear to where it had been, listening to the frantic fluttering of my heart. My head bends forward, my lips brushing the border where her hair meets skin, and I breathe her in. Bitter green and dangerous.

Her head lifts.

"So fall," she says, her mouth a leaf's breadth from mine, "and let me catch you."

Chapter 19

Julia

THERE IS A DARKNESS IN MY HEART. I KEPT IT CAREFULLY hidden beneath coiffeur and tailleur and demure, but it was always there. Now, lying on a thin, hard, narrow pallet in an unheated, unlit cabin in this raw and wild place, I watch my werewolf strip above me and give in to that swelling darkness.

As gentle as he tries to be, he is dangerous in a way Cassius never could be and I want it. I wrap my foot around his ankle and pull. He lets himself fall over the foot of the mattress, his shoulders flexing as he catches himself above me. I let my hands wander up the sinew and bone of his arms.

"I won't risk getting you pregnant," he whispers as he lowers himself to me, his weight hard on my body, "so I will not fuck you." The word burns into my dark mind as hard as his cock burns against my belly. "But show me how and I will chase your...your bright ache? I don't know how you say it."

I don't need a translation.

"Bright ache will do," I whisper, pulling him down so that more of his skin touches mine. "When you danced with me that night...had you had lessons?"

"No."

"Then how did you know what to do?"

"I just paid attention."

"Exactly. Then do that now."

At first, he follows my lead—when my lips touch his, he mirrors what I do—but soon he strikes out on his own, trying things.

I've always thought I was a closed book, that no man could tell when I was enjoying something or when it made me uncomfortable or when it hurt.

Apparently, though, I wasn't closed. I was simply a book in a language that hadn't found a reader.

Even as I moaned at his teeth against my nipple, he stopped.

"Why did you stop?"

"You didn't like it."

And suddenly a whole well-rehearsed script opens in front of me.

Our scene opens as CASSIUS takes JULIA'S hand and puts it to the seam of his pants, eyes half-closed, smile half-cocked.

JULIA
Just a second. I've got to brush my teeth.

CASSIUS
(exasperated)
You're fine.

JULIA
(smiling hopefully)
I want to be more than fine for you.

JULIA runs to the bathroom, brushes her teeth, and digs out the lubricant hidden in the bottom of her makeup bag. She heads back.

CASSIUS
You're so wet for me, baby.

CASSIUS pushes his mouth to her breast, biting her left nipple three times. Her right, three times. He continues back and forth while pistoning with his cock. JULIA thrashes about.

JULIA
(praying to get to the end)
Ahhh. Ahhh. Ahhh. AHH.

CASSIUS rolls off, again with the half smile.

CASSIUS
Tell me again how much you've missed me.

FIN

I almost cry because he's right and I hated the way Cassius treated my breasts, my body. Like a collection of sex toys that had nothing to do with me and everything to do with him.

"No. Not like that. Not biting. With your tongue. Slow and flat and then with your lips—" A sharp breath and a low groan put an end to whatever I was going to say.

Yes. Like that.

Arthur has no map to go on, no porn-born preconceptions. I thought I had nothing left to learn, no innocence to be stripped away, but that's because I have never experienced the watchfulness and adaptability of a hunter.

He undoes my own assumptions, making parts of me that I'd never thought of once become magically carnal. He laves the skin at my lower back, bites the tendon at my neck, or sucks at the thin skin over the pulse point of my inner thigh, though that mixes confusingly with the pressing of his cock against my leg and I jerk against him, my hips tilted.

He strokes his hand down my belly, pausing briefly above the heat of my core, where the skin feels especially tight. I hold my breath, waiting as his hand moves lower, cupping between my legs, and I twist myself against him, sucking in one breath after another as though I can breathe in relief from the emptiness.

One finger slides in and it is glorious, then another, then another, and I fuck myself on his fingers and against his palm pressing hard to my entrance.

When he takes my mouth again, he doesn't have to tease me open. I pull his tongue into the slickness of my mouth, and he fucks me with his tongue, and a wire that had been wound tight inside me unfurls and stretches taut and play-able by the rhythm of his fingers until my lungs falter, my breathing shreds, my legs stiffen, and when I come, I suckle at his tongue, tasting blood.

I pull him closer, sliding along the erection pressed so tight against me I can feel the heartbeat of it, see the drop shimmering on his crown, and I know from long experience how close he is.

His thickness makes it impossible for me to make a full circle but close enough. I hold my thumb tight along the underside, and when his coming is inevitable, I press my belly hard into him, so I can feel the throb and warmth of his release against my skin. So that when he falls, I will catch him.

He is the antithesis of the men I have had. They were top dogs: burly, macho, and egotistical. He is the Omega wolf: lithe, controlled, and attentive. I hold him tight against me, suddenly aware not just of my body. Not just of the way skin that had felt used and hardened feels new again. But aware of the way the starved and shriveled and ignored heart of who I am has expanded to fill that skin.

I know that no matter how many men may have touched my thighs and my mouth and my breasts, only my werewolf has ever touched *me*.

Chapter 20

Arthur

"WHAT ARE YOU DOING?"

"Heating it up." I test the towel that had been soaked with rainwater and chilled through. Hopefully, it's warm enough now. "How does it feel?" I ask as I press it to her hip.

"Fine," she says with a shiver. "Okay, a little cool but it's fine."

With slow strokes, I wipe away my release from her skin, then I use my tongue to lick away the last remnants from the curls between her legs, from the gentle ebb and flow of her belly, from the hard line of her ribs, and from the swell of her breasts. I continue all the way up her sternum to the notch at the base of her throat.

"What are you thinking?" she asks.

I shake my head and hop up, taking the towel to the bathroom.

"You were looking at my throat," she calls from the bed.

The face in the mirror across from me tightens. I turn on the water and begin to rinse the towel.

"Should I be afraid, werewolf?" she says.

That stops me. Not because I mind her careless use of

werewolf—it is what I am. It's her careless use of the word *afraid* that brings me back, kneeling beside her.

"Julia…"

"Don't look so worried. I was just teasing."

She's on her belly, watching me, her legs bent so I can see the soles of her feet.

"I'm not going to pretend this life is easy—we are vulnerable to bullets, hooves, claws, a mistimed jump… There *are* many dangers here but I am not one of them. Not to you anyway."

The ball of her foot at the base of her toes is darker, thicker, because that is what hits the earth of Homelands when she runs.

"Julia, I…I am—we all are—hardwired to hear the Alpha's voice; the need to listen to her is almost a…a physical thing. But when I needed to, I couldn't hear her." She swallows and I look away from her throat. "The voice I heard—the voice that saved me from myself—was yours. It cut through everything and for the first time, I thought: Here was someone I could trust myself with. Someone who whatever happened, could bring me back."

She lays her cool hand to my face. "Look at me," she says and sweeps her hair up and away, holding it with one hand on top of her head. A single wave falls down and curls around her neck.

I turn my head slowly until my lips are buried in her palm.

"Trust has to go both ways, Arthur."

Under my lips, I feel the slightly rough skin on her palm, knowing that the longer she's here, the rougher it will get.

"Arthur?"

I put the tips of my fingers to her throat. "This is where we are most vulnerable. When a wolf exposes their throat, it means, 'I trust you.'"

She lies down, her hair spilling across the pillow. "Like this," she says, smiling.

"This is the most intimate thing we do, Julia. More than fucking. It's not something we take lightly."

She drapes her head over the back of the pillow and raises her chin, making her throat impossibly long and achingly exposed.

"What happens next?" she asks, all teasing gone.

"The other wolf—" For some reason, my voice chooses this moment to crack. "The other wolf uses their jaws…" I clear my throat. "But it's so gentle. It means 'I see that you're vulnerable and I will not hurt you.'"

Leaning on my elbow, I smooth her hair back but can't bring myself to take her throat.

"So, wolf, do you not trust me or do you not trust yourself?"

"If you are slighted?"

The fire will not burn.

"If you are angry?"

The fire will not burn.

"If you are in pain?"

The fire will not burn.

"If you are in love?"

Gran Sigeburg didn't ask that but I already know the answer. That other fire cannot burn because all the fuel in my soul is taken up with this one.

Tossing one leg over her hips, I put my hands on either side of her shoulders. She waits for each slow second while I hold back, giving her time to change her mind.

Her hands slide along my torso and over my shoulder blades and toward the nape of my neck and pull me down. I trace the pulsing path of her blood with one dull excuse for a canine until I reach the base of her throat. I open my mouth wide, setting my jaws on either side; not a single tooth touches her, and I ache for the tenderness of it.

In the time it takes for a copperhead to strike, she wraps her thighs around my hips and pushes my head down hard, forcing my carnassials to scrape her skin. The harder I try to back away, the tighter she holds me.

"Stay," she growls, and that single word vibrates through my skull and I fall from the precipice.

Chapter 21

Julia

ARTHUR SAYS IT'S MILKWEED, THOUGH THE TIGHT PINK heads and spear-shaped leaves look nothing like the milkweed behind the lodge that we rented for Thanksgiving weekends back when my father was alive.

I poke the milkweed with a stick.

Nothing happens.

In the fall, I'll come back and then when I hit the spiky beige pods with a stick, they will explode.

Hopes and wishes, my father called the fluffy seeds flying into the sky.

Not so long ago, my only hopes and wishes had to do with flower arrangements and dresses and linens and chandeliers and invitations and the Windsor Grand's kitchens. When did that give way to an engrossing interest in the ripening of snap peas and mulberries and the phases of the moon?

When were my dreams of the Mille Carré replaced by milkweed?

"*Rowp*?" asks a pup, appearing from nowhere, his muddy paws on my leg, his teeth tugging on my stick.

"You want it?" I ask, pulling my arm back. "Fetch."

The pup cocks his head and watches the stick sail into the trees. We're both kind of shocked by how far it went.

"*Rowp*?" asks the pup again, his head cocked, looking between me and the bracken where the stick landed.

"Sorry, *chiot*, but that's the way fetch works: You get the stick, you bring the stick, then I throw the stick *again*."

One little ear turns, followed by his head, then by his whole body. He runs toward the trees, his fickle fascination with the stick already gone.

A woman with pale-blue eyes and dark-brown waves and full curves pushes from the woods, the pup over her shoulder. I don't recognize her, though I have the uncomfortable feeling that I should, a feeling that becomes stronger and more uncomfortable with every step.

"*The Pack*," she says in an icy voice, "does not train its pups into games of mindless obedience."

"Beta?"

"The Alpha will see you now," Tara says. I don't think I've ever seen her in skin.

"But...I didn't ask to see her."

Tara's frown deepens and her eyes narrow.

"You will see the Alpha now."

"Are you telling me that the Alpha would like to see me?"

"'Would' and 'like' have nothing to do with it, Shifter."

As she strides off, she puts her hand to her shoulder where my would-be playmate watches me through the thick wall of hair.

"Traitor," I mouth.

"*Rowp*," he says.

Pack protocol having not been part of the matrons' of St. Ailbhe's deportment lessons, I find myself frozen outside the Alpha's office, fist raised to the door, when she calls me in.

"I'll be with you in a minute," she says without taking her eyes from a pale-green ledger.

I look around the office that I haven't seen since that horrible, miserable, phantasmagorical day when my already tenuous grip on reality was completely untethered by the sight of a wolf ripping Arthur open. That day when I was herded into the Alpha's office, I looked for—and found—brutality everywhere: in the gloomy room, in the walls spotted with skulls and grimoires, in the Alpha who sat glowering from her wooden throne, in the werewolves who hated me and Cassius, who wasn't fond of me either.

A lifetime later, I see the office for what it is: a large wood-paneled room with windows overlooking the water on one side and darkened by the inconstant shade of leaves on the other.

The Alpha's throne turns out to be nothing but a big, wooden chair like bank clerks used to have. Bent over a long ledger in the middle of a desk with chewed drawer pulls and clawed wood, the Alpha grimaces, pencil in one hand, metal ruler in the other, swiveling back and forth on the wheels of her "throne."

The grimoires turn out to be years-old cardboard file boxes: *Getæl. Namboc. Gewiss. Weaxbred.* I don't know what they mean, but I am now familiar enough with the sounds of the Old Tongue to recognize their origin.

A thick binder saying *Gafolpenig* along the spine tilts on the shelf, displaying the disappointingly mundane translation. *Property Taxes*.

My memory was right, at least, about that shelf of skulls, though I remember them as being larger, fiercer. They are all, in fact, quite small. I pick one up and touch the ferocious tips of fangs that meet a matching pair below. The teeth look fearsome but the curved bone under the empty eye seems remarkably fragile.

"Squirrel," the Alpha says from the desk. "Most First Kills are. Squirrels. Or rabbits. Be careful with it." I set the squirrel gently on its shelf. "They are important to us. They mark the moment our young start the transition from being takers to being providers as well."

For some reason, a chill runs through my back and into my thigh.

"The Iron Moon begins tonight," the Alpha continues, looking back at her ledger and her long ruler and her pencil. "We will have no fingers or words in Homelands so you must be wild, but my wolves must hunt and I will not have them slowed down. Your bedfellow…" She holds her finger at a spot and drops the pencil, picking up a highlighter instead.

"Who?"

Taking the lid off the highlighter with her teeth, she looks toward me with one eyebrow raised.

"You mean Cassius?" It took me a moment to come up with his name, like he was a kindergarten playmate I hadn't seen since first grade. Technically, I suppose, he is still my fiancé. It's hard to imagine that I once highlighted and categorized his every like and dislike as carefully as the Alpha does with her ledger. He hates asparagus. Tolerates artichokes alla Romana. Likes creamed spinach. Can't stand fleece or wool, though vicuña is fine. Two buttons, not one and, god forbid, three. My heels should be two and a half to three inches. Possibly two.

My smile should show no teeth but never look forced or smug.

"Yes, well. Your *bedfellow*," the Alpha says, "has chosen to remain at Home Pond for the duration of the Iron Moon. We will guard him. Provide him with sandwiches. You may stay with him if—"

"*No!*"

The word explodes with a violence that shocks me. I look down at my arms, clenched around my waist; my shoulders, bent forward; I feel the tremor of the nervous smile on my lips and I shake out my arms, roll back my shoulders, and grit my teeth.

"You know food is not cooked and brought to you. During the Iron Moon, we hunt or go hungry." The Alpha scratches at her scalp with her pencil.

"I understand, but no," I say, expanding so that there can be no misinterpretation. "I do *not*. Want to stay. With my fiancé. Eating sandwiches."

My thumb and forefinger fidget with the ring that isn't there, as though trying once more to unscrew it from my finger.

"*Ever.*"

She moves the ruler once more.

"Alpha?" someone says from the hallway.

I pull the screen door closed behind me. The 12th has been preparing the Summer Gardens for the Iron Moon, preparations that seem to involve the males drinking a great deal of iced tea and walking the perimeter of the pears and pea pods. More than that, I don't want to know.

Sitting on the low steps at the back door, I look out over the cold frames and into the verdant chaos. Something shuffles through the beds and then bolts out heavy and furry and low to the ground, followed a few seconds later by a tortoise-shell wolf.

Arthur sits next to me.

"What was Ulrich chasing?"

"Groundhog. Once they've built out their burrows, they're hard to get rid of. Too many tunnels and rooms and back doors. Hold out your hand?" He hands something to me. "I found it by the stream."

It is an aspen leaf; the softest parts have been worn away, leaving a silhouette of veins and branches and a hundred cells gilded by a few remnants of bronze.

"Cassius is staying here," I say, smoothing the leaf made of lace on my thigh. "Near Home Pond. With a bowl of sandwiches apparently. The Alpha asked if I wanted to stay too. With him."

Arthur frowns and looks at his fingers intertwined between his knees.

"What did you say?"

"I said no." A wind starts. "She says I have to hunt." I cover the filigree with my hand so it won't blow away. "I've never killed anything before."

He drops his chin on top of my head. When we're wild, he does this—puts his chin on top of my muzzle—after I've tried to do something difficult; it's meant to remind me to take time.

"We're not allowed to hunt moose," Arthur says without moving his head. "We need to wait until their population is self-sustaining. But there's one that seems to have brain worm and the Alpha says we can hunt that one."

Nestled into the notch under my werewolf's chin, I chuckle. The night before I met Cassius at the airport, we'd had dinner at Chronique. I'd ordered lamb with a mint and verjus chimichurri. It came with a side of fig crostini.

I ordered it but didn't get it.

"Are you sure that's what you want?" Cassius had said, holding one imperious hand up for the waiter while he looked at me expectantly.

Instead I got the beet and carrot salad with walnuts.

"Hold the chèvre," he'd said.

"Oooo: Moose with brain worm. *Orignal à la ver du cerveau.*"

I press tightly gathered fingertips against my budded mouth and deliver a chef's kiss.

Mwah.

"Is that sarcasm?"

"More facetiousness."

"Does that mean you'll be eating sandwiches with Cassius?"

"No." I lean back into the curve of his neck. "Nothing

could stop me from eating brain-worm-infested moose with you."

―――――――

The Pack usually assembles outside on the grass that spills down toward Home Pond. Cold, wet, muddy, hot, it doesn't matter; the one exception is blackfly season, which is why we are all crowded naked in the Great Hall.

There are some men and women I don't recognize. They are Offlanders, I presume, those wolves who Arthur has said best approximate human behaviors and represent pack interests in the larger world as lawyers, lobbyists, money managers, and accountants. Better groomed than most, they stand with their noses pressed against the glass, scratching— sometimes violently—at their skin.

Arthur isn't here yet but I pick my way toward the corner where the 12th is gathered.

"Jules."

I hadn't noticed Cassius when I came in. Hadn't looked for him either. Tucked away under the slope of the staircase, he is fully dressed in running pants and a sweatshirt that says something about St. Elizabeth's College of Nursing.

"*Jules,*" he hisses again, more loudly this time. "*Here.*"

I suppose the Alpha didn't bother to tell him my decision, so Cassius assumes that I will be joining him for three days of stale sandwiches and grievance. He points to a space beside him; he either didn't notice or didn't care that I would have to crouch down to fit under the steep slope.

That I would have to make myself small.

Things have changed, though, because I now know him for who he is: a small man with a small mind who needs someone smaller than he is to make himself feel big.

What he doesn't know is that I was just pretending. Yes, I'd done it for years, and like any costume worn for too long, it had started to fit.

But not anymore, it doesn't.

I take off my clothes slowly and deliberately, folding them with unnecessary flexing and tightening of muscles that have hardened after hours of working in the Summer Gardens and running wild. I put my folded pile on top of other folded clothes belonging to the 12th Echelon.

Cassius glares at me, but I turn my back and I sit with my wolves, because I am no longer a girl trained to games of mindless obedience.

Arthur opens the screen door. I know it's him by the scent of blood and woodsmoke that wafts down the hall past the med center, past the kitchen, past the Alpha's office, and past the library, into my lungs and body and coils around my spine.

As soon as he reaches the hall, he undresses quickly, shifting his hips to release his jeans. They slide down revealing the indentation at the top of his thighs and the base of his spine. When he pulls off his shirt, his ruined torso arches the way it does when I pull him deep into my mouth and make him groan.

He bends over to retrieve his clothes, his hair falling forward, and he looks up at me with silver deep-set eyes fringed by impossibly long, dark lashes. The 12th shuffles around, making room for him.

He squeezes in between Hakan and me, his knees up, arms loosely clasped around his shins.

A fight breaks out behind us. I didn't see the start, though I do see the end when the Alpha grabs Constantine's arm and, with a sharp yank that makes even him groan, grinds his shoulder back into its socket.

Then she gives him a sad smile that if I'd seen on anyone else, I would have said was loving.

"Just so there is no misunderstanding," she says with a pointed look for Cassius and for me, "the Iron Moon takes us as she finds us and makes us wilder. If we are in skin, she makes us wild. If we are wild, she makes us real wolves." There is a hitch in her throat that she swallows before adding, "Forever wolves."

A sigh flows through the pack, and the wolves of the 12th lower their eyes.

"Arthur? What is a forever wolf?"

He props his chin on his knees, a bleak look on his face. "A real wolf. A wolf who will never be part of the Great North again, though the Pack will do everything we can to protect her."

"I think I asked the wrong question. *Who* is the forever wolf?"

"Varya Timursdottir," he says.

I've heard that name. It was a name that made people listen, not like "Oh yeah, she's August's niece or Otho's daughter or Cassius's fiancée" but like "Oh yeah, she's Varya Timursdottir" and that was enough.

"August Leveraux sent someone to kidnap Tiberius's pups. They were supposed to take Silver too, but they took Varya by mistake. She managed to make it back and warn us about…"

He looks out toward the orange and lavender sky reflected in Home Pond.

"Warn you about us," I finish. "About Cassius and me and the old farts with the guns."

"Yes. But we didn't know you—they—were coming from the north, and Varya's mate, the one who was hidden in Westdæl, changed so he could howl a warning. It was like it is now, when it was too late, and if she changed, there would be no going back, but that's what Varya did. She gave up everything so she could fight for the Pack when we couldn't."

Cassius is arguing behind me. The Alpha answers.

"Was one of them white with blue and green eyes?"

"Yes."

"Was one of them gray?"

"Yes. It's why we call her the Gray now."

"And did she kill my uncle?"

"Yes," Arthur says.

So this was the one, the one Constantine had watched kill my uncle. "She shoved a metal bar through his throat," he'd said and I hadn't believed him. Couldn't believe a girl could kill August Leveraux.

"Well, good for her," I say, and at that moment, a table explodes toward the wall.

"Pick it up," the Alpha says, and I hear in her voice that Cassius has pushed her too far. I'd been ignoring Cassius, because that is what he hates most, but *this* I watch because I want him to know, when his body sails through the air, that I have seen him too, beaten by a woman.

The Alpha crouches down for one more look through the window before turning to the Pack and yelling something I don't understand.

Eadig waþ, Arthur says. "It means happy hunting, happy wandering."

Then the Pack says, "And be yourself not hunted!" their voices coming together like thunder.

Inna taps the back of her head, and Lorcan pulls out the rubber band that holds his ponytail. Ulrich gently turns the leather braid around Gwenn's neck.

A pup balances on the back of the sofa, little haunches trembling. She jumps into the adults who gather her up and nuzzle her before letting her escape under tented knees like the pups in the den on the video in my mother's "study."

"And be yourself not hunted," I tell her.

"Do you feel it?" Arthur asks.

Just as I am about to say "no," something prickles at my sternum, an odd pull, as though the line attached to a hook sunk deep in my heart is being reeled in. I feel an impatience in my bones that Arthur sees.

"*Wait*," he says, his hand on my arm. "Wait for it to take you. I've already lost one wolf to the wild. I can't lose yo…" He slumps to the floor. I try to catch him, but my arms dangle helpless and the strength of my spine fails me and I collapse on top of him, and for a long time, I feel not only the turmoil of my changing body but his too.

With a final twang, my eyes open to hundreds of wolves

jumping excitedly, rubbing and licking and greeting [It's you! It's you! It's you!] before running for the door. When the first ones get jammed up, the second wave clambers over their packmates' backs. A few of the bigger wolves are still changing, including Tiberius, who lies under the watchful eye of the silver wolf. A little way off, another wolf lies on the floor, a pair of running pants and a St. Elizabeth's College of Nursing sweatshirt sagging around him.

I run toward the blockage of the door and sail over the top, my back foot slapping a broad forehead. I am gleeful until I skid toward the stairs and skitter back from the edge. I've never negotiated steps before. It's not like the three steps at the cabin that I clear easily enough. Arthur joins me and shows me how to take them at a diagonal.

Before running to the trees, I take one last look toward the door to the Great Hall and the end of "inside" for the next few days. On the porch, Cassius struggles to stand, his paws tangled in running pants and sweatshirt. He looks sullenly at a huge metal bowl filled with water that is already gilded with pollen and the big, open Tupperware box, crammed with avocado and jelly sandwiches.

Arthur and I break into a run.

At first when I was wild, I was wild because I didn't want to be left alone, but now I can't imagine ever feeling alone like this. I am like a milkweed pod, and when I am wild, I burst free, dancing with the world and with every life that calls this place home.

While Arthur and I have run together, he has always hunted alone. Now, with the coming of the Offlanders, the entire 12th will hunt together. As I am not a hunter, I putter around, taking the long way to avoid a porcupine snuffling for roots, following the smell of rot that turns out to be a strange sticky flower on a log.

A little further on, I catch the musky scent of an animal I don't recognize. I track him, trying to make sense of his story. He stands in front of leaves that he does not eat. He hides when nothing threatens. He puts on displays when there is no one to see. He circles water but doesn't drink. It's like a puzzle I keep trying to piece together but nothing fits.

Until I see the silhouette among the high weeds near the Spruce Flats. A moose walks round and round, stumbling then stopping, its hind leg hitched up unnaturally high as though kicking some invisible enemy.

Spinning in the air, I run back for the echelon, circling them excitedly. A few wolves spare me an irritated sidelong glance, but I don't know how to tell them, *I found the moose with the brain worm! ME! ME! ME!* I jump up, bringing my front legs down repeatedly, trying to convey urgency and my weird exhilaration.

Arthur stands facing the way I came from, his nose to the ground, then he looks over his shoulder at me as though asking, "Well, are we going?"

We haven't been gone long before Lorcan pulls up beside us, sniffing around, trying to figure out what I'm up to. Now it doesn't make sense, because I'm no longer following the pointless meanderings, just my own direct path.

Except then my straight line intersects the moose's meander and Lorcan stops, lowers his nose and his muzzle and finally his whole body, rubbing one way, then the other, his legs up in the air. With a quick flip, he races back the way we came.

I trot over to sniff at the musky, moosey spot.

Next time, I'll know.

Soon after, Arthur heads toward the trees where the 12th has gathered. Silently, using only the movements of his eyes and head and the display of teeth, Lorcan splits the echelon in two, one moving to the upper part of the slope, the other around to the potential escape.

Sticking under the shadows of the trees, I move away. I don't want to see this because he is my moose and now they're going to kill him.

Then I remember Constantine standing with his arms folded in front of him, watching waiters move our table so I wouldn't have to see my dinner waving at me as it was pulled from the lobster tank. Later, after we'd all been served, Constantine stared at me. With an enormous knife, he broke open the claw, twisted it off, dragged out the meat still shaped like what it had been in life. He held it up to his mouth. I still remember the emptiness of his eyes as hot butter and juices ran down his chin.

I lost my appetite after that and pushed my own lobster away.

"You may not have seen it, but it's still dead," Constantine had said, wiping his fingers on a hot towel. "There are consequences."

August told him that was enough.

"Pass it to me," Constantine said and ate my untouched lobster.

All my life was private schools and ski vacations and ballroom dancing and closing my eyes to the guns and Krugerrands and midnight calls and the bloodstained shirts in the trash can.

Look where that got me.

I'm not going to do that again. I'm not going to pretend that Homelands is just puppies and Summer Gardens and explosive orgasms.

If I didn't want the damn moose to die, I shouldn't have fetched wolves.

The poor creature can't do much more than pick up speed moving in the path the worms have etched into its brain. By the time I get back, four wolves have converged on it, and with a well-timed leap, Inna tears out its throat. The moose's eyes dim but don't close and it almost seems to relax into her jaws while a shimmer of steam rises from its torso into the cool night air.

The sound of fangs ripping hide, of back teeth grinding against bone, is too much for me and I start to back up, except then I am hit by the coppery, musky scent of the earth's power made flesh. I move closer to where the warm blood flows out darker and redder over the reddish-brown carpet of pine needles. Something is damp and sticky under the pads of my paws. My mouth waters, my stomach rumbles, and Arthur, my attentive wolf, leaves off from eating to make room for me.

There's a lot to learn: how to hold down the leg, how to tear with fangs and cut with carnassial, and how to angle my head to swallow. How to cut sinews so Arthur and I can drag our leg away from the overcrowded kill and gorge until my belly is full and Arthur licks away the last gobs of blood on my muzzle.

In the end, the echelon is fed; a moose who needed to die did; and my werewolf finds me charming even with my mouth full.

Eventually, Lorcan throws back his head and howls. It's not the one full of longing or the one full of questions. It's a shorter, more staccato one, met with more of the same howls moving in waves across Homelands, and within moments, other wolves break through the brush to take what has been left by the 12th.

Full and content, I curl into Arthur, my head on his shoulder.

———

Qu'avez-vous fait pendant vos vacances? the maîtresse would ask the first day back at school.

What did you do with your summer vacation?

Her tone always implied that she knew we had squandered this gift of time. So one by one, we would stand and give long mendacious recitations of the way we had improved ourselves.

Studied Florentine architecture. Memorized sonnets. Played through *The Well-Tempered Clavier.*

They were all lies.

I imagine going back now and telling the maîtresse exactly what I've done with this summer life.

I would tell her the truth: that I ran. I hunted. I slept. I ate. I heeded. I fucked.

I was.

Chapter 22

Arthur

THE LAST NIGHT OF THE IRON MOON IS INTERRUPTED BY the sound of shooting. It's not near us—closer to the flat spaces to the west of Beaver Pond—but Julia is not used to being hunted and she freezes.

I bite her hind leg to get her moving toward the High Pines. This huge forested area that floods down from the northernmost mountains and across the foothills is dense and irregular, crisscrossed with windfall trees and tangled vine and hobblebush and water-worn gullies. Another shot echoes and I nip her again and again until she shakes herself awake and surges forward, clearing rivulets and gullies and racing past fallen trees.

She even runs past four adults herding our six littlest pups.

Francesca scratches her ear with her hind leg while looking at me for an explanation, but I have no idea why Julia would run past pups who clearly needed help. Francesca bends her head toward me, and along with other wolves of the 9th, they grab four of the pups and race for the High Pines, the little bodies swinging limp in their mouths.

I nudge Solveig and John forward. They are old enough

to understand the need to stay with an adult in an emergency. They are not, however, old enough to understand that the ravine up ahead is too wide, and I have no way of telling them to stay and wait. I will come back. With a growl, I push John back, then leap across with Solveig; I turn around as soon as I drop her, but John is already there, perched on the other side, his hind legs jittering, ready to jump.

A gray wolf races past me and flies over the ravine, barreling into John, tumbling away from the edge with the little pup cushioned in the curve of her body. Solveig and I watch Julia shake herself off, then sniff around John's muddy fur before she finally takes him primly in her teeth. I can barely stand to watch, terrified that her reticent grip won't hold as they sail back across.

I curl my lips away from my teeth, showing her how I take Solveig gently right below her shoulders, my fangs forming a cage around her little body.

When another shot rings out, Julia doesn't hesitate. She lowers her head to John, her teeth creating a gentle vise around fur and mud, and runs.

Other wolves race past us on their way to the High Pines, though Elijah breaks south, running all out, probably to find Thea. The Alpha heads west toward the Gray and the Bone Wolf.

Two more shots.

We run faster toward the border stream that marks the edge of the sanctuary of the High Pines. It has settled into its more sluggish summer banks, though the rocks are still slick from spring and a rand of mud marks either side.

Wolves are everywhere here, though humans would never know it. As soon as we arrive with the pups hanging from our jaws, they emerge from the trees, begging Julia to let them take John because they don't trust her with him.

Julia ignores them and carefully makes her way across, setting John down with the other pups in the deepest part of the forest. Relieved adults try to keep him still while they clean him.

Usually during the nights of the Iron Moon, when hunts are done, someone will announce leftovers or the Alpha will sing a song, but it is eerily quiet as we all sit, waiting and irritable. A wolf from the 8th snaps at Leelee for playing with his tail.

Finally the Alpha returns, pausing only briefly so that her wolves can smell the life of Westdæl, the Gray's territory; of Beaver Pond; of the Clearing and know that it is safe to start again for the Great Hall as the Iron Moon continues her journey, taking her blessing with her and leaving us in skin again.

When Järv leans down to take John, Julia leaps forward, snarling. The 7th's Beta mate takes a shocked step back, watching as Julia trots away, the pup eyeing him contentedly from the safety of her mouth.

———

We call it *Morgenswea*. Morning Woe. It's the disoriented feeling that comes after three days of wildness.

Leonora calls it a "Hang Over," though she never does

say what we are supposed to be hanging over. I'm not sure she knows.

All of us suffer the loss of our four-legged quickness and sharp senses and the unspoken connection but some suffer more than others. One wolf lies on the floor, arms crossed in front of him, staring sullenly at his thumbs. Another sticks out her tongue, forgetting it's not long enough to reach her nose.

A juvenile raises his back leg to scratch his ear and topples over backward. Nobody lends him a hand to get up because we've all forgotten we have them.

Julia sits at the table with her head propped on her upper arm, absently picking pup fur from her tongue.

Her shirt is on backward.

No one hunted last night, so there is a pileup of short-tempered wolves at the serving table. Pack jostle each other to reach plates. The Alphas stand at attention, snarling and gnawing at scones. I didn't see how it happened, but someone got a fork in the arm and bled into the oatmeal.

I load up plates—one for me, one for Julia—paying special attention to rich dishes filled with butter and cheese and cream to make up for the fat of summer prey we missed last night.

Once all the wolves have filtered in, the Alpha signals the official start to the Iron Moon Table, the one time each month when the whole Pack is together with thumbs and words.

"In our laws are we protected," she says in the Alpha voice, the voice that wraps itself around our hearts and makes us want to obey.

"And in lawlessness are we destroyed," we answer as wolves have since the days of the Ironwood.

Elijah's mate, Thea, starts. She is human, a human who knows what we are, but she has the trust of the Alpha and Elijah is not to be crossed, so here she is. She cradles one arm around a lump nestled under her shirt, then describes her version, the human version, of what happened last night. She'd heard the shooting and was already making her way toward Beaver Pond by the time Elijah came for her.

The hunters were two young men who were neither sober nor local. I wouldn't say we have a good relationship with locals, but most want to avoid the lengthy and expensive law proceedings that always seem to come with bringing firearms onto land controlled by Great North LLC.

Apparently, they flapped what they called a "furbearers" license in front of her as though any furbearer is hunted in summer when our fur is thin.

When she's done, Elijah accompanies her back to her cabin near the old fire tower.

Unfortunately, the Alpha says, taking a deep breath, she was unable to stop them before they killed the Alpha female coyote. The pack groans, because we all know that when the time comes, every female coyote will go into heat and this time next year, we will be eating coyote—nobody's favorite—to restore balance.

They also shot up all the beaver lodges. We don't know if some adults survived. If not, Beaver Pond with all its prey-rich habitat will disintegrate.

"If you feel like shit, it serves you right," Cassius whispers. He smells oddly like turnips rotting in flooded soil.

Julia covers her head with her arms and groans.

"And what the fuck have you done with your rings?"

I look around. Elijah has left with Thea, and Lorcan is trying to break up a fight between Tonia and Ulrich.

"She didn't have fingers," I answer. "She *couldn't* wear them."

"I didn't ask you," Cassius says, voice dripping with disdain.

"What did you do? Lose them? Or," he starts, looking pointedly at the cheese grits, "do they not fit anymore?"

The sun is brightening and I rub my eyes.

"Arthur?" Julia says worriedly.

I wave her off: it really is nothing, just the angle of the light.

"I'll take care of it," she says quietly and turns back to Cassius.

"Arthur?" Cassius brays a humorless laugh. "If you need her to take care of anything, you are in serious trouble. It's Princess Julia, here, who needs the tending and I doubt you can afford her."

Julia stands between us.

"Do you remember, Cassius?" Her voice is quiet but not at all gentle, like the hiss of a snake. "Do you remember those enormous boxes of chocolates from Fond de Lait?"

"Of course I do. Those things cost a fucking fortune."

"Hmm," she says. "They had such interesting flavors: soy sauce and goat cheese and ketchup and tobacco. When you came, my mother would always look at the beautiful white box with the lavender ribbon and say, 'Such a gentleman.'"

Why is she talking about chocolates? Is this something she misses?

"Where are you going with this?" Cassius asks, because clearly, he doesn't know either.

"Every time," she continues more firmly, "I would ask what kind of chocolate you liked and you would tell me. Orange-filled or raspberry. White chocolate with mint crunch. And I would tell you my favorites: plain truffles. Salt caramel. Walnuts.

"And the next time you came, I bought you a box of orange-filled and raspberry and white chocolate mint crunch. You brought me another big box of chocolates from Fond de Lait with interesting flavors like soy sauce and goat cheese and ketchup and tobacco, and my mother again called you 'a gentleman.'"

"Jules," he says.

"*Don't*," she snaps. "*Do not call me that.*"

"I've always called you Jules. You always liked it before."

She says nothing, and during the long silence that follows, I look toward her. Every muscle is tight, but not like she's trying to make herself smaller. More like she's trying to hold herself back.

"Do you remember what that woman said when I bought your rings?" Cassius says.

"What woman?"

"The one at Harry Winston."

"I don't remember. She said a lot. Most of it about how lucky I was to have such a generous fiancé."

"She said she thought it was cute. That I was buying jewels for my Jules. And you *are* lucky to have such a generous fucking fiancé. *Were* lucky."

Now she releases the tension just enough to take a deep breath.

"You've always been so careful to tell me how expensive everything was."

"Because you're spoiled, Julia. For you, money grew on trees. I needed to make sure you understood their value."

"Believe me, I knew exactly what your gifts cost. Do you?"

"What?"

"How much did my rings cost?"

"Talking money is not the kind of thing a man does with a woman."

"You don't know, do you? You liked to beat me over the head with it, but you don't actually know. Well, I do. All together they cost a little over $1.5 million American. *I* know because when my mother needed a receipt for insurance, Uncle August sent it to her. The receipts were in his name, because *he* bought them."

Her arms are crossed in front of her chest, but her hands are not tucked away. They are splayed across her biceps.

"When did you find out?"

"A week after you gave them to me."

"And you never said anything?"

"I was doing what I could to make us work."

He stares at the bare finger of her left hand.

"Why? If I was such a nightmare?"

"Because I'm a Canadian werewolf and my options are limited."

There is a long silence.

"*Shifter.* You're a Canadian Shifter," corrects Inna. Someone murmurs something. "What? It's true."

I'd been paying such close attention to Julia that I'd failed to notice that the Pack had grown silent, watching. Some are moving quietly toward the door. I search out the Alpha, who is leaning into her legs, ready to jump, her head cocked, questioning.

"Omega?"

I breathe deep and shake my head, so she'll understand that I see her and know who she is and know who I am.

And the fire will not burn.

She nods and takes her mug, getting another cup of coffee, turning her back to me, a sign to the Pack that I am not a problem. The Offlanders take markings from pack-mates and Alphas, then they unroll their shirtsleeves and the males tighten nooses around their necks and the females clip shining metal into their ears, and when they leave, they clasp palms to cheeks, as though to keep that precious sense of belonging safe until next moon.

"What happened to you?" Cassius says, backing away. "You were a beautiful woman and I was proud to call you mine, but now you're nothing but a…" He glares over his shoulder toward Elijah, who is fighting his way through the exiting wolves.

"A what? You can't even say it, can you, Cassius? You're still clinging to the idea that we are somehow better. Well, I'm not. I know what I am. I am female and I am a wolf and I am better as a bitch than I ever was as a woman."

"*Shifter!*" Elijah bellows and Cassius storms away.

Julia watches him, her fists tight beside her, until the door to the mudroom closes and then the screen door closes too. Finally she sits down, pulling her plate closer.

"It's cold now," she says, pushing her spoon through cold cheese grits.

"You still have to eat it."

"I know." She loads up her spoon and holds it in front of her. "He is going to make me pay for that. Somehow, he is going to make me pay."

Chapter 23

Julia

IT WAS ULRICH'S RESPONSIBILITY TO KEEP THE SUMMER Gardens free of rodents, but it turns out that the occasional peeing of the perimeter isn't enough and now we have a groundhog. An aspirational groundhog with a McMansion consisting of multiple tunnels and rooms and exits too numerous to count.

The 12th has spread out among the old fruit trees and meandering beds of tender greens, digging at every exit. At this rate, they'll have obliterated the whole of the Summer Gardens before they finally corner the groundhog in its burrow.

Lorcan assigned me to an old collapsed hole, thinking, I suppose, that this was where I could do the least harm. What he doesn't know, and I can't tell him, is that I didn't spend two hundred hours at Taverne Cobra playing Whac-A-Mole for nothing.

Something moves in the dark soil. My muscles are so tight, I can't believe the wind doesn't make my tendons twang. First comes a whisker. I don't move. Then comes a twitch. Then a nose. I wait just a fraction longer than I think I should and my body uncoils.

Every day I learn something new.

Today I learned that unlike whac-a-moles, groundhogs scream. The warm torso beneath my teeth deflates with a loud and high-pitched *Weeaaaaaaahhhwww* that pierces my ears. I don't let go. If I'd grabbed its head, it'd be dead already instead of scraping at my cheek with its claws.

Weeaaaaaaahhhwww, it screams again and I shake my head just to get it to shut up. I guess I did it too hard though, because on the third shake, I feel a crack against my jaws and the groundhog goes still. I lower it gently, worried that if I let it go, it'll race back into its burrow.

Inna comes closer and nudges the still body before tapping my muzzle.

I slowly unlock my jaws from fur that smells like broccoli and Lorcan yelps toward the trees. Within minutes, pups come running, jumping over one another, swarming the groundhog. Arthur bumps at my jaw with his nose and licks clean the torn skin while pups fight over the still hillock of fur.

———

I don't think I have ever been so proud.

———

"Tristan is just going to say it's a flesh wound," Arthur says as I head toward Medical.

"It's a flesh wound," Tristan says, digging through a bowl

of peanut-butter-filled pretzel rods while staring at a comic book. "And I am very busy."

"How do you know it's a flesh wound?"

"If it doesn't shatter bone or damage internal organs, it's a flesh wound."

"Supposing it scars?"

"Supposing it does," he says, turning a page. "Every wolf has scars. Look at him." He bends his head toward Arthur, who backs away, his hands held up. Keep me out of this. "I'm not sure what you want me to do about it."

"I want you to stop reading your stupid comic book—"

"It's not a stupid comic book," he says, lifting it so we can see the cover. "It's *Swamp Thing*."

"Whatever it is, put it down and look at my face."

One eye floats up.

"Are you going to give me something?"

He heaves a sigh and reaches into his pocket. He shakes two pale-green pills into my hand, then pushes us out.

"Take two and don't darken my door again."

Arthur clutches at my hand and almost makes me drop them on the floor. They taste like breath mints.

"Spit them out! Spit them out!" he hisses and pulls me toward the kitchen sink. I spit them out. "Rinse out your mouth. I'll get some iced tea."

"Are they poison?"

"They're not poison, they're Tic Tacs. Tristan gives them to anyone who comes in for something minor. If a wolf smells wintergreen on you, they'll know you went to Medical for a flesh wound and you will lose respect."

Arthur looks toward the door.

"They're coming," he says, flushing more water down the sink before leaning against the edge, handing me iced tea. "Drink this quickly."

I gulp down the tea, listening as something comes down the hall making an eerie flapping sound, like a burlap bag filled with bats.

Six children trip in on shoes that thock awkwardly against their heels. Their clothes, even when they are the right size, don't seem to fit. Every move they make is awkward, uncomfortable. They stand too close to one another.

"Say hello to Arthur," says a tall woman wearing high heels. Almost as an afterthought, she adds, "And to the Shifter."

"Hewo, Artur. Hewo, de Shister."

"Hello, wolflings," Arthur says stiffly before nodding his head toward the woman. "Hello, Leonora."

"Everyone take a seat," Leonora says, waving her hand toward the table.

Distracted by my accidental ingestion of Tic Tacs, I'd failed to notice the enormous scarred and sanded table that is usually either empty or surrounded by wolves chopping has been spread with a tablecloth and set with six places, each with plates, glasses, and cutlery atop neatly folded napkins. In front of each chair is a piece of printer paper folded in quarters that says MENU in bold script on the front.

"What's going on?" I whisper to Arthur.

"Intro to Human Behaviors. Probably practicing for a field trip to Pizza Barn."

"They need practice for pizza?" I ask.

"You'll see."

Leonora eyes the children. "'Take a seat' means put your bottom in the chair." Then she takes an apron from an iron hook on the door to the pantry and holds it high. "Now," she says, "remember, when I put on this apron, I am no longer Leonora. I am a human and I will judge you as a human does. That means anything out of the ordinary will immediately alert my suspicions. You have all the tools you need to do this, but you must concentrate. We only have three weeks to get ready for the trip to the Pizza Barn."

Arthur mouths "Pizza Barn," then turns toward the door.

I grab onto his arm because I want to know why baby werewolves need three weeks to prepare for pizza.

"So does anyone have a question before I put the apron on?"

A little girl asks a garbled question that I don't understand.

"We will go to the Clearing afterward."

Another boy asks something about trolls.

"If everyone concentrates, this will take less than an hour. Any more questions?"

Two hands shoot up.

Leonora sighs.

"Any questions that are *not* about voles?"

The two little hands sink.

"Now," she says, tying on an apron. "Look at your menus."

The children glance furtively at one another while Leonora slices a round loaf of dark bread into rough chunks and loads them into a towel-lined basket.

Finally one of the children leans forward, staring at the

closed menu as though trying to make sense of it by sheer force of will. Seeing this, the rest of the children do the same.

Leonora frowns and scribbles something on the back pages of her notebook. She brings over the basket of bread and sets it in the middle of the table.

A boy and a girl both reach for it, but the girl is faster and drags it away. The boy manages to keep hold of it until the girl bites his knuckle. He yelps, and she scuttles toward the corner of the kitchen floor next to the pantry, crumbs flying from her mouth.

The boy flies toward her, grabbing for the basket again. Bread scatters everywhere. Chairs topple as children pluck up the chunks bouncing along the floor.

I squat down, my arms loose on my knees, watching the children gathered under the table, eating bread with muffled growls. They reach for each other, nuzzling cheeks, snuggling into laps and shoulders. The girl who bit the boy's finger now licks his hand.

Despairing, Leonora asks the deserted table if they've had time to look at their menus and are ready to order.

There is no way they are going to be ready in three weeks.

I take a seat at one of the empty chairs, ostentatiously shaking out the napkin and spreading it low across my lap so the children under the table can see.

As I lift the menu in one hand, little heads pop up above the level of the table. A few climb back into their chairs, some on bottoms, some on knees, others standing.

Lifting the napkin, I pretend to dab my lips, then spread it once again over my lap. The bread girl shakes out the napkin and spreads it low over her knee. Others follow suit. Then she holds the menu in one hand in a precise imitation. I pretend not to see her studying me.

"I'd like a scone square à la butter, please," I say, skimming the menu that for all its flourishes is breakfast leftovers. "And an eggy cake. Is there any meat in that? I'm a vegetarian."

"There is no meat," Leonora says with a sigh of relief. "Would you like any dessert with that?"

"No, thank you. I'll wait and see if I'm still hungry."

Leonora takes off her apron. "Eyes here. We got off to a rocky start. So let's repeat the rules for eating Offland. Xena?"

> *Eats up nicey, when you done.*
> *Use you nabkin, nod you tongue.*
>
> *Tabow's where you keep you glass;*
> *Chaiw is where you keep you ass.*
>
> *Teetheses are fo eading nod fo biding.*
> *Paws are fo fowks nod fo fighding.*
>
> *Foodes dat faws on de floor*
> *S'not good for eading ninee more.*

"But wheyey?" Xena cries.

"It just is, wolflings," Leonora says. "It just is. Now you're almost done, so let's finish up."

Moutheses muss shuts for when you shew
But open up for peases and tinks you.

"Yes, well, knowing them is not the same as doing them. So who can tell me how many of those rules you broke today?"

The children look at each other. One scratches nervously at her leg and then smells her nails.

"All of them, wolflings. All of them."

The pups run in, sniffing around the legs of the table. Two have found a piece of bread on the floor and start to tussle over it.

Little claws tickle my calves. John props his paws up on my legs, his head cocked to the side. I reach under the table and draw him into my arms but he doesn't want to be held. He's just using me to get at the bread on the table.

When he tries to put his dirty paws on the tablecloth, I bop his nose gently and begin the little rhyme that must have been recited by every St. Ailbhe's matron since the school's founding.

The tablecloth I must not spoil,
Nor with my food my fingers soil;
Must keep my seat when I have done,
Nor round the table sport or run;
When told to rise, then I must put
My chair away with noiseless foot.

The children freeze, cowering like prey hoping to avoid a hunter armed with a new and terrifying weapon in the arsenal of manners.

Leonora, an eyebrow cocked in my direction, beats a *tat-tat-tat* with her pen against her notebook.

"Shifter," she says. "You will help us prepare for Pizza Barn."

"Wolf," I say. "I will help you, but *you* will call me Julia."

She looks at me for a moment, her pen suddenly silent, then laughs. "Why not? I already have to call the other one Constantine. It seems there is only one Shifter left."

While Leonora puts her apron back on, the children sit at the table, sliding their eyes around at their packmates. I shake out my napkin once more, and they all follow suit.

"Now," Leonora says, her pen poised once again above her notebook, "look at the menu and tell me what you would like to eat."

The children look at the menus and at each other before one girl raises her hand.

"Voles?" she asks hopefully.

———

"Do you want your rodent bag?"

"My...?"

Arthur holds out the mud-spattered, spiky-furred bucket bag of custom-dyed, wolf-gnawed mink.

"I'm not carrying anything, and besides it doesn't really go." I trail my hand in the air, indicating my attire of jeans and brown Henley with rolled-up sleeves. Leonora offered to let me choose from her collection of Offland costumes, but this is Arthur's shirt and I find I love the smell of blood and woodsmoke.

"Are you sure you don't want to come?"

"I really can't," he says.

Leonora is leaning over the driver's seat, talking to the First Shoes. "One seat belt for *each* wolfling," she says. "Julia? The buckle is on your side."

"You go," Arthur tells me. "I'll see you when you get back."

All five of our charges have managed to squeeze themselves into one seat belt, the shoulder strap covering Aella's face. When I free them, the grateful Aella licks my cheek.

"I love you too," I tell her, "but you can't do that Offland, remember?"

"'Kay," she says and chomps her teeth together, her lips pursed to keep her traitor tongue from escaping.

"And, Leofric?" I catch up his little dirty sock-clad foot banging against the seat. "Where are your shoes?"

He pulls out his hands, which had been tucked under his thighs, and proudly displays his shoes.

"On your *hind* paws. Until we come back to Homelands, shoes have to stay on feet."

I finally get them all settled and climb into the passenger seat. For three weeks, I'd been thinking of this as a vacation, the possibility of central air and pepperoni looming as large in my imagination as one of those interchangeable private beach resorts where uniformed waitstaff on rope-soled shoes silently served bittersweet jewel-colored drinks on the verandah of my bungalow overlooking raked white beaches and endless teal water.

Now, the belt presses against my lungs and the smell of the car makes it hard for me to breathe. I roll down the window and look in the side mirror at the Pack who are there to see us off. Arthur stands tall and slim among the tall, slim trees. He lifts his hand, my stupid rodent bag tucked under his arm.

OBJECTS IN MIRROR ARE CLOSER THAN THEY APPEAR

I wave back to him and the mirror does make him seem so far away and I have second thoughts about pepperoni and central air, but then the car bumps and tilts precariously downward and I don't see him anymore.

A foot kicks the back of my seat, and when I turn around, I see five little faces trying to hold it together. Their burden is so much larger than mine. They know, because Leonora has told them often enough, that the Pack is relying on them. If they get it wrong, if they don't seem plausibly human, those who actually are will start to question.

"And for the continued survival of the Pack, they must never question."

The rough drive gives way to macadam and then to even smoother and more open roads and finally to another road where the trees are gone. The wolflings stare through the window at the strange world of strip malls promising cheapness and convenience and cling to one another.

To distract them, I suggest a human game. The wolflings get the idea of twenty questions pretty quickly, but their knowledge of animals, plants, and minerals is so much more sophisticated than mine ("Gots pinnate leafes?") that I quickly find myself unqualified to referee.

"Leonora?" I ask, watching the abandoned strip mall

disappear in the distance. "What happened with Arthur at the dollar store?"

She looks in the rearview mirror at the distracted wolflings and purses her lips.

"Who told you?"

"He did. Or he tried to. He doesn't remember much and what he does remember doesn't make a lot of sense."

We turn onto a wider road. Four lanes with low greenery on either side and a median that smells like fresh-cut grass.

Leonora taps rapidly on the steering wheel with her thumb. "You know, I come here every year, and every year I forget whether it's Exit 40 or 41. I think it's 41."

"Leonora."

"I don't take my beginning class places like that anymore. It's too much. The lights are too bright and come from everywhere. Same with the sounds. And the smells... Paper smells like chocolate, bottles smell like lemons, pens smell like blueberries, women smell like rutting bucks. They were all having a hard time. Obviously, I wouldn't have taken him if I'd known what he was."

"A werewolf."

"We don't use the word anymore. They were the only pack most humans had ever seen, and they used it to paint us all as monsters in a fairy tale."

"So what do you call him?"

"Arthur," she says decidedly. "We call him Arthur. We hadn't had one for generations. Maybe never in the New World. Only Gran Sigeburg knew the old stories." She stops for a moment and then starts in a gravelly, oddly accented voice. "'The eyes dim, the fire burns, and the Pack dies.' Honestly," Leonora says, her voice her own again, "sometimes Gran Sigeburg needed as much interpretation as humans do."

She sniffs twice, then looks into the rearview mirror. "Who used their teeth?" she asks, and immediately four little fingers point to Xena.

"Xena, what did I say?"

"No, teefs," she says. "But 'Dmund—"

"Debride your packmate, Xena, and don't do it again. I don't want him walking into Pizza Barn looking like a cheese chew."

"And?" I press her once Xena starts licking Edmund. "What happened?"

"Inna took a compact from a woman's handbag. She didn't know. I'd told them they could bring me things to ask about as long as they were gentle and put them back. I'd forgotten to tell her that things in carts were off-limits. She wasn't hiding it; she was just showing everyone. Mirrors are hard for First Shoes to understand. Then the woman grabbed her by the arm and started screaming that she'd caught a thief and needed security.

"It was chaos. I was trying to calm the woman down; the speaker goes off saying something about security, and there's a screeching sound…"

"Feedback."

"Feedback." She repeats it slowly. "Anyway, then a security guard shows up. He's dressed in black and wearing black glasses. I remember that so clearly because why was he wearing glasses inside?"

"Drugs?"

"How did you know?"

"Educated guess."

"We didn't find out until later when the lawyers had to settle. Anyway, he shows up and I thought he was going to tell the woman to calm down, but he didn't. Instead he reaches behind him and pulls out metal restraints and snaps one on Inna's wrist and Arthur flies at him. He was as little as they are"—she motions with her head toward the wolflings in the back seat—"but he flies through the air. Grabs the guard's neck in his teeth."

She shakes her head, her knuckles white on the steering wheel.

"There was so much blood."

"He killed the guard?"

"No, it was Arthur's blood. The guard shot him."

"The guard shot Arthur?"

"Sure, you can see the scar here clearly..." She puts her hand to the upper-right corner of her chest. "No, I guess you can't anymore." She lets out a long breath. "Arthur still held on to the man's neck. I needed the help of four humans to hold him down. I shoved an antler into his jaws to break his grip.

"We paid the guard off—"

"*Why*? He was high. He shot a *child*."

"In what way do you imagine that trial coming out well for us? Blood tests, investigation into his schooling? No, but Arthur would never leave Homelands again."

She pushes her hair back.

"Julia?"

"Hmm?" I say, distracted.

"Arthur has worked hard and been so careful ever since then. You know the way he holds his arms around his waist sometimes?"

"Hmm."

"I think he started doing that because he was afraid something was going to fall out. He knows how important it is that the Pack trust him to control himself. Even during his Clawing, the Alpha trusted him. But now it's happened again."

She makes a turn onto a county road.

"We do not use the word 'love' as thoughtlessly, as carelessly as humans do. I want to make sure you understand that more than any other, that wolf's love comes with consequences. It is not easy and it is not safe."

Your voice cut through everything and for the first time, I thought: Here was someone I could trust myself with. Someone who, whatever happened, could bring me back.

"I don't believe he would hurt me."

"Maybe not, but if he felt you were threatened, it might unleash something that is very hard to restrain, and for the safety of the Pack, we will do *whatever* must be done to stop him."

Then she clears her throat. "Almost there, wolflings. Is the blood gone?"

———

At Pizza Barn, we park under a maple tree to keep the car cool. The restaurant itself is a prefab red shed with three broad doors, two of which have been partly boarded up by red-painted particleboard and turned into windows. A "silo" surrounded by corrugated steel disguises what must be a vent, leaking small wisps of yeast-scented dough and burned tomato sauce. Two ragged plants in plastic barrels stand guard, one on either side of the three concrete steps.

Not exactly Soir or Bouileau.

A little hand slips into mine, reminding me that while this is well outside my native range, it is worlds away for the five worried First Shoes. Taking a deep breath, I hold the door and pray that this doesn't end up with blood on the floor.

━━━━━━━━

I am so proud of them. Our wolflings were no worse than really sloppy and awkward children. Knowing that children this age will be forgiven a great many missteps if they mind their pleases and thank-yous, that's what Leonora focuses on.

"Tink you for de nabkin," says Leofric, handing the waitress his crumpled napkin. "And tink you for de fork. And tink you for…"

I scratch my nose with my finger, the sign we have to indicate that it's time to put hands in lap and close mouths, which Leofric does promptly.

As Leonora says, it isn't always easy for them to keep their wild in check, but they are not like human children who are raised with the luxury of disregarding an adult's warning.

Baby wolves do not have the same expectation of safety, so when an adult says go still, they do. When an adult says run, they do that too.

"I gots to go to the tree," Edmund says, holding his crotch.

"Trees not fo' pees, 'Dmund," Aella recites loudly.

"Thank you, Aella," Leonora whispers. "So who else needs to use the toilet?"

Every hand goes up.

Leonora hands me the car keys and a prepaid card. "You need to add money for the server."

I can't help but chuckle. "Yes, Leonora. I may be Canadian but I do actually know about tipping."

"Good. Good. I like to tip well," she says before shepherding her charges toward the back where the spotted chrome doorway says RESTROOMS FOR CUSTOMERS ONLY.

I check the bill. How much is on the card? $150? $200? Whatever it is, between this and the car, Leonora must know that I could walk out of here and drive to a gas station with a phone. Within three hours, I'd have a replacement card, a new phone, a mani-pedi, and a reservation at Soir for those lovely Wagyu tournedos with a tart cherry reduction.

Holding the bill and the card in one hand, I signal to the waitress. She takes it, stopping at another table to write something down. As she makes her way to the wait station, a young man snatches our card from her and holds it high. I watch him with my hunter's eyes as he waves his hands around—abracadabra—and slides it into his pocket.

The young waitress isn't afraid, just tired.

"Give it back, Carston," she says.

With my hunter's ears, I hear Carston's whispered reply to his companion about "those weirdos up near Wolf Pond."

"Give it back," the waitress says more urgently. "I don't care where they come from. They're nice. When they come, they eat, they say please, and they tip. Not like you and Kenny. Coming in once a week stinking of weed, eating a single big bowl of baked ziti, and missing the toilet."

That last makes the men laugh, and they keep right on laughing as they head outside.

"Carston!" she yells, her eyes swinging from the retreating men to me before dashing through the swinging doors into the back of the kitchen. "Charlie, they..."

I have no idea who Charlie is, because I'm already out the door, walking through the parking lot, led unerringly by my hunter's nose.

"You have twenty seconds to give me my card back."

"What card?"

"Twenty, nineteen, eighteen..."

"Or what?"

"Eleven, ten, nine, eight..."

"C'mon, Kenny. Let's go."

"Four, three, two, one."

My hunter's legs propel me to the hood of the car, a Chevy Cavalier painted matte black. I'm bigger than I was and heavier, and the hood crumples beneath my weight. Down the other side, I push Carston against the door and shove my hand into the back pocket of his running pants.

"If you want to grope something, grope this." I feel the

excited flutter of his pulse as he pushes my free hand against the inseam of his sweats.

"Move your hand, Carston."

"Move yours, pretty lady," he says and tightens my hand around his cock.

"Do you have the keys?" Leonora says behind me.

I hold up the card in one hand.

"Having a little trouble," I say calmly. "Haven't paid yet."

Leonora plucks the card from my hand. "Children," she says in that deep voice they know to obey. "Stay by the car until Julia is done here and lets you in."

Out of the corner of my eye, I see the wolflings watching me intensely. They're studying me like this is an object lesson in the way the world works.

A lifetime ago, a man in line at the movie theater repeatedly touched my ass with his dick, but every time I turned around, he pretended to be looking at his phone. When Cassius came back with the popcorn, I weighed my options: have Cassius turn him into a melodramatic pulp on the sidewalk or watch *John Wick 3*.

I really wanted to see *John Wick 3*, so I said and did nothing. Even when Cassius realized he hadn't gotten napkins and the man did it again.

What do I want Aella and Rainy and Xena to take away from this? That this is simply an occupational hazard of being a human woman? That they are going to have to learn how to purse their lips and say nothing? That they must learn to smile nervously and mutter something about "my boyfriend"?

"Tighter, baby," Carston says.

My fingers, hardened in the soil of Homelands, tighten until he whimpers.

"Is that tight enough for you?" I ask and let him drop to the ground.

The wolflings stand on tiptoes, their necks stretched, watching.

"You fohgots you peases and tinks you," Edmund yells toward Carston. He turns around toward Rainy and shakes his head. "'What? The mans didn' say pease may you touch my peens!"

I feel for the keys in my pocket, shoo the wolflings into the back of the car, and remind them that there is one seat belt for each.

Slamming the door shut, I lean against it, arms crossed in front of me. I can't see Carston, hunched on the ground, but I see Kenny standing frozen between trying to comfort his buddy and making a horrified assessment of his dented hood.

"I hope you noticed," Leonora says as soon as she settles into the driver's seat and adjusts the rearview mirror, "how a human handles conflict. What was the most important thing?"

"NO TEEEZZZ!" the little voices yell.

"That's right," Leonora says. "No teeth."

I smile at the little faces in the side mirror.

OBJECTS IN MIRROR ARE CLOSER THAN THEY APPEAR

Back on the highway, we pass a parking lot and a big

sign advertising a craft store, a fast food place, a dollar store, and a—

"Leonora, wait! Turn in here. I need to—"

Leonora has already made the sharp turn into the parking lot. No suspicious questions about why or what I'm up to. It's like when we're wild and we turn together, stop together, hunt together because wolves trust other wolves not to lead them astray.

"I won't be a minute," I say, unbuckling my seat belt. I swing my legs out, then stop and slump. "I don't... Leonora, I don't have any money. You can have my rings. They're worth—"

But just like her turn into the parking lot, the prepaid card is already outstretched in her hand because wolves trust other wolves not to lead them astray.

"Did he tell you to get these?" says the young woman at checkout as she squats down to retrieve a box from its hook along the wall.

"No. But I've seen enough to know."

She struggles up, the black box in her hand.

"Just saying, 'cause my boyfriend? Andy? He told me to get the Magnums too. That thing just slid right off, and that's how I'm working here while my mom takes care of Leo."

She tugs on the teal vest with the drugstore logo embroidered on the left breast.

"And Andy?"

"Alaska. On a trawler? He's supposed to be making money to send back? I haven't heard from him for six months. No Wi-Fi, he says, it being Alaska."

I hand her the prepaid card. "Is there enough on there for the thirty-six?" I ask.

"Let's see." She swipes the card. "Sure."

I take the box.

"You don't want a bag for that?"

"I can carry it."

"Have a good day?" she says, not as a statement, more as a query, hoping that someone will confirm that the possibility of a good day still exists.

"Yeah. You too."

I don't know what to say.

After clambering back into the Rover, I stuff the condoms into the center console and belt up.

Then I hand the card back to Leonora, who puts it into her billfold. She snaps her purse shut and starts the car.

I lean my head against the window, staring at the march of auto body shops and fast-food places and more weed-choked strip malls with more dollar stores and wonder if one of them was where a man with dark glasses shot a little boy with black eyes.

"Leonora," I ask as the trees grow thicker around us, blocking the late afternoon sun, "how much is on that card?"

"There was $1,500 when we left Homelands. So $1,350 minus whatever you spent."

Seeds from the maple tree at the Pizza Barn parking lot scuttle across the windshield as the wind picks up.

"How did you...?" My voice fades.

"Yes?" she asks.

"How did you know I wouldn't leave? You handed me

$1,500 and the keys to the car. What made you think I wouldn't simply head for home?"

She taps at the whirligigs on the windshield.

"Samaras don't look like much—a bit of paper and a tiny seed. Inside each one, though, is the possibility of a maple tree, but to become more than a possibility, they need to escape the shadows cast by bigger trees."

With a click, she turns on the windshield wipers.

"I don't believe you would ever willingly return to the shadows."

Just as I rest my head against the window again, a sharp bang fires from the back, and a moment later, the inside of the car is flooded with the smell of latex.

Curving my arm behind my seat, I wiggle my fingers, looking expectantly at the shocked faces in the rearview mirror.

Aella puts the opened box of condoms into my hand.

"Da badoon popt," she says.

Chapter 24

Arthur

IN THE BASEMENT, DIAGONALLY ACROSS FROM DRY STOR-age and next to the root cellar, is the closet where Leonora keeps the props and costumes and stage sets that provide a backstory for a wolf's transition into the human world.

It's larger than it had been before the old Great Hall burned down, big enough to accommodate things Leonora once stored in her own cabin. On shelves behind the can-dlestick that is used to teach juveniles respect for fire at the dinner table are the albums for each of the echelons.

I pull out the one for the 12th and flip through to the early picture of my echelon as First Shoes. One line of wolflings is seated in the front. Another group kneels behind and a third stands in the back. Lorcan was already larger than anyone. Varya had not yet made that desperate journey from her Arctic birthplace to the Great North. And it would be months before anyone knew that one of these wolves would never be allowed out again.

Like everyone else, I was nervous and awkward, sitting at the very front, holding the wood-framed sign with its black felt that we tussled over for the right to slide the little letters into their places. "Mr. Weston's First Grade. Lelou Lower School."

There was no Mr. Weston: Leonora simply drafted whatever presentable adult wolf happened to walk by when she had to take the picture. In this instance, it was the silent, stern, and mountainous Sten, which goes a long way to explaining why we all look so terrified.

Turning the page, I find another photograph with all of us in front of the water-stained linen and glue banner for "Camp Mahigan." There's a new one—this professionally printed—rolled up in the corner. "If anyone asks," Leonora had said, "this is where you spent your summers."

The pages that follow show different configurations of "children" and "parents" and "family" but that was the last one with me.

Putting it back on its shelf, I dislodge a ribbon of white from one of the hangers. As soon as I pick it up, I know what it is. Somehow the laundry wolves managed to remove all the traces of mud and blood. I slide to the floor and hold it soft and heavy to my cheek, feeling the coolness of the strange costume Julia wore when she broke my life into the time before and the time after Julia.

The break in her life is so much more wrenching. I know it. She lost her family and her friends and the world she knew. Now, for the first time, she is out there again and I am here, hiding terrified in the basement, trying to prepare myself for the possibility that the pull of that world will be too much and she will draw away from me. I will lose her. Maybe not physically but I will lose her all the same.

Partly hidden beneath the row of clothes is a stack of milk cartons with Leonora's collection of magazines. Holding the white silk to my face, I begin to leaf through them.

Pages are marked with bright-colored stickies, no doubt part of some code that only Leonora knows.

"Fall in Love with Cute and Cozy Sweaters!" says one article.

"Fat-Melting Entrees We Love!" proclaims another.

"He'll Love These Party-Pretty Styles!"

All the women on these pages are so happy. They hold things—a bottle of perfume, a can of beer, a box of something called tampons—and leap into the blue sky in a world filled with exclamation points!

I try to imagine Julia jumping for joy into cloudless skies.

Despite the joy caused by tampons, they are not included in the article on "30 Presents That Say I Love You!" The shiny pages got damp, dried out, and are now stuck together. One by one, I pry them apart, revealing leopard-print slippers, a candle warmer, a pink camera, a watch, a cheese board.

"Gifts," the article says, "that show the way you really feel."

A leather-bound calendar says *365 Days of Love*. On January 1, someone has drawn a big heart with the words "I love you" written inside.

I put the magazine away and stare at my empty hands and I don't come out until the first wolf howls.

They are all moving by the time I run up the stairs. Finally, those of us in skin hear the scrunch and thump of tires on the rough access road. The gate is already open and wolves who are wild lope alongside the Range Rover, sprinting the last yards so that they can be waiting as it comes to a stop.

As soon as the doors open, pups fall out. Sick of having been in skin so long, they have already stripped off shoes and clothes and throw themselves naked into the roiling fur and the rough tongues that clean the last traces of anxiety and garlic butter.

Within seconds, the Pack dissipates, shepherding the pups away from the parking lot to our wilder spaces. I stand back among the trees, watching Julia retrieve the little clothes from the back of the car, passing them to Leonora who will take them to the Laundry where other wolves will do to the wolflings' olive-oil-and-tomato-stained cotton what they did to Julia's blood-and-mud-stained silk.

Before she slams the door closed, Julia reaches for a black box. She turns to me with a sad smile and the fibers of my heart, as tough as they are, fray.

I try to read her silence as we walk back to the cabin. Her pace, her breath, the direction of her eyes, the tilt of her head, the posture of her back, but all of it is colored by my own terror.

I wish I could tell her I understand about the blue skies and the jumping and the tampons and that I have just the thing to make up for that loss, but I don't.

When I close the door of the cabin behind me, I cling to it, hand on the lever.

The sun is at that point in its downward descent when it seems to race toward the horizon. Shadows whisper across the worn floor, across the old metal bunks with their sagging springs and flaked pale-gray paint, across the chipped porcelain sink, across the faded roller blinds on the windows opposite.

Homelands looks so dark and raw and rough compared to the shiny jewel-toned ecstasy of Offland.

"Leonora gave me money," Julia finally says. "She gave me $1,500 and the car keys and left me alone."

My hand tightens on the lever of the door.

"It was on a card. Prepaid. It would have been so easy to get into the car and drive back to the life I knew. The safe and comfortable life I knew."

Dreorigmod, dreorigferþ, hygesorg, freorigferþ, wintercearig, winegeomor, geomorfrod.

They all rush up to me, all the words wolves have for sadness.

Mind sad, soul sad, heart sad, sadness that freezes the soul, winter sad, old with sadness.

"Why didn't you?"

Sorglufu.

Sadness born of love.

The wood frame of the door feels cool against my back.

"Homelands is not safe." She drops to the thin mattress, then hugs the hard pillow to her waist. "It's not comfortable either. But I feel stronger here than I ever did when I was safe and comfortable. And I *know* beyond the shadow of a doubt that if I went back, I would wither away to nothing."

Dreorigmod, dreorigferþ, hygesorg, freorigferþ, wintercearig, winegeomor, geomorfrod. My sadnesses tremble like drops on the tips of leaves when the rain is over.

I pick up a bag from the back of the chair and hand it to her.

"It's for you."

She runs her finger over the pink canvas with the white embroidered logo. "Halvors, Sorensson, and Trianoff," she reads and looks up at me. "Is it a present?"

"I don't think so." I settle next to her. "I mean, I didn't buy it."

She reaches her hand in, hesitating as her fingers try to make sense of the cool, smooth shape with such sharp points.

A loose string catches around one of the teeth as she removes the skull from the bag. She turns the groundhog around slowly. The bone glows gold in the low light, the teeth glint, and the eyes are hollow and shaded.

It's hard to read her expression, but she does not look like a woman who has been given a box of tampons.

"It's your First Kill," I say before adding hopefully that I'd made sure it was clean.

She turns it around. Her hair is covering her face so I can't see her eyes, and I can't help but feel that I've made a terrible mistake and that a groundhog skull in no way resembles leopard-print slippers or a pink camera or a cheese board or any of the other presents that say I love you.

I feel again how empty my hands are.

"The Alpha told me," she begins. Her voice trails off. "She told me that First Kills mark the moment when young wolves move beyond being simply takers."

She puts the skull gently on the bed and reaches around,

her hand to the back of my head and her lips to mine. Relief makes me laugh against her mouth.

"That's the best thing I've ever gotten, but this"—she searches around behind her until she finds a box—"this is the second best."

The black box has the outline of a jowly man in a helmet.

"I offered Leonora my rings for these," she says. "She didn't take them—the rings—but it would have been worth every penny."

The smell coming from the opened box burns my nose like creosote.

"What are condoms?"

She gives me a smile that is so big and bright, the kind that makes me think she's going to jump into the blue sky and that maybe condoms are as wondrous as tampons.

"Get naked and once you are, I'll—" She raises an eyebrow. "Okay, that was...really fast."

"I'm pack. Getting naked fast is what we do."

"Lie down," she says, pushing me back. She takes off her own shirt, binding for a moment her arms above her head, exposing her breasts. It is colder in the cabin and she shivers. I am used to the cold and reach out to her to warm her body, to take the pebble of her nipple in my mouth and swirl with my tongue, silk on one side, velvet on the other until I start to bury my fingers inside her—

She pulls my hand out and sucks the slickness from my fingers before wrapping my fist around the base of my erection. "Hold yourself. Like that." She extracts a gold packet from the box and tears it open with her teeth, taking out a thin ring. She pinches the tip before slowly, excruciatingly slowly, unfurling it over the length of my cock. A smile plays on the corners of her mouth while the tip of her tongue traces her upper lip back and forth in concentration until finally she is done and I am encased.

"I love what you do with your fingers," she says and scrapes her fingers across my palm and up my arm, sending an icy shiver up my spine. Then she leans over, her breasts soft against the plowed furrows of my chest. My head falls back as I feel the heat of her breath against my throat.

"I love what you do with your mouth." Her lips brush mine. "But…"

She pushes herself up from my shoulder, all the gentleness and softness gone. Tightening her grip, she swings one leg over, straddling my hips.

"But now…" She slides, riding along the ridge of me. Then she stops, poised at the crown. I try to push her off, or at least that's what I will tell myself. The grip of her hands on my shoulders and her thighs around my hips were impossible to break, or at least that's what I will tell myself.

Then Julia strikes and I gasp and my hips jerk forward and I'm buried inside her, feeling her pulsing around me, and I stop telling myself anything at all.

Chapter 25

Julia

This would be Ælfrida's fourth and last attempt. The Pack at Essex had refused, as had Anglia. Even the tiny remnants of the Pack at Gyrwe had sent her away empty-handed.

Now staring at the strong and plentiful wolves of Wessex, her heart sank. She'd even caught sight of a pup staring at her from under a dead oak, the first she'd seen in England in over a decade.

Her own Mercia Pack hadn't had a pup since Halwende, and he was almost an adult. As she waited to be announced, subordinate wolves circled Mercia's Alpha, sniffing her curiously and gathering her scent to take back to the dominants. Others, still in skin, watched from a distance.

"Ælfrida, Alpha of Mercia. Wessex þu wilcumaþ swa beódgæst."

Ælfrida, Alpha of Mercia. Wessex welcomes you as table guest.

I CLOSE THE BOOK, MY FINGER HOLDING MY PLACE. GWENN is the only other member of the 12th who is reading. Ulrich is sitting, arms resting on the library table. Editha, Tonia, and Kyle are lying on the floor. The rest stand alert at the opened windows that look out onto the trees and Home Pond and an enormous sandbox of packed earth that no pup has ever used.

"What *are* we doing here?" I ask.

"Waiting," Gwenn says.

"I know that. But what are we waiting for?"

Arthur shrugs. Editha's eyes circle toward me. Gwenn starts a big yawn but suddenly remembers she has cheeks and cuts it off.

"Does it bother you to wait, Shifter?" Inna asks.

"When I don't know what I'm waiting *for*, it does."

"When I was Offland," Hakan starts, "I had a boss— which is like an Alpha, but without—"

"We know what a 'boss' is, Kappa."

"Well, my boss played many random games of domi- nance. Assigning meaningless tasks. Imposing rules that served no purpose. Punishing workers for unimportant infractions like being ten minutes late coming back from lunch, which was because of fire engines. Making us wait to prove that he could. Perhaps the Shifter fears that the Alpha is playing random games of dominance?"

Luckily, Lorcan comes in, putting an end to all talk of the random games of dominance played by Offland bosses.

He holds up a wire and plug. "Had to find a charger," he explains and kicks the door closed behind him. Nudging his wolves away from the outlet, he plugs in the charger, then plugs in a phone. He sets it on the table and waits.

The little battery icon blinks. As soon as it's charged enough, Lorcan passes the phone first to Editha, his Beta. Two by two, the wolves crowd around the phone. My hand itches for it.

Finally, it is our turn. I hold the phone because Arthur never has. It's on Instagram, and at first, I am distracted by the thought of hundreds of unseen responses on my Art_ Tarts account and the followers I have no doubt lost by not responding.

The phone times out and Arthur stares at the blank screen until I swipe again.

Now I pay attention, not to the number of followers or likes but to the photograph, blurred and shadowy, but still identifiable as a dark-gray, moon-gilt wolf only partly hidden by trees.

Gingerly, I scroll down to see the comments.

BangBang.
🐺 💀
🐺 ☠️
🐺 🩸
Guess I'll be getting a new rug! LOL
👉 👉 Check it out @NYSPredator!
#ADKWolf #ADKPredatorParty

Arthur stares at this little box with its little app and its little picture of a little mistake that could be fatal.

He bends his head and rubs his cheek against the screen as though marking her. The image disappears, replaced by someone's breakfast burrito.

"She usually stays clear," Lorcan says, taking the phone, "but the last night of the Iron Moon, when the hunters came, she veered a little too close. One of them got a picture."

Lorcan holds the phone loosely in one hand. "Thea has tried to claim it is a coyote, but…"

His voice fades. Not that he needs to finish the sentence. We've all seen the comments and it won't take long before someone who knows the difference confirms it.

"We need the lands to the north for the Gray," Lorcan continues. "The lawyers are working on getting them from August Leveraux's estate."

It's odd, hearing this name that had once been so important to me. That I had lobbed helter-skelter whenever I wanted money or respect or a reservation. Now it is indistinct and distant, like a name shouted from a boat far out at sea.

Lorcan glances at the image once more before flicking it away with his thumb and looking around at his wolves gathered in the library. No one is lying on the floor now. Now they all stand at attention, a current coiling through the little crowd that needs to be released in action.

"Until we get that land, the Gray is the 12th's wolf and we will protect her. Friday night to Sunday night are, for whatever reason, always worst. The Alpha and I will patrol the Homelands side and Thea has offered to monitor the boundary on the Offland side, but we need one more Homeland wolf who completed Advanced Human Behaviors to help her."

As one, the 12th looks down. Gwenn sniffs at the spine of a book, then opens it, pretending to read.

Lorcan stares at each disconcerted wolf who refuses to look at him.

"Hakan?" Lorcan says to the Kappa, who just minutes ago was talking so authoritatively about bosses.

"I… If there's no one else, I can try," he says, "but you remember what happened—"

"Right, never mind," Lorcan says. "Did anyone at least graduate from Intermediate?"

Reinholt's foot pounds the floor in furious rhythm with the hand scratching his scalp.

"I can do it," I say.

Lorcan stares at me as though I'd just materialized through solid brick.

"Alpha, no," Gwenn says. "She is not Pack and the 12th is responsible for her. If she goes Offland and—"

"'She' is right here. Look, I get why it's hard to trust me. I am August Leveraux's niece, though I no longer get any pleasure from saying that. But I've already been Offland. Alone. With $1,500 and a car. I could have been miles from here in the safe and easy life that was served up to me. But I am not there. I am here. In a life I know is *not* safe *or* easy and never will be. And I am offering to help."

Lorcan looks from Gwenn to Arthur to me.

"Did you pass Advanced Human Behaviors?" he asks.

"I did not pass Advanced Human Behaviors, but I spent five years in an all-girls boarding school."

"Intermediate?" he asks hopefully.

"Humans don't teach human behavior, Alpha. Maybe they should but they don't. Here's the one thing I can promise you: Nothing prepares you for the darkest corners of the human heart like five years in an all-girls boarding school."

Lorcan shifts the phone from hand to hand.

"Editha?" he says, looking at his Beta.

"Gwenn's right," she says, scratching at her thumb. "She is not one of us."

Lorcan shakes his head slowly and turns to his wolves, hoping, I suppose, that one of them will miraculously look like a convincing human and offer him some other solution.

I turn to my wolf, hoping he can miraculously come up with the words that will make them trust me. Arthur doesn't say anything. Instead, he puts both hands to the hem of his shirt. A moment later, it hangs loosely in one hand. He lifts his chin toward the ceiling, his hair falling behind his shoulders.

See me, I am exposed.

The wolves stop and watch. I should have known that the thing they needed to hear would have no sound. That the thing I needed to say would have no words. I lean into him, my breasts against his torso, teeth against neck, my heart beating in time with the fluttering of his vein under my tongue.

I see you at your most vulnerable and will not hurt you.

I feel the weight of the Pack's eyes on us as clearly as I feel the whimper in his throat tight against my stretched mouth, responding to the distant howl in the far-off mountain of the wolf who was once theirs.

I took my book from the library, writing the title on the list on the clipboard that hangs from the nail pounded into the wall beside the doorway. Attached by a length of red and white butcher string, the pencil had been thoroughly gnawed by sharp teeth. Arthur warned me that Gran Jean could smell water damage and the glue of a cracked spine and gave me a bookmark.

The same bookmark I carefully slip between the pages before putting the book into my backpack as a woman in a deep khaki shirt and pants strides quickly up to the path toward the large rock facing Westdæl where I have been sitting since early this morning. There is a black tape that says VILLALOBOS on her upper left-hand pocket, and the handle of a gun is visible in a holster attached to her belt.

"You go that way," she says, pointing down the narrow dirt path marked by an artfully roughhewn sign that says WOLF HILL—2.8 MILES. "Stop anyone coming," she says and heads back the way she came. "I'm handling the trailhead."

Thea is human but she acts like a wolf. Gives commands like a wolf. I don't know why she's saying what she's saying, but I trust her. Like a wolf. Even as I turn toward Wolf Hill, I hear a familiar scuffling from the tree-covered hill above. Wolves hunting are always silent; fighting, not so much. Lorcan yelps loudly.

I jog south, following the path marked by crushed grass and mud stamped with heavy treads, picking up speed as I catch the sound of women talking. I am well out of earshot of Westdæl before I slow down, trying to look casual as I round a curve on two young women in their twenties. Local, judging by their sweatshirts (Northern Adirondack Central

School—Home of the Bobcats!); would rather not be local, judging by their hair color (one blue, one green). They know enough to wear hiking shoes and backpacks, not the compression leggings and athletic top with convoluted straps that I wore hiking in Rougemont.

They smell like citronella oil.

"Hey," I say. "We have to stay back."

"What for?"

"I don't know but I talked to a ranger. She said there was some trouble up ahead and give her a minute to sort it out."

"The one with the black hair?"

"Yeah, I guess."

"What kind of trouble?" asks Blue Hair.

"She didn't say exactly, just someone acting up?"

The blue-haired woman tightens her lips and shakes her head. "See, Caro? I knew it. The moment we saw Devin and his dad in the parking lot, we should've gotten back in the car and headed to Pinnacle."

"Who's Devin?" I ask, less because I care and more to give Thea time.

"He's just a guy we know from high school," continues Blue Hair. "Most of them aren't from around here."

"Tracey's cousin was there too, Nat," says the green-haired Caro, who is quieter and reminds me of myself. I smile at her, offering encouragement. Still waters run deep and all that.

"I said most," Nat snaps. "Anyway, they're all there with their camp chairs and coolers. Couple of them were already drinking."

"What are they? Birders?" I ask as though I didn't already know.

Caro and Nat stare at me blankly.

"You know, like, bird watchers," I add when they don't answer.

"I know what birders are," Nat says incredulously. "But they're not looking for birds. They're waiting for the wolf. You know from the picture? You'd have to live under a rock not to have heard about it."

"Close. Montreal."

Nat nods. "I went to Montreal for a senior trip. Rained the whole damn time."

"That sounds like Montreal." I try to smile but it's hard to pretend that I give a fuck about the weather in Montreal.

Caro holds out her phone and shows me the now-familiar fuzzy picture of the wolf who was once Varya.

"Yup, that's it. So this picture gets posted and suddenly every guy in the North Country is gearing up like the Russians are invading," Nat says in disgust. "You watch, it'll turn out that one of Uncle RonRon's coydogs got loose, but he's too chicken to admit to it."

Nat sniffs. "You got a tissue, Caro?"

I watch the whole process—the digging out from the backpack, the picking out from the little plastic package, the unfurling, the dabbing at the nose—with my teeth gritted, my jaw clenching and unclenching.

"I mean honestly, what do I care if there's a wolf up there. We've got too many deer anyways. Too many ticks. Let them deal with it." And she points with her chin toward Homelands.

"Who are 'them'?" I ask.

"It's 'they,'" Caro says. "Who are *they*."

Nat rolls her eyes and points to one of the huge yellow signs the Pack has posted all around the boundaries of their land. "See those? Trust me, you don't want to go there. To start with, there's no trails or anything. Then…wait, you don't have a gun, do you?"

I shake my head.

"Good because it's like they can sniff them out. And if you come into their land, they don't like it, but if you come into their land with a gun? You see at the bottom it says something like yada, yada, yada 'fullest extent of the law'? Turns out that the 'fullest extent of the law' is an oceanic shit show."

"When Al Anderson went in a couple of months ago, he didn't have a gun."

"He had traps, Caro. And besides, I don't trust Al. He's got this thing about them. Even when they paid for the new fairgrounds, he said we shouldn't let them because they were only doing it so the fireworks would be farther away from their land."

I think of the First Shoes' terrified faces when the condom popped and think that sounds about right.

"Me, I'm, like, fine, whatever," Nat continues. "Let 'em pay for it."

"Grandma says they're satanists," Caro says, and I start revising my assessment of stillness-to-depth ratio. A mud puddle can be pretty damn still.

"Your grandma thinks Presbyterians are satanists," Nat

says. She looks at her phone again and slaps it lightly against her palm. "How long did that ranger woman say it was going to take?"

"Environmental conservation officer," Thea says, turning the corner with an unnaturally bright smile. "Thank you for waiting."

"Was it those guys?" Caro asks.

Thea gives a single shake of her head, which could be "no" but looks more like "not at liberty to tell" or some other official non-answer answer.

"I knew we should've done Pinnacle," Nat says before turning to me. "It was nice to meet you...?"

"Jas," I say, because weirdly it's the first name that comes to me.

"Maybe next time I'm in Montreal."

"Sounds great," I say, though neither of us bother with last names or phone numbers or anything. I find myself flagging under the effort of making conversation.

At the bend in the path, Caro turns around and signals to me, shouting.

"Maybe you should come with us. I know these types. What with the beer and the Captain Morgan and the guns, it's not really a safe place for a woman alone."

I shake my head. "Thanks, I'll be fine," I say.

I don't tell her the reason I'll be fine is that I am neither a woman nor alone.

Thea waits. Only when she is sure that I can no longer hear them do we head back to Westdæl. I tell her about Nat and Caro's divided opinions as to whether it's a wolf or one of RonRon's coydogs. I tell her about their dislike for the Great North and its litigiousness and its secrecy.

"What can they do? Nothing will make the Pack acceptable except being normal, and that's the one thing they'll never be."

I reach out, holding her arm and taking a deep breath until it rattles around like rust inside my head.

"Someone's bleeding," I say.

"Lorcan. The Gray didn't like having him on her territory. She ripped up his shoulder."

"We need to get him back."

"Elijah will go with him as soon as he brings Arthur."

"Elijah is bringing Arthur?" I ask. "Why Arthur?"

"The Gray seems to have some residual memory, and the Alpha hopes she'll recognize him."

"She didn't recognize Lorcan and he's her Alpha. Was."

"That seems to be the problem. Lorcan has changed over the past weeks, but Varya never respected him as Alpha. Never felt he was strong enough."

"If she didn't feel Lorcan was strong enough, what is she going to do to Arthur?"

"The pack has great respect for Arthur's strength even though he is not highly placed. Varya did too. She only ever marked two wolves in the Great North. One was Evie, the other was Arthur."

I pull my book and my thermos from the backpack and settle them on my stone. "How do you know all this anyway?"

"Elijah spent three decades among humans," she says. "He picked up some bad habits. Like gossip. He's a terrible gossip."

Maybe we both imagine the 9th's mighty Alpha leaning across a white picket fence with a housedress and a furtive look. I doubt it, but for whatever reason, we both laugh.

Thea's fingers play lightly across the leather band around her neck.

"What is that?" I lift my chin toward her throat. "The necklace you're wearing… I've seen a lot of wolves wearing them."

"It's not a necklace, it's a braid. It's the symbol of a mated wolf: the three strands symbolize the connection of land and pack and mated pair."

"So you're married to Elijah, even though you're human?"

"I'm not married. We're not mated either. Not officially anyway. If I had been pack, our echelon would have hunted the deer and tanned the hide using the oaks of Homelands. Then it would have been cut into a long strand and anointed by the blood of the Alpha and the sex of the couple." She touches it with a soft smile. "Elijah took the law into his own hands and made it himself. I wore it at first, not understanding what it meant. Then Elijah insisted I take it off until I did. Understand." She looks toward Westdæl. "He's here," she says.

Shading my eyes with my hand, I search the near-vertical western slope of the Gray's mountain territory, scanning the trees that cling precariously to the mountainside by long exposed roots. Finally, I see them, two wolves: one black with eyes the color of amber, the other graphite with eyes the color of silver. The black one turns away and waits, giving the gray one the privacy to say what he needs to even though he has no words. A few quiet, distant moments later, he closes his eyes. When he opens them again, he whips about to follow the Alpha.

I turn toward Thea, my fingers toying with the empty space at the base of my throat.

"What did he want you to understand?" I ask.

"What?"

"Elijah. About your braid."

"Oh that. He wanted to make sure I understood that I was leaving certainty behind, that I was choosing another life, a dangerous life. A life lived"—she nods toward the precipice of Westdæl—"on the edge."

———————

Turns out that Elijah's gossip is solid, because the Gray accepts Arthur's presence. It's quiet where I am along the trail, I suppose because the hunters are jammed up closer to the trailhead and most everyone else is opting for Pinnacle instead.

Between my reading and wandering, I found a pencil nestled in the tall grasses and Queen Anne's lace ringing the back of the boulder. It's weathered, but I can still read the color embossed on the side.

Periwinkle, it says.

I slide it into the backpack, put the backpack under my head, and stretch out on the warm rock, listening to the chir-ring of crickets, a bird singing *welewooowelewoo*, squirrels running over branches, and the soft rustle of wind through the leaves, the distant *tat-a-tat* of a woodpecker. My eyes flutter closed to the rough cry of ravens.

When I wake, it's with a bad feeling of something not quite right. The wolves of Westdæl are silent, which is good, but so are the squirrels and birds, which is not. A hawk circles the swathes of weeds and high grass that bend as something moves through them. I jump up on my rock, watching a man dressed in gray and black camouflage who's hunkered down behind the artemisia. He has a backpack and a rifle slung over his shoulder.

Seeing me, he stands upright.

"Hey, little darling," he calls. "What're you doing out here?"

"Reading. You?"

"Came out to stake a claim away from the crowds. There's some bitch with a badge saying nobody's allowed along the trails with guns. Which is bullshit. If you can walk on the trails, you can have guns on the trails."

"She's an environmental conservation officer," I say coldly. I'm going to have to warn Thea.

The man struggles forward until he stands in front of my rock, his hand to his forehead, blocking the sun setting behind me.

"You should be careful," he says. "Haven't you heard? There's a wolf out here. You'd make a pretty tempting target. All alone, by yourself."

I understand the menace in his repeated emphasis— *alone, by yourself*—and the way he stands so close. I think briefly about saying that I'm waiting for my boyfriend, but then what? Supposing this hunter says he'll wait with me. Keep me company, as though any woman alone must be in want of male companionship.

"I'm okay, thanks."

"You don't know what you're talking about, darlin'. When those things start hunting, you can't run because running makes them more excited. They kill just to kill."

My heart beats faster and my molars grind and I feel the desire to lash out bubbling up in my blood, but I told Lorcan I knew how humans worked and I could handle them.

"And why do you kill?"

He reaches behind, pulling a dinged metal thermos from the pocket of his backpack. He unscrews it and offers it to me. Whatever is inside is sweet and acrid and isn't coffee. I shake my head and he slugs it down, smacking his lips.

"I hunt to make the world safer for Little Miss Riding Hoods like you." Now he's close enough for me to feel the heat of his legs.

"It's Little *Red* Riding Hood or Little *Miss* Muffet," I say.

He lowers his thermos, his lips tight. A drop with the color of syrup and the smell of ruin runs down his chin. As he opens his mouth to answer, I hold up my hand.

"*Shhhhhh.*"

He stops in the middle of screwing the top back on and stares at me in disbelief. "Are you *shushing* me?" Then he takes an ill-advised step closer.

I hear it, a slow growl rolling down the steep slope.

Shit.

"You need to back away. Slowly."

He slides his thermos back in the pocket and does the opposite. He leans his body against my knees.

The growl comes again, distant still but closer.

"It's going to be okay," I say loudly. I've got two conversations going on: one with a man who means nothing, and another one with a wolf who means everything. "I've got this."

"What is it you think you've got?" the man asks. Stretching out his sweaty, mosquito-bitten arms, he puts his hands on the rock on either side of me, touching my thighs.

I am trying, Leonora. I'm trying to use my words and not use my teeth, but right about now, teeth feel like they'd be so much more persuasive.

"I'm trying to warn you. This is not going to end well."

"Oh, but I think it will," he says with a sly smile.

Something is moving high among the trees, a shadow among the shadows, and only when the leaves move does sunlight pick out his fur. His eyes are black pits surrounded by a thin silver ring like the night after a new moon. I don't have time for more words.

It seems to happen so slowly. A push, a stumble, a toe to the temple, a disconcertingly contented sigh. His rifle slithers from his shoulder, followed by the *thunk* of a heavy body. I take the rifle, holding it casually as though I've grown up with guns, which I have. As though my father taught me how to protect myself, which he never did.

"Where the fuck do you get off, touching my rifle?" he yells, scrambling to his feet.

"And where the fuck do you get off, touching my body?" I snap back. "Now get out."

"Not without my gun."

I jam the narrow shooting end into a wide crack in the rock and push to the side. The thing bends and snaps.

"My father gave that to me!" he shrieks.

"Fetch," I say and throw the pieces impossibly far.

And the howling man, trained in games of mindless obedience, chases after them, promising to report me to Thea, "the bitch with a badge."

As soon as he is out of sight, I scrabble up the hill, holding branches and bracken, anything rooted into the steepness. The low sun has painted one side of the trees gold while plunging the other side into darkness.

Up above me, the Alpha growls a warning.

And that's when I see him, gray fur shimmering like a silver birch among the patches of deep shadow.

Other wolves appear—large wolves, Alphas—forming a half circle, watching, a growing wall of fur and fang, and I remember what Leonora said.

For the safety of the Pack, we will do whatever must be done to stop him.

I know by the way they hold themselves, by the grimness of their eyes, that they are ready to tear him apart, the man-wolf who cannot be trusted not to kill his own.

"Arthur." My voice echoes in the quiet. Now, even the leaves seem to want to avoid notice. His head whips around toward me, lips pulled back tight, snarling below those impossibly dark eyes.

He moves slowly toward me, head swaying as though he is hunting for some sign, some sight, some smell, some sound that will remind him who he is. He stifles a growl between clenched jaws, his hind legs trembling in effort. Maybe the wolves of the Great North see their Omega losing control, but all I see is Arthur trying so hard to hold on to it. Begging for help to hold on.

My eyes meet the Alpha's over his shoulders.

Please, Alpha, I beg her silently. *I can do this myself.*

It's exactly what Arthur said, right before Silver tore him open. And as at the Clawing, the Alpha sizes up the situation. Maybe she decides that if Arthur tears into me, it will be distraction enough for her to take him down. Whatever her calculations, she doesn't move and I drop to my knees in front of him.

He leans in, and the heat of his breath on my skin sends a chill up my spine. My weight shifts and my foot slips and I start to fall backward in a tumble of dead leaves, air, bark, and green until a shadow leaps over me and I come to a stop against the Alpha's stiffened body. She stumbles slightly when I hit but then holds. Arthur is above me, blinking against the sunset, his lips curled back from long fangs.

I feel Arthur teetering, and I have to pull him back from the edge. With Cassius, I would have used an eager-to-please smile or the coy glance, but submission isn't what Arthur needs. I know my fear will only drive him farther in.

Scrabbling back up the hill, I grab him by the thick fur on either side of his jaws and force him to turn away from the Alpha.

"You told me," I whisper, "that no matter what you were, you would always know me." His too-black eyes turn toward mine. I don't turn away.

"So, wolf, know me now."

I put my head against his cheek and mark him the way wolves do. Then I stop and listen to the rumble in his chest and in his throat that doesn't break out through his mouth. I feel the shiver of his muscles as they tighten and hold.

Everything stops: the wolves above, the Alpha below, the sun, which by all rights should have already set but seems to wait, breathless on the horizon.

Arthur's heart beats against my chest and I whisper to him.

Arthur leans in to me, the growl fading.

Ahhh, you heard that, didn't you, my werewolf.

Letting go of his fur, I wrap my arms around his head. The Alpha starts away, though when Arthur straightens his back legs, she skitters, still tense, and the wall of wolves steps back.

At this moment, he is the most dangerous thing in this place. More dangerous than the drunk men with guns; more dangerous than the wolves; more dangerous, even, than the Alpha—and in some primal part of my brain, I want him. Like this.

"Change, werewolf, and fuck me."

Chapter 26

Arthur

Madness is not dark.

Madness is a constant swirl of too much. Dizzying and endless and too fast to grab hold of, to make sense of.

Except something cracks the maelstrom with the sound of command that I want to obey and that I have to obey.

Change, it says.

Change.

And *fuck me*, it orders.

I look down, surprised to see a hand with fingers that follow my instructions to claw at the mulch. I know I look human though I have never been less.

She puts her hand to my face, watching me unblinking, unafraid and unclothed, her thighs draped across mine.

Come, says the voice. I know that voice. I need that voice.

Come into me.

I need you.

My body struggles against itself, straining forward and holding back, all the violence of fire burned up on stasis.

I cannot find the words in the welter. I cannot put them

into order. I cannot talk to her, tell her that I am rough, I am raw and can't now be anything else.

Yes, she says.

"Julia." It is the one word I can find. The one word I can say. It cracks from my mouth, a warning that I don't remember how to break inside her and keep her whole.

"Yes," she says.

Her hand runs down my chest like blood and honey, warm and sweet, wounding and feeding.

"Yes," she says.

By the time she comes to my cock, it is overfull with all the excesses of my mind. I am too far gone for kindness and gentleness. She circles her fingers around me, and I am hard as bone pushing into her hand.

She pulls me. Hand on my shoulder, thigh on my hip. "I can't do it all. Lift me. Use your hands. Like that. Like that. I will not break. I need," she says. "*I need.*" She takes my lip with her teeth. There is blood on her tongue. I suck at it, drawing more, and she grinds against me. She throws her head back and I take muscle that stands out strong between neck and shoulder and pin her there while I lift her, settle her on my hips, burrowing, burying impossibly deep, as though somehow, some way, I will be able to fuck my way to clarity.

She comes in great powerful spasms that demand everything I have and consume everything I am. And when I open my eyes to the fluttering of her heart, the stuttered breaths and the scream of *Yesyesyes!* and fall into the softness of her breasts and the hardness of her arms clinging to a rough trunk for her life and for mine, I look beyond her to nothing but an abyss.

Chapter 27

Julia

I COULD HAVE SAT WITH HIM, PETTED HIM, SOOTHED HIM, waited with him until he was calm and he recognized me and we walked back to the cabin or ran for the forests. I would have berated him gently, reminding him I could take care of myself.

But I needed him dangerous and rough and wild. I needed the trembling of barely contained fury. I needed to know I could ride the violence of fire and escape unscathed.

And I did. Almost.

There is a place not far from the ruined farm with its wild-ling lilac. It is a small clearing bordering a sluggish stream. At night, a thousand lights puncture the black sky above and a thousand fireflies sparkle among the laurel below.

We were to go there on our way back from Westdæl. I had even slipped a condom into my backpack.

Now, I slip the condom's remains into my pocket.

I don't know exactly what happened... I wasn't careful, we weren't careful. We were too hard, too rough, too wild, too much, but I do know that...

The balloon popped.

Chapter 28

Arthur

SOMETHING HAPPENED AT MOVIE NIGHT. I HAD THOUGHT of taking Julia, but there was a touch and then another and we didn't. Now all of us who weren't there are gathered around the wolves who were, collecting accounts, mostly in the Old Tongue because the Old Tongue has so many words for anger: anger of the mind, anger of the soul, fake anger, anger from pain, anger from offense, anger of impatience. Anger of the heart. The fury of a woman.

I try to translate for Julia as quickly as I can. Poul, the Alpha of the 10th, is a strong unmated wolf and has always assumed that when the Alpha became receptive again, she would choose him. Apparently, she not only did *not* choose Poul. She didn't even choose a member of the Great North. She chose Constantine. A Shifter.

Poul was *ierreþweorh*—insolent in his anger—and the two of them fought *handlinga*—in skin, with hands—which left Poul with what one wolf describes as a *heolfrig hleor*—a gory face—though another wolf insists it was no more than *blodig næs-gristle*—bloody nose cartilage.

Whatever the extent of the damage, it caused an

immediate loss of respect and that made Poul *gyrst*—teeth-gnashingly angry—so he challenged Constantine to a fight for *cunnan-riht*—fucking rights—except Silver said he couldn't because Constantine was neither pack nor a *beod-gæst*—table guest—of the Pack. Poul took a flyer on demanding a *mæþ holmgang*—an honor challenge—but predictably the Deemer shot that down because if Constantine was not wolf enough to fight for fucking, he was certainly not wolf enough to fight for honor.

The only legal challenge, she said, would be a *hyrdunggaderunggefandung*.

"A *what*?"

I look around the table. Inna shrugs. George holds up his hands.

"A strength-encouraging bringing test...ing?"

Julia scratches at the corner of her mouth.

"Back when there used to be other packs, dispersers would sometimes make their way here hoping to join the Great North. But the Pack has never had room for weakness, so those wolves had to fight a *hyrdunggaderunggefandung* with a high-ranking wolf to prove that they brought strength to the Pack."

"Constantine is not a wolf," Julia says, her eyes brightening.

"And Tiberius is only half-wolf, but no one would argue that he hasn't brought strength to the Great North."

"I take it that's Poul?" Julia whispers, lifting her chin toward the 10th Echelon's Alpha, who is readily recognizable by his swollen plum-colored nose.

"Hmm."

"Seems to me like they already fought and that Constantine won," she says, looking down the length of the table.

I pull the cheese plate from behind the bread basket and hand it to her.

"Fighting in skin is play fighting. Outside the law. You can't move up the hierarchy, so it's meaningless."

She cuts off several big hunks of cheddar and spoons out the house cheese with honey and thyme before passing it down.

No one reminds her anymore that she needs to eat everything she takes.

A new whisper starts as a wolf of the 11th leans in to our table.

I tell her that Constantine has apparently managed to convince Elijah to train him. They've already started sparring, which explains why Constantine is eating with his left hand while his right shoulder seeps blood through his shirt.

Only the Alpha is a better fighter than Elijah. Not only is Elijah an Alpha, but he spent thirty years Offland, making him a prime target for wolves who thought an Alpha's place was at home.

No one was able to unseat him then or when he declared that he was mated to a human either.

Julia looks thoughtfully toward Elijah, who is talking to Tiberius. Silver's mate leans against the back of the sofa with Sigeburg on his crooked arm. The pup is watching Elijah gesticulate with a breadstick until he waves it a bit too close and Sigeburg takes the opportunity to leap, grabbing the breadstick in her little jaws.

She skitters under the sofa and Tiberius laughs, his long, sharp, inhuman fangs shining brightly.

"If we had children," Julia says out of nowhere, "would they have teeth like that? Like Tiberius?"

"I don't…I don't know."

"He's half-pack, half-Shifter."

"I don't know, Julia," I say, tension settling hard in my stomach. "This is why we're using condoms, so we never have to find out."

"Never is a long time," she says.

I pick up my plate.

"Not long enough."

Chapter 29

Julia

WHEN THE TIME CAME, NO ONE IN THE GREAT NORTH seemed to think Constantine had a chance. Poul had been fighting fang and claw his entire life. Constantine had had a month.

Remembering what my mother said, I wasn't so sure.

Death walks in that man's footsteps.

Wolves nudged each other and pointed each time Constantine walked in with a new injury, except for the Alpha, who avoided looking at him at all. I barely knew him but I did know he was not an easy mark, and sure enough, a few days before the Iron Moon, Elijah was the one who was limping.

Death walks in that man's footsteps.

On the last day of the Iron Moon, Constantine, now a gray wolf with eyes the color of moss, measured off the rectangle of packed dirt surrounded by low wood walls where Pack fought their challenges. I saw in him something that transcended my mother's talk about death and footsteps. I saw in him bleak determination: losing wasn't an option because leaving wasn't an option. I understood what pushed him to take this slim chance at staying in this forsaken for-ested corner of upstate New York, forgotten miles away from even Plattsburgh. Of throwing his lot in with its doomed Pack and the Alpha of the haunted eyes.

I needed him to win because if he had a chance, maybe I did too.

It all fell apart shortly after Poul jumped into the pad-dock. Constantine started to panic, racing back and forth as though he was searching for a way out, then he shot the Alpha a look of despair and leapt over the side. He clam-bered across the backs of wolves before disappearing into the woods.

We all watched stunned and silent as he vanished. Wolf by wolf, their mood changed from curious to confused to furious. I could hear the snarls, feel them even in the wolves near me.

Poul followed Constantine, his head low to the ground, tracking him.

It didn't make sense to me. That was not who Constantine was. He'd never run from anything. I searched through the wolves of the Great North, looking for Tiberius; he would know. Even Cassius would…

There had been a time not so long ago when I put on perfume Cassius liked and threw out the one I liked. A time when I ate a jambon-beurre before dinner so that I could order a salad and not starve. A time when I pretended to like horror movies because he liked the way they made me tremble.

How could a man who had taken up so much real estate

in my mind have vanished so completely? As completely as he has from his sullen spot on the edge of the Pack.

I knew Constantine would not run away, but he would definitely run after.

I pushed my way through the wolves still milling around the paddock and began tracking Cassius's sour scent. Before long, Arthur arrived at my side.

When there are no words, wolves must trust, and Arthur trusts me absolutely. Trusts that even if he doesn't understand what it is, there is something I need. Finally, I found what I was looking for. After rubbing my face into the spot, I whipped around. Arthur cleared a path back to the Alpha, his teeth tearing along the flanks and muzzles of any wolf who didn't move fast enough.

When I reached the Alpha and offered up my muzzle, she stilled. I feared at first she would dismiss me as another problematic Shifter, but as she leaned into my face, the heartbreak in her eyes changed.

She jumped on the wall of the paddock, her head held high, ears turning, nose searching the winds of Homelands.

The Great North stilled, looking for guidance from their Alpha, though my echelon, the 12th, sniffed my muzzle and knew.

The Alpha turned toward the Boathouse just in time to see Constantine leap from the end of the dock.

And the tail end of a canoe disappearing behind the trees on the opposite side.

"Here's another bowl, just in case."

I eye the ancient turquoise Duralex bowl through the slits in my lids, then hiccup. Like every hiccup since the last night of the Iron Moon, it is fetid with the taste of my former fiancé.

A splash followed by drops. Arthur wrings out the cloth and presses it first to my cheek and neck and then my forehead. It does nothing for the nausea but it makes me feel a little cleaner.

I didn't see what happened after Constantine dove into the water. There were too many wolves, moving too quickly. Arthur would fill in the details as he tended me with cool cloths.

The Alpha had given Constantine his phone back, a gesture of trust or maybe of the love hinted at on that day when I refused to take Cassius's note.

Anyway, Constantine had hidden the phone in the cabin he was using, and Cassius had found out about it somehow. He'd taken advantage of the Pack's distraction to take the phone, then steal the canoe to row across the lake. He obviously hadn't counted on Constantine noticing and his determination to swim after him.

The two of them fought in the boggy Southlands that eventually give onto NY State Route 3.

By the time the Pack found them, the battered Constantine had collapsed, the worst of his many injuries a ruptured spleen and broken collarbone.

The worst of Cassius's injuries was a hole where his throat had once been.

While the Alpha stayed with Constantine, the rest of the Pack pulled Cassius back toward a tiny island in the middle of Home Pond, and there we set about eating him because the law requires that wolves eat what they kill and the Pack wasn't about to force Constantine to do this alone.

Inna was right about one thing: we taste just awful.

"You didn't have to eat so much," Arthur says, moving his cool hand to my belly. It gurgles loudly in response to his touch.

Someday it will be safe to open my mouth again. Then I'll explain to him that I did it because I felt responsible. Like maybe if I hadn't spent all those years giving in to Cassius, pretending like he was always right, he might have been able to imagine that there was value in lives that didn't revolve around him.

The floorboards squeak. "I'll be right back," Arthur says.

I listen to the sounds of voices, lulled by the growled cadences of the Old Tongue, until Arthur returns with something that smells like the consolation of new-mown lawn.

He sits on the floor because even the slightest bend in the mattress makes my gut lurch.

"It's sweetgrass," he says, holding out grassy stems. "Wolves chew it to soothe the stomach."

I look at him, bleary-eyed, as he holds it closer to me.

I open my mouth and let him feed me the blades.

As I grind it between my molars, the freshness of wild summer grass begins to cut through the hard lump of Cassius's heart slowly dissolving in my stomach.

Time had become increasingly fluid, dripping unnoticed through my fingers until one day, as I peruse newspapers on long poles that hang from hooks on a wood strip along the wall in the Main Hall, I realize that yesterday was September 12, St. Ailbhe's Day, the day emblazoned in gold script on the white, leather-bound book my mother gave me.

Underneath, in more gold script, were the words *My Day*, as though a woman could only be afforded one.

That book had sections for dresses and flowers and food and guests, and I filled it up with pictures and notes and contacts.

Somewhere in Montreal, there is a dress made of white silk that is so heavy it feels like chain mail with an overdress of lace, hand-beaded with pale-blue seed pearls. In some hothouse, someone grew lilacs of the palest blue to hang from the ceiling. In some textile factory somewhere, damascene linens were woven with our initials. A large "C," curled protectively around a smaller "J." In a custom glassworks studio outside Toronto, sheets of stippled mirrors were cut to the measurements of the Windsor Grand ballroom, so that they would reflect the hundreds of candles and the hothouse lilacs of the palest blue.

What did they do with all that?

If I'd followed the plans laid out in my wedding journal, I would have spent the night in a flurry of orgasm-free tongue-jabbing, nipple gnawing, and penis pistoning, then woken in the Royal Suite of the Windsor Grand Montreal to the rattle of a breakfast cart. I would have sat on overstuffed chairs with itchy flocking and uncomfortable gilt rails while the waiter set the table with shirred eggs and caviar with a side of bacon and toast for Cassius.

A fruit parfait ("hold the granola") for me.

I polish off the eggy cake, which has nothing to do with cake and everything to do with cheese, wiping my fingers carefully on the stiff, line-dried napkin.

Arthur halves the huge biscuit slathered with butter and the first of this year's elderberry jam and holds it out to me.

I slide my feet under his ass. Later, when I finish with the biscuit but not the story I'm reading, I burrow one heel against the seam of his jeans. I nestle it closer, feeling it grow harder against my ankle until Arthur leans over and pulls away the corner of the newspaper. He can't help but see the smile that I can't help but have. The newspaper falls to the floor with a swoosh of paper and clump of wood and he crawls the short length of the worn and cozy sofa, unleashing a tiny dusting of pup fur. He brushes my hair back and takes in my eyes like he has just seen a miracle.

He licks away the butter and the first elderberry jam of the year from my fingers and my mouth and makes me laugh and slide my legs apart, so that I can feel the lovely, slow dry hump of denim that makes me ache and burn.

All the should've and could've and would've have disappeared, leaving what is.

I have only one regret. I would have liked to go back to Monsieur Trenet, the terribly posh and oily on-site coordinator at the Windsor Grand Montreal.

I would have liked to have seen his expression when I asked for my money back.

"*Malheureusement, j'ai mangé mon fiancé, alors… Puis-je récupérer mon acompte?*"

Unfortunately, I've eaten my fiancé, so…

Can I get my deposit back?

It's getting cooler. The cold rolling down from the peaks turns into fog that snakes between trees as it hits the warmer air down below.

Color is everywhere now—not just the gaudy red maple, but the neon yellow of tamaracks and the orange sheep's laurel weighed down with pink berries and the goldenrod dotted with orange and black monarchs as they make their way south.

The little red newts.

Efts, Arthur says.

We skirt Westdæl, careful not to come too close so we don't disturb the Gray, though with Arthur, she doesn't retreat into the depths of her territory. She watches us carefully, drops dotting her muzzle from the stream that flows down before sheeting out across the rock face. Her mate is a few feet above her, looking wary.

She comes a little closer to Arthur, her nose twitching. She stares at me. She doesn't know me, so I lower my head and begin to turn away. At that moment, one of those cool breezes rolls down the mountainside.

Instantly, I know something about her, because it's a secret we share.

———————

"The Alpha wants to talk to you about the Gray," Arthur says, slinging the bag with dried peas and overlarge zucchinis that we will use to harvest next year's seeds over his shoulder.

"I didn't say I *knew* she was pregnant," I answer. "I just said I *thought* she *might* be pregnant. She looked a little, I don't know. Different." It's a lie. All of it. It's not "might be"; it *is*. I don't "think"; I *know*. How I know, that's trickier; it's an instinct born of a kindred condition.

Having spent so much of my life being discounted, it startles me to make some vague conjecture and watch it booted all the way up the chain of command, until the Alpha calls me into her office. Not Lorcan, not Arthur.

Me.

When I get there, everything is chaos. The furniture in the Alpha's office had been moved to the side to accommodate a huge map. It's hard to make out as most of it is green and blue interrupted by contour lines but few roads and no cities. There is a thick line marked in blue that I presume is Homelands. A man with a pencil kneels forward, gently sketching another line, while two women stare intently at a laptop and call out coordinates.

Constantine and Tiberius and other wolves who are dressed in the costumes of Offlanders hover nearby. One of them sits cross-legged, poring over the seventeenth edition of *Ontario Estate Management* in her lap.

"How well do you know your aunt?" the Alpha asks. A woman leans over the Alpha's laptop, pointing out something on the screen. She nods and types something before turning to look at me.

"Me?"

"You're the only one in this room who knows who her aunt is."

"I've never met Drusilla. Well, I did when I was very young and I don't really remember her." I pause for a moment, wondering if I should tell her about my father in the drain of the Racquet Club but decide against it.

"She is not a good person, Alpha."

"So I gather," she says with a quick look to Constantine. Of course he would know and of course he would tell her. "We should approach her using one of the shell companies. Maybe Platinum Paper or North Country Gas."

"TransCanNA, Alpha," says another woman who has just entered wearing a black pantsuit. She pulls a folder from a briefcase and hands it to the Alpha before rolling up her jacket and sliding it carefully among the First Kills. She pushes the sleeves of her white knit shirt up to her elbows. "This is exactly why we arranged for the self-dealing investigation. So we could have a company with just the right whiff of corruption should we ever need it."

The man with the pencil leans back onto his calves, hands pressed against his lower back.

"I think this is it, Alpha."

She moves to the map, leaning over the man's shoulder. Everyone else gathers around, looking anxiously.

Constantine's fingers curl around the Alpha's shoulder, his thumb stroking the base of her neck. Her hand goes to her mouth.

All I can see over the scrum of bodies in front of me is a few inches of gray pencil marking, herky-jerky in the sea of pale green and blue.

"All the way up to Chateaugay?"

"Nearly," the man says. "And here"—he bends down to point to the invisible map—"as far east as Champlain."

"If it's anything like as large as this, it will be enough," the Alpha says. "It will be enough for the Gray and the Bone Wolf and"—now she looks to me—"all the wolves to come."

Chapter 30

Arthur

I THOUGHT SHE'D RECOVERED FROM CASSIUS WEEKS AGO. She seemed to, at least. Recently, though, when we caught a goose, she ate almost nothing before scratching a nest for herself in dry leaves that smelled like spikenard and hops and fell asleep.

"You worry too much," she said the next night before cradling her cheek in the crook of her arm. Her free hand skimmed over my skin, pretending that she was not tired, and reached for my inconveniently hard cock, pressing her thumb to the tip.

I sucked in a breath and pulled her hand away, trapping it instead to my heart, waiting while her breathing slowed, each gentle touch of the rise and fall of her chest against my ribs making me panic.

The next morning, she refused to go to Tristan.

"You worry too much," she said again.

Yesterday afternoon, we took a late run. Everything now is sepia. It's not just the brown and gold and orange of fall. It's the sound of parchment leaves under our paws and the smell like old paper that was damp once and is now dry.

We reach the High Pines when the low sun streaks through the dark green and the soft balsam carpet called to her, and once again, she lay down and slept. I let her until I tasted the unmistakable crispness of the air, mineral and sharp like a knife. It's early in the season for snow. I'm used to it; Julia isn't and her undercoat isn't fully in yet. I nip at her flanks to get her going again, but she refuses with a snarl and whips her fang against my teeth and lies back down. I nudge her tail over her nose, then curl my body around her, knowing that when we wake up, it will be to a sun filtered by a layer of snow.

"It's time to see Tristan," I told her the next day as we sorted through the clothes just returned from the Laundry.

"Arthur, you worry too—"

Tristan kicks the step, loosening dirt from the deep treads of his boots.

"What's he doing here?" Julia asks as he sits in the chair at the desk and unties his laces.

"I hear you're feeling poorly," Tristan says, coming toward her, hand extended sideways, almost as though inviting her to dance. Julia appears to understand the invitation and extends her own. Tristan jerks her hand up and down and up, and she seems fine with that.

Not so fine when he yanks her close and sniffs at the hollow between jaw and ear.

And not "fine" at all when he falls to his knees, hands on her hips, pulling her close.

What do you think you're doing?

"A vaginal sniff?" he asks.

She jumps away, looking at me.

"It's either that or you have to come down to Medical for an ultrasound."

"Arthur?" For the first time in months, her voice sounds anxious, questioning.

"How?" I ask, staring at her belly.

"Well, my youngling," Tristan says, clasping his hands tightly together in front of him, "when two wolves love each other very—"

"*Go*," Julia snaps, her voice distant and harsh like a tree cracking in an ice storm.

"If I go, will you come for the ultrasound?"

"*Yes. Now leave.*"

The woodpecker starts in—*dhok, dhok, dkdkdkdkdkdk*—and Julia's hand clutches my wrist, stopping me. I hate the look in her eyes as she stares into mine to see if I'm losing myself.

I'm not. I am so fully me, only more despairing, knowing that whatever happens, I will remember everything afterward.

Julia twists the fading furrows left by the rings that were Cassius's claim to her. If she had not come to Homelands, she would have added another ring to all the others. She would be married to Cassius, surrounded by mirrors and hothouse lilacs in a hotel somewhere far away.

She would not be pregnant.

"I don't understand why you're so upset," she says. "Women have babies all the time."

"But. You. Are. Not. A. *Woman*."

Seconds later, the door bangs behind me. I crash full on into the trees, dropping clothes on the red elderberry though it's been weeks since the vireos and sparrows plucked it clean of any fruit.

In the darkest heart of the deepest forests of Homelands, the howl that I've been holding in finally breaks through the column of my throat. It reverberates against the sounding board of the Pack's wooded core, and within seconds, the Great North joins in. They don't ask why. They only know that there are a thousand words for sadness and all of them are contained in my keening and as long as there is one wolf left to join me, I will not sing my song of sadness alone.

I want to stay here, stay wild, but I can't. My only responsibilities as an unpaired werewolf at the bottom of the hierarchy have been working hard and keeping my shit together, except that's not enough anymore. I may not have wanted it to happen, but it did, and Julia is a long way from home. I can't desert her.

Under an overcast sky, I move quickly, making it back to the cabin just as the storm starts. Julia left the lights on and they spill out low and gold and smudged by raindrops.

I kneel beside the mattress. There's a thick book beside her. On the cover is the drawing of a woman barely older than a girl. She has a smug smile and her hands are propped proudly on her belly. Behind her is a clean and tidy quilt made of purple and white.

There are sections here about Red-Meat-Free Diet and Junk Food and Cell Phones and Hot Tubs and Stretch Marks and Body Image and Labor and Forced Labor and Forceps. There's nothing, though, about how to clear food from your mate's trachea so she won't choke to death on undigested food while her mouth changes.

Nothing about what to look for in the ultrasound so that if the pups change during an exhausted nap, the mother can be wakened before the presence of their alien bodies sets off an immune-inflammatory cascade.

And not a single mention of how to convey to a female at the end of her lying-in not to give up. To keep fighting.

The front page has a note written by Leonora that says "Advanced Human Behaviors."

I close it and drop it to the floor, then quickly slide next to Julia, staring at her sleeping face, at the hair stuck to her damp cheekbone. I loose it with my finger and smell the salt and remember that other time when her cheek was wet and she called them tears.

Oh, Julia.

"You smell like pine and rain," she says sleepily. "And fur."

She snuggles closer, her body—smooth and blanket-warm and perfect—next to mine, which is not.

"When you asked about Tiberius, about his teeth… Did you know then?"

She sighs and turns over onto her back.

"I wasn't sure."

"Why didn't you say something?"

"You seemed to hate the idea of children. Do you remember what you said? 'Never is too soon'? Something like that."

I pull the blanket over her shoulder. It's getting colder. Snow will be coming soon. Real snow, not the casual visitor of fall but the snow of winter that comes and stays.

"I don't hate the idea of children. Every child is a *wuscbearn*, a wish child, beloved by and belonging to the entire Pack. So, no, it's not about wanting children. It's about wanting *you*. It's about needing *you*. It's about"—my voice breaks—"losing *you*. This"—I lay my hand over the image of the smiling young woman and the lavender quilt—"has nothing to do with you. There's nothing about the lying-in, when the pups begin thinking for themselves, going back and forth. There's nothing about what happens if the mother doesn't change in time and her body rejects them and they all die. *All* of them. There's nothing that explains how to help a mother who stops fighting because she's just too exhausted."

Pushing the book away, I lie down next to her, looking into her autumn eyes.

"I was cut out of a wolf who stopped fighting."

I feel the heartbeat of Julia's fingers as she settles them against my pulse.

"Tell me you know me better than that."

I curl my leg across her thighs and bury my head in her hair, listening to the rain tapping against the windows.

"Arthur. I will not stop fighting, but if that book has nothing to do with me, it would help to know what does."

I would sugar coat it if I knew how but making hard things palatable is not really in our nature.

It's not bad at first, I tell her. In the beginning, pups will react to the mother's hormones, changing when she changes. It's when they start reacting to each other that the lying-in begins. That's when the whole Pack steps in and steps up.

I tell her about the Meeting House, how the Great North

cleans it from top to bottom. How we pull out the carpets and curtains that are used only for this occasion to mute sound and light. There is also a special bed for the female that goes up and down as well as a cot and chair for the male. A refrigerator is filled with foods that are easy to eat and high in calories.

Surgical lights are suspended from a thick eye screwed in the ceiling exactly for this purpose. Machines I can't even begin to describe are brought in from Medical.

And there is a metal cabinet with drawers filled with things to cut the mother open and other things used to try to sew her closed.

Finally, in the culmination of the proceedings, the female herself is laid across the interlaced arms of the strongest wolves, a symbol of pack support during this difficult time. Then she is brought to the Meeting House in a ritual that—judging by the look of the females' faces—is more terrifying than it is comforting.

Once she is settled in the bed, surrounded by her echelon, the Deemer says the blessing.

"*Wes þu gebledsod,*" I whisper, remembering the last lying-in when Victor hesitated before delivering the traditional blessing in a strained and angry voice. "Be thou blessed. Be thy body as strong as the tree. Be thy will as hard as the mountain. Be thy young as wild as the storm. Be thy land as plentiful and untouched as the stars. Be the lead of men as soft as snow upon thy fur."

She takes my hand and presses it to her belly. I try to pull away, reluctant to show any tenderness to these pieces of me.

"Be thou blessed," she says.

Chapter 31

Julia

FINAL SEMESTER AT ST. AILBHE'S, WHEN GRADES WERE notional and the matron's threats comical, we went out a lot. We gathered in Jas's room—at the end of the hall, it had an extra window, extra space, and a sink—and there we would trade lipsticks and backless bras and shapers and clothes and jewelry until we hit the magical balance between an edginess that pretended we didn't care and attention to the restaurant's smart-casual dress code, because we actually did.

There was a lot of laughing.

There is no laughing in the Great Hall, just a handful of juvenile wolves nervously trying to prepare themselves to slip unnoticed through a hostile world.

Homeland wolves and other juveniles who didn't make it into Advanced Human Behaviors surround us, making suggestions based on extremely perverse understanding of the signals sent by a studded vest or a puffed-sleeve Laura Ashley garden party dress. I snatch a shiny red-and-green-plaid clip-on bow tie that a one-eyed wolf from the 7th Echelon keeps trying to put on Adrian and stuff it in my pocket.

Whatever my lack of proper educational credentials,

the Pack has come to accept that I know something about human behaviors. When I explain how plaid pants with double zippers and chain detailing signify suburban punks and are not at all the look we're hoping for, Leonora feels the fabrics and takes notes.

She also takes notes as I clean and polish Margaret's nails to hide the crescent-moon stain of raccoon blood that won't scrub out. As I trim Kevin's beard, which is weirdly mature on his gangly teen body. As I show Avery how to wear black tights that will hide the hair she refuses to shave because winter is coming and her legs will be cold when she is wild.

There is no giggling about being transgressive, because they are wolves and that is transgression enough.

Linnea stands naked and resolute as we try to find something to accommodate the broad shoulders and muscled arms that make her the Alpha presumptive of her echelon if she doesn't end up Offland. I take another run down to Leonora's closet in the basement, rejecting clothes that are too outdated, too formal, too small, too casual. I riffle past what at first I think is a tablecloth hanging from the bottom bar of a hanger, but when my fingernail catches on it, I immediately recognize the white silk as heavy as chain mail that I never thought would be wearable again.

At the top of the steps, I hear the grunting and growling and mewling coming from the small crowd gathered around Avery. In my absence, Leonora put on the pearl collar that had been fitted to my neck, but it is tight around Avery's. The juvenile's eyes are wide with panic, maybe because the nacreous beads feel like teeth.

Leonora keeps whispering to her—*Gestille, wulfling. Gestille*—while she tries to undo the latch.

Unfortunately, the necklace is expensive and the catch is designed not to come undone easily. Avery pushes her fingers between skin and pearls and the strands pop, sending the pearls down to the floor with sharp taps like hail against a rooftop. She breathes a sigh of relief but then looks at me abashed, maybe remembering that I once thought of the necklace as mine and humans like their things.

I reach out for her and pull her close.

Gestille, wulfling, I say. *Gestille.*

Be still, wolfling. Be still.

She relaxes into me, her cheek to my collarbone.

John and Sigeburg dart out from under the sofa and bat the pearls around the floor. They stick their heads between the railings that protect them from falling down the stairwell to the basement, watching the batted beads bounce down the steps. *TikTikTik.*

I shake out the white pantsuit in front of Linnea.

"Try that."

The palazzo pants fit loose over her strong thighs, and the halter doesn't bind the shoulders that make her so appealing to wolves.

"The Grand Isle Ferry leaves in two hours," Leonora says.

I drape a shawl around Linnea's back so humans are not disconcerted by her power.

The pups bat more pearls down the steps. *TikTikTik.*

Unlike the First Shoes, the juveniles do not cling to one another during the three-hour trip to Champlain, a restaurant on Grand Isle. Instead they sit stiffly, hands folded tightly, while Leonora peppers them with questions.

"You start eating immediately upon being served while the food is hot. Yes or no."

There's a little discussion before Avery answers that it is polite to wait until all of your packmates have food in front of them.

"Yes, but again, we have to get out of the habit of saying 'packmates.' 'Friends' or 'family' only."

There are some more questions about big spoons and little spoons and big forks and little forks and napkins and slurping and not eating big bites and the importance of not handling a knife like a weapon.

Leonora rehearses once more the importance of pleases and thank-yous, and I think of all the waitstaff I've waved off without a single thought and vow to be at least as good a human as these teenage wolves.

Champlain seems both so familiar and entirely other-worldly. It takes me a moment to remember all the markers: the way this man relaxes into his chair while the other two across from him lean forward. That table over there with the two couples? One woman is perfectly groomed. The other used to be but now the expensive dress stretches tight over her hips. Something sticky mars the material at her back. Her husband either didn't notice or didn't bother to tell her.

His wife is talking and he listens with a small smile, his leg pressed against the other woman's thigh.

This is close enough to my native range and I know how to act: holding my head high enough to look like a woman who knows her value, but not so high that I will be mistaken for a bitch. Wearing the soft smile that says not that I am happy but that I am obliging. Swaying my hips enough to get men to notice but not so much that the women will.

I know how, but I don't bother.

The entire restaurant gapes at us. How can they not? Every one of us is well over six feet even in stocking feet.

Some of the faces are hostile, and for the first time in my life, the maître d' shepherds me past the golden tables where the rich, important, and beautiful people sit, past the arguably acceptable tables where I sat once when Cassius came late and the restaurant—a new place that did not yet understand Who I Am—settled me. I could have said something, but I didn't. Instead, I waited for Cassius because he enjoyed seeing the panic on underlings' faces.

So for the first time, I am ushered to the way back, the place usually reserved for people who the gatekeepers prefer to keep out of sight.

Tucked away alone in the corner are four tables squeezed together into a square big enough to accommodate us all. Even under the tablecloth, I can see that the edges don't quite meet up and there's a ridge that will definitely cause some young wolf's drink to spill. Leonora has noticed it too. She pushes against the far corner and I fear that she is going to strip the table, turn it upside down, and screw the damn thing in herself.

I turn to the maître d'.

August, my father, Cassius, never bothered listening to whatever came between "My name is _____" and

"I'll be your server/host tonight." They were men, rich men, powerful men. They didn't have to. I was a St. Ailbhe's girl, and we knew that if a waiter hated but didn't fear us, the cook would spit in the soup.

"Lleandro." I tilt my head slightly to the side, my knees bent so I will be shorter than he is. "Would it be possible to fix this?"

His eye goes to the stack of diamonds from my digested fiancé that I'd put on for exactly this eventuality. "Of course," Lleandro says. "One moment."

Within seconds, a group of waiters swoop in, stripping the table, turning and remaking it. We all sit.

Adrian has written sweetbreads, chitlins, foie gras, and haggis on his palm so he won't make a mistake and order some more obscure form of carrion.

Most of them have ordered flageolet salad with artichoke velouté and lemon, thyme, black garlic creme. Those who haven't ordered the pumpkin soup with truffle oil and crisped sage.

I order the lamb chops. Tiny little ribs served bloody with a Bandol and tart cherry reduction, because it reminds me of the tournedos from Soir.

"*Avery*," Leonora says sharply.

The golden tables line triple-paned plate glass that gives out over Lake Champlain and the brightly lit marina. Our window—the one Avery is staring through—gives out onto trees that only just shield the dumpster from view. A flurry of leaves loose into the bright streetlight.

"Avery," Leonora hisses again. "Humans eat carri—I mean, *people eat meat*. You cannot look away."

Her jaw set, Avery turns quickly, her elbow hitting the

spoon sticking up from her bowl and sending pumpkin soup down the front of her shirt.

If she could cry, she would.

I take her to the bathroom where there is a bottle of lavender soap and a pile of thick, sturdy paper towels stacked against the gleaming black subway tiles. I dampen one and hand it to her while I peer over the tops of the stalls.

"Playing human," I say quietly, "is not about learning a part and dressing in a costume and having a photograph taken so you have a scrapbook. It's about being able to—You can't take your shirt off, Avery."

"But I have a bruiser on."

"It's brassiere, a bra, and humans will still be shocked to see you in a public place in your underwear. So button up."

"It's not a public place, it's a toilet. A toilet for *females*."

"Button. Up. Then dab at the spot with the towel. You can't get rid of it, but you need to look like you've tried. Not so hard. You'll tear the shirt."

Now, the towel barely grazes her front.

"Here, let me." Dampening the towel, I begin to wipe away the pumpkin soup. "What I was saying, Avery, is that humans eat carrion. They eat baby carrion. I'm not saying you have to eat it, but you have to be able to look like it doesn't bother you when they do. Here." I give her my lipstick. "Pretend you're putting it on. Someone's coming."

I turn to the mirror and pat at my face with the powder from my compact.

"Avery? Julia? What are you doing here?"

Avery drops the lipstick and throws herself at Josi,

tucking her head under the lawyer's chin, trying to climb into her embrace.

"You can't do that here, wolfling," Josi says, petting Avery's hair before pushing her away. "Field trip?" she asks me.

I nod, then point at my lip to remind Avery that only one half of one lip is red.

"I spilled it, Gamma," Avery whimpers.

"That's nothing. During mine, Torsten dumped a pitcher of water on a waiter who'd come to light the candle." She heads into the stall. "How many glasses have you broken so far?"

The lock turns.

"Two. And a charger that cracked when Oliver put his soup dish down."

The toilet flushes and Josi comes out, washing her hands in the square above-counter sink.

"So what are you doing here?" I ask.

She sucks on her front teeth with a disgusted *tchk*. "Elijah and I are failing to talk the trustee into selling us the land."

The trustee.

I'm grateful she doesn't say your uncle's trustee, who is acting on behalf of your aunt. Not like she's being coy but rather like she has forgotten that those people were once my people.

"I thought the offer had already been accepted?"

"So did we. Everything had been arranged remotely though. This was supposed to be a chance to meet in person for a celebratory dinner. Then we got here and things started to go wrong... I honestly have no idea. Unless Elijah has managed some miracle in my absence, we are going back empty-handed."

"Gamma?" Avery cocks her head to the side with a mournful expression.

"Watch the door, Julia." Josi says before drying her hands and tossing the towel into the basket under the long, wall-hung counter. While I lean against the door, Josi Dianasdottir, Esquire, Gamma of the 3rd Echelon, marks a juvenile wolf made sad by lamb chops.

After Josi leaves, I tell Avery that I want to check something out. "Hunt with me," I tell her. Avery may be a terrible restaurant patron, but she is a fine wolf and falls in step behind me, matching my speed, my direction, the volume of my footfall, as we walk out among the golden tables. She pays attention to what I notice and what I just pretend to.

It doesn't take long to find Josi's table. There has been no miracle. The waitress is laughing at something Elijah has said. Across from him is an older man who was handsome but no longer in his prime. He has yet to come to terms with his change in status and watches Elijah resentfully. Watches as Elijah plays the field so freely. What he can't see is the leather braid around Elijah's neck, the one that he made and he wears and he presses to his skin whenever he thinks about the woman he loves.

The trustee watches with lidded eyes, his mouth narrow, his index finger scratching against the thumb of his fisted hand.

Elijah is too used to playing Alpha and the older man feels the loss. Feels disrespected, underappreciated.

"Go back to Leonora," I tell Avery. "I'll be there as soon as I can."

I run my fingers through my hair, then hold my head high enough to look like a woman who knows her value but not so high that I will be mistaken for a bitch. I shape my mouth into a soft biddable smile and gently sway my hips.

At the table, I greet Josi with an air kiss before turning to the trustee.

"If you're looking for a lawyer, I cannot say enough about Josi, Mr…?"

"Grenier," he says and stops picking at his thumb, "but you can just call me Cédric."

"Ahh, Cédric Grenier."

I use the name I used whenever the St. Ailbhe's girls were doing something that would get us expelled if anyone traced it back to us.

"*Moi, c'est Amandine, mais tout le monde m'appelle Ama.*"

There was something about saying Ama, a word so close to *amour*, that made men say it with a sigh, and Cédric's no different.

"Ama," he repeats with a small smile. He leans back into his chair, looking at me as I watch only him. Pay attention only to him. A warning rumble in Josi's throat is inaudible to humans but Elijah hears it and sits back in his chair with a squeak.

I don't flirt, not exactly. I don't want him to think I'm offering sex. He sees the rings on my finger after all. A person without subtlety thinks there are only two things that a man wants: sex and money. But really sex and money are stand-ins for the much more important things that everyone wants: attention and agency.

That's what I give him. Attention. Not so much that he feels cheap, like something he'll have to pay me for, but enough so he feels his strength returning. Enough for him to feel himself Elijah's equal, to show me that he indeed has agency.

"Oh, I'm so sorry, I lost track. You were in the middle of something. I didn't mean to interrupt—"

"No, no, no," Cédric says. "We were just finalizing some details, weren't we, Mr. Sorensson?"

"Yes, Mr. Grenier," Elijah says. "Thank you," he says.

I excuse myself, again. Apologize again. I take Josi's hand and tell her we should get together some time in the way of someone who knows they never will. Then I turn to Elijah with a nod and another "Excuse me." I don't want Cédric to suspect that Elijah is worthy of my attention so I don't ask his name.

"You know, Mr. Leveraux's estate has another bit of land a few miles away," Cédric says as I leave. "It's just five acres, but there's an access road. You could use it to store equipment or…"

Chapter 32

Arthur

CHANGE HAS RARELY BEEN GOOD FOR WOLVES. FORESTS are replaced by split levels. Arrows and spears and pikes are replaced by guns. Then faster guns. Skittish and tasty horses are replaced by cars, which are neither.

So when the Alpha arrives late one breakfast in a dark-gray pantsuit, white shirt, and shiny beads around her throat, the Pack immediately becomes nervous. She brings with her the scent of Offland and a stiff, formal bag from which she extracts something and wordlessly drops it to the table where the 9th Echelon sits.

Then she swings back around on her heel and bolts for the door. There Constantine takes the bag while she claws at the stiff jacket. He helps her get it off and smooths his hand along her back.

When the door closes, the Pack gathers around, staring warily at the big expandable file festooned with tabs as though it is a bear trap. Sigegeat, the 7th's Gamma, bends over to sniff it until Elijah pulls out a thick stack of papers.

He runs a finger down the first page, then the second. Quickly, he moves to another tab and then one more before finally turning it over and flipping through the last pages.

For a moment, he puts his hand to his chin until Esme growls and hits him in the shoulder. "Well?"

"It's ours." He holds up a map that no one can read. "All of it. She did it." He shakes his head. "The Junkyard too. She did it. It's all ours."

There is stunned silence as the Pack absorbs the meaning of what he's said. By the rights understood and obeyed—more or less—by humans, we have added huge swathes of land to our territory. Land that will allow the Gray and the Bone Wolf and their pups to expand and grow and form their own pack.

The sound started with a deep *whoosh* of wolves inhaling or exhaling depending on where they'd stopped breathing, then a few nervous titters, then laughs and the sounds of benches scraping and mugs banging and loud voices congratulating one another.

Godes wyrdes, they say, meaning both "good words" and "good wyrds," the fates those words conjure.

Julia's hand relaxes where it had been clutching mine, and my fingers tingle as the blood flows back. Oddly, Elijah looks up from his reading and rereading of the pages and seeks out Julia and lowers his head.

The door opens and shuts again, interrupting the chatter. The Alpha and Constantine stand at the entryway, both of them dressed in work pants and flannel jackets and muck boots. Constantine knocks the thick handle of a pitchfork against the floor one more time.

"*Heh, Wulfas. Ic beo gearo,*" the Alpha says, turning to show the huge bolt cutters resting on her shoulder. "*Beoþ ge?*"

Hey, wolves. I'm ready. Are you?

Almost immediately, pack tumble over one another in their eagerness. The Alpha assigns echelons to various tasks. Sten sends for tools from Carpentry. Lorcan empties out the gardening shed. Elijah takes the map so that we will be sure to mark our land in the ways of men. Other pack—males mostly—fill up on iced tea, preparing to mark the new land, the land to the north, in the way of wolves.

The 12th joins the Alpha and the 7th in the walk to the Junkyard. The Pack has been trying to buy this disused human farm for years. We'd whittled away at it over the centuries, but no matter how much money we offered the previous owner of this remaining five-acre plot, he refused for no reason other than spite. Al Anderson hated everything about us. He hated that we bought land and did nothing with it. He hated that we posted it and kept hunters from wandering drunk to take prey we needed. He hated that when he emptied used motor oil into the soil, we reported him. The human sold it to August for cash and the promise that he would keep us from ever having it.

Even though the mountain of doorless refrigerators, shredded tires, leaking barrels, and rusted air conditioners had been cleared away when August took possession, we still call it the Junkyard and keep the pups away from it because it smells of antifreeze.

The Alpha pauses at the edge of the barbed-wire-enclosed trapezoid. A doe that had been chewing on a few mangy grasses leaps over the fence because she knows that whatever we look like with our shovels and old spackling pails, she should be afraid.

Facing onto the empty lot are large bright-yellow plastic signs that read:

**Private Property
Hunting, Fishing, Trapping,
or Trespassing for Any
Purpose Is Strictly Forbidden.
Violators Will Be Prosecuted to
the Full Extent of the Law**

With the phone numbers of both Elijah Sorensson (JD, LLM) and Josi Dianasdottir (JD).

A wolf has already cut away one of the cords securing the sign. The wind blows underneath, and after one more snip, it is ready to be moved to new boundaries.

Hanging from a gate at the front is a decrepit metal sign left over from when humans owned the land.

Trespassers Will Be Shot

The Alpha looks at it for one long, grim moment before shrugging the bolt cutters from her shoulder. Whipping them in front of her, she cuts through the thick shank of the padlock.

The chain slumps to the ground and the Alpha kicks the gate open.

It's hard to look at this plot of land without remembering everything that has changed since it was piled high with old cars and cans and broken appliances. John is gone now, leaving it to Evie to see through his vision with Constantine by her side. We have lost Varya but gained a gray wolf who will roam a territory that extends north toward Canada and east nearly to Champlain.

Without Varya to rely on, Lorcan has grown into his role as Alpha. He assigns a handful of his echelon's wolves to work on the fences, and they move purposefully with pails and staple pullers, tearing out the fencing staples from the line post. Other wolves follow behind, rolling the barbed wire onto spools. Finally, another group attacks the line posts themselves, loosening the earth around each base with picks, then setting a small boulder beside it to act as a fulcrum, allowing one wolf to stand on the stone and pull the four-by-four up and away.

Julia and I join those wolves who are assaulting the ground with pitchforks and hoes and shovels and anything that is sturdy enough to break up the poisoned and compacted earth. Each thud releases a whiff of sick-sweet and acrid. Pack who are wild, whose noses are so much more sensitive and closer to the ground, skitter away.

More pack follow, adding compost to each hard-fought meter of land, and slowly the bitter fug of oil is disguised at least a little by the richness of black earth.

When we are done, some pack leave to put away the tools. More change so that they can run through the new territory up north, marking only the boundaries but not the land itself, so that the Gray will lay claim to what she needs.

Julia doesn't want the others to see her weakness, so she waits for them to go before collapsing onto the pile of four-by-fours. I sit behind her, holding her. Fatigue is normal at the beginning, Tristan said, though it will subside. He put a thick circle around a week in the spring in red grease pencil.

The woods around the Junkyard have the thin, crowded sameness of young forests. In time, trees will fall and rot and new trees, different trees, will more closely re-create the profusion of Homelands. Still the low autumn sun bleaches the already pale bark of birches and makes shadows of the few spindly spruces that will eventually tower above them.

A squirrel darts onto the freshly tilled earth, a nut in his mouth. He stops, looking at us guardedly, while he scrapes up the soft earth, drops his treasure in, and carefully pats it down.

"I need to call my mother," Julia says wearily. "We don't talk often, but it's been too long."

"What will you tell her?"

"I've thought about it a little. I think the best thing is to tell her Cassius left me and that I can't come back to Montreal. Tell her that too much there reminds me of him. She'd expect me to fall apart without him."

One finger taps her belly, picking up the same rhythm the squirrel does to bury the acorn, repeating the ritual of generations of squirrels whose forgotten seeds have raised up trees that have sheltered future generations of squirrels and birds and wolves.

"I'll tell her I'm traveling. Not that I think she'll care once I tell her she can clear out my old room for her pottery wheel."

She lifts her hand, creating a shadow arm in the late afternoon autumn sun that stretches across the whole of the newly tilled earth.

I raise my shadow arm and meet hers.

Chapter 33

Julia

"Most of Homelands is a dead zone," the Alpha says. "Here, you're closer to the modem and you can have some privacy. I'll make sure no one comes in," she says and closes the library door.

The door clicks behind her, leaving Arthur and me and my phone on a window seat stippled in loose wolf fur.

I turn the thing over. It feels familiar—red-gold and emblazoned with a loopy diamantine J—but also outlandish, flimsier than I remember, like the screen would break if I put just a little pressure. I gently swipe through the texts. There are a few from actual people: a text from M. Luddy saying how inconsolable he was to hear about August's death but glad I was taking this time to "heal."

One from my building manager asking that I call about a leak.

Aside from that, I have repeated thanks for monthly payments from the gym, from Telus, from the parking garage, from my home insurance. As though in some other place, there is a Julia Martel who is running on treadmills, texting her friends, driving to restaurants, doing dangerous things in her apartment.

It's all normal until I see the thirty-two voicemails. Only my mother leaves voicemails.

Some in English and some in French as though she wasn't entirely sure she remembered what language I spoke and wanted to cover all bases.

"August is dead. Where are you?"

"Call me immediately."

"*Où es-tu?*"

"*Appelle-moi tout de suite.*"

Before adding for emphasis.

"*Immédiatement.*"

Arthur curls his hand around my shoulder, making me realize how tense I've become. I take a deep breath and call my mother at home because her mobile is almost always on silent. As the call goes through, I try to remember the name of the new housekeeper and fail and feel shitty that in the tiny pack that made up my mother's house, I hadn't bothered to learn her name.

"4UC3," says a stiff robotic voice. "The client you are trying to reach is temporarily out of service or not equipped for incoming calls."

I get the same thing the next time as well. There's no chance I got the number wrong: it's the number that's been programmed into my phone since I first had a phone. I try her cell.

"Where have you been?" she says, sounding genuinely upset. "I've been trying to reach you forever. *August has died.*"

The old tightness binds my chest and chokes the words in my throat.

"Julia, are you listening?"

"What happened to your home phone?"

"*I don't have a home phone.* I don't have a *home*. Did you know the house wasn't even mine? It was a *rental*." She spits out the word like it is profanity. "August rented it. In *his* name and now he's dead and the landlord said he was going to increase the rent. I couldn't pay that. I moved into your guest room."

"Mine?"

"You weren't here. Somehow, it's still being paid for. I don't know how since the payments stopped on mine."

"It's…it's coming from my account."

"How do you still have money?" she asks, her voice accusatory.

I hear the slap of the Venetian slippers my mother always wears inside.

"It's the money from my inheritance."

A cabinet door opens and I hear the light tink of a glass. I can picture that glass and that cabinet so clearly.

"I'm going to need that back."

"What do you mean 'back'? That was a bequest from Papa to me. Besides, you have your own money. He left you a fortune."

"Clearly you do not have any idea how much it takes to raise and educate a child—"

"August paid for my school. Everything else I put on a credit card that *he* gave me."

She opens the freezer and fishes ice from the bin, and I can picture that freezer and that bin too.

"Aurelian left me," she says, changing the subject. Her bitterness spits across the line like a cobra.

Can't say as I'm surprised. After my father died, my mother had called August almost daily. Two weeks later, Aurelian showed up at our door with his handsome face and his single skill: the ability to make my mother think she was the center of the universe.

"I'm here now," he'd said, pressing down the switch on the phone before August had a chance to answer my mother's latest call. "I'll take care of everything."

She was the only one who thought his passion was taking care of her. Even I knew that his *job* was taking care of August.

"*Alors, donc.* Are you going to tell me what's going on? M. Trenet from the Windsor Grand called here trying to find you. I had to tell him I didn't know where you were. And where is Cassius?"

"He left me too," I say, knowing she will find vindication in this lie. "After August died."

Then Sabina Martel does something I cannot picture. She gets water from the faucet. I'm not sure I've ever seen her standing at a kitchen sink.

"*On fait la paire, tout les deux,*" she sighs, sipping at her tap water.

What a pair we are.

Not exactly. Aurelian is no doubt making some other rich Shifter widow believe she is the center of his world, while Cassius has been eaten, digested, and shat out or vomited up in discreet piles around Homelands.

"If you had called me," she cajoles, "I might have been able to get at least some of your deposit back, but M. Trenet said it was all forfeit."

The wind is picking up, pushing steel-gray clouds above the steely gray of Home Pond, making the fringed reflections of tamaracks ripple bright gold.

"Drusilla asked where you were," she said.

I look at Arthur, then at the wall separating the library from the Alpha's office. On the clipboard with the pencil with the red and white butcher string, I scribble

CONSTANTINE
ALPHA

Arthur leaves without a noise.

"And…and why would you talk to her, Maman? You haven't talked to her for years."

"I called her because she's family. Because August didn't leave a will so everything went to her. I wanted to make sure she was aware of the nature of his…of our understanding."

The door opens again, and this time Arthur returns with the Alpha and Constantine, moving in that silent way that only wolves can.

"Maman, I'm doing my nails. I'm putting you on speaker."

"You know they never turn out well when you do them yourself," she says disapprovingly.

"It's just my toes, and besides, it's too cold to go around barefoot."

The Alpha looks at my sock-encased feet, clearly not

understanding how a conversation about toes and socks could require her attention.

"What did you tell Drusilla?" The Alpha's eyes slide toward Constantine. He nods and leans against the edge of the table, arms crossed.

"We had a long talk. I told her how I'd lost my house and had to let both Yolanda and the new girl go."

The "new girl" who had been with my mother since before I graduated from college.

"I told her that after Otho died, August had promised I would never want for anything."

The Alpha glides silently to the door and pokes her head out. One second later, she's back.

"She didn't even know you were engaged to Cassius. She was so considerate. She wanted to send you a wedding present but I told her I didn't know where you were. Do you know how embarrassing it is? Not being able to say where my own daughter was? I promised to call her as soon as I heard from yo—"

"No!" I snap. My mother sucks in a shocked breath. Constantine whispers something to the Alpha and she nods, watching him leave. "Maman." I have to think what to say. "With Cassius gone, I... I've decided to make some changes. I want a simpler life. So—"

"Oh, don't do that. All that *vie simple*. Rosamunde Thibaut did it. Got rid of everything that didn't spark joy, absolutely everything. Next thing you know, she's buying it all back. *En fait, la vie simple, c'est très compliqué,*" she says and laughs at a punch line that couldn't have been that funny when it was new.

I start again. "Yes, well, I want to turn over Papa's bequest to you."

She goes quiet for a moment.

"How much do you have left?"

"Most? I don't know what it is now. Twenty million? Thirty? August's people had been managing it, so I presume it's been earning?" I stop, feeling suddenly awkward about the bubble that cocooned me so thoroughly that I can't tell my mother how much money I have within the nearest ten million.

"That much?"

"Yes, and it's all yours, but don't ask for *anything* from Drusilla."

A drawer opens on the other end of the line, followed by the sound of my mother rustling through the utensils.

"She is *family*, Julia."

"*Maman.*"

I look around the room at Constantine, who has returned and now holds the Alpha's hand. At Silver leaning against Tiberius's broad body that is bent around her. At Lorcan. At Leonora. At Tara.

At the pup who pulls up short at the sight of so many adults and loses his footing, landing splayed out on the floor.

At Arthur, my wolf, who has had to be so strong to be least of them all.

Drusilla may be my sire's littermate, but this…

This is family.

The corkscrew clinks against glass, then squeaks through the cork before lifting out with a small pop. "*Alors,*" she says, pouring wine out with a gentle burble. "*Ça m'est égal.*"

All the same to me.

"You will call Ulysse?"

"*Pfff.* Ulysse retired years ago. His son has taken over the firm now. Charlus is nowhere near as charming, but he is a very competent lawyer."

In the distance, a howl breaks through the stillness, and with one hand on the table, the Alpha leaps across quickly, closing the inevitably open windows against the rising answer of the Pack that has become such a comforting part of my soundscape but must be protected from strangers.

"Where *are* you?" my mother asks.

"Like I said, with Cassius gone, I had to get away. Far away. You know I was thinking… Why don't you move your pottery wheel into my room? You can rearrange it however you think best."

Wine burbles down the narrow neck of the bottle.

"I've never had the proper setup," she muses as the glass clinks against the phone's mouthpiece. "Maybe I could turn your closet into a damp room?" She goes on about storage shelves and lighting that I know she'll never do, but it has distracted her from the sound of wolves that is still rolling across the hills. And at the mountains beyond, the wind that bends the tops of trees and releases leaves and caresses fur and eager noses, and my wild rails against this glass box.

"Julia? How do they look?"

Arthur gently taps my toes with his, reminding me of the nails I was supposed to be painting. I look into his silvered eyes, mirroring my wild self, my better self, my loved self.

"Beautiful," I say.

"*Bon*," she says approvingly. "You never know when a new man will come along. You must not let yourself go to the dogs."

The Alpha is the last wolf to leave, after scribbling down the email address of a pack lawyer who will deal with drawing up whatever papers I will need to sign. When eventually I hang up, Arthur opens the window and, in the heavenly cool and damp, holds me, rocking me back and forth like our first dance.

Back when Cassius was alive and I still thought I was a girl of the Mille Carré.

Before I had gone to the dogs.

Chapter 34

Arthur

"Ow!" Julia jerks against my legs.

"This would be easier if you stayed still."

She doesn't stay still. She moves her head from side to side, peering into the mirror that usually hangs above the sink. "They're all over!"

"It happens." I separate another strand of hair. I don't tell her that it only happens with pups, because adults know to avoid the cockleburs.

If it had been summer, we might have just cut them all out, but she can't run around shorn in the cold, sharp air of fall. Julia puts the mirror down and settles between my knees while I slowly and painstakingly pull burrs from hair the weight and color of deep forest honey.

"So...who is Drusilla?" I ask and feel her tense between my thighs.

"My aunt. My father's sister."

I turn to a comb to attack a nest of five burrs. "Why didn't you want your mother to talk to her?"

She doesn't say anything and I keep working, loosening one dark filament after another.

"Julia?" I set the cockleburs beside me, part of a ragged mountain of hooked seeds on the porch.

"I don't know her. Not really. I met her when I was very small and I don't remember much."

I let my fingers roam, coaxing out the hidden tangles until she starts again.

"The only thing I know is that something happened between my father and Drusilla. I heard my mother on the telephone once talking about how August had betrayed Drusilla with 'that bitch.' I remember it because it was the only time I'd ever heard my mother curse. It wasn't until years later that I figured she wasn't cursing. That she was talking about a wolf. About Tiberius's mother."

"Mala," I say. I didn't know Mala. But Tiberius took her name when he put aside Leveraux and took a pack name, becoming Tiberius Malasson.

"I never knew her name," she says, plucking a loosened strand of hair from her shoulder. "All I knew was the next day we were packing for a new house with thick walls, bulletproof windows, steel doors, and a safe room. Good sight lines. My father rarely came home after that. A couple of years later, he was dead—heart attack, we were told. My mother asked why Drusilla didn't come to the funeral. August didn't tell her."

She holds the single strand up in the air, and when she lets go, the autumn wind scoops it up and carries it away to tumble with falling leaves.

"He told me though. When I was fourteen and ran my mouth at him. That's when I found out two things about her.

He told me that unless I wanted Drusilla cutting me into tiny pieces and flushing me down the drain of the Racquet Club like she had done with my father, I needed to remain 'exquisitely inconsequential.'"

I slide the brush through her hair, searching for any final cockleburs.

"What was the second thing?" I ask, and Julia looks up absently. "You said August told you two things about Drusilla."

She shakes her head. "He *told* me only that one thing. The other, I just knew. By the words he chose, by the sound of his voice. Even at fourteen, I could hear that he was terrified of her."

———————

"Are you?" the Alpha calls on the first night of the Iron Moon.

And her wolves call back.

"We are."

The Evening Song is when the holes in the Great North are made audible: the small unraveling left by the death of Hildy, the easygoing, careless Theta of the 13th who hadn't had time to make her mark on the Pack; the gaping tear left by the loss of John, Solveig, Orion, and Paula who had.

It's like listening to a chorale that has been part of our consciousness forever and realizing that the harmony is broken.

Constantine and Tiberius were not raised as wolves, so their voices are less like parts of the chorus, more like traffic noise coming in through the window of the auditorium.

Not something we really miss.

I wouldn't think much about it except when I search for the Shifters' scents, they are old, buried by a damp layer of late fall leaves.

A car is missing from the parking lot.

As soon as I walk into the small cabin in the middle of the woods, Silver looks up for one anxious moment before slumping back into her seat.

"Where are Tiberius and Constantine?" I ask, looking at the cell phone on Silver's table. Homeland wolves rarely need cell phones. As soon as she sees me looking, she opens a pad of paper, covering it.

"You are the Deemer. It is your duty to think about the law. I am the Omega. It is my duty to pay attention to the Pack."

"Sometimes," she says, rolling a pencil back and forth between middle finger and thumb, "you pay *too much* attention, Omega."

Her head bent over the pad of paper, she begins tracing lines that curl around the page like the leafless woodbine on the tree outside the window.

"Where are they?" I ask again.

More vines gradually encroach on the page, until only one small corner is left free.

"Is Drusilla coming?"

Silver looks up but says nothing. She doesn't have to. I can see it in her eyes.

There is a sharp turn in the access road, and from that point on, it's all Homelands. Or almost. On the ridge above the turn is an abandoned fire tower, a spindly reminder of the outside world.

Once the big gray wolf scrabbles down the hill, I leave my hiding place and head toward the trees next to the fire tower. I smell the woodsmoke before I see the cabin. Then I smell the wolf markings that mean I've come for the first time since that one time to the border of our territory.

And for the first time since that one time, I am Offland.

Thea sits on the porch, her legs hanging over the edge, a cup of tea sitting on the wide wood planks. She leans over, belly to thighs, brushing at her pants leg.

I knock on the post support.

"You only have to knock when the door is closed," she says without sitting up. "Elijah just left."

"I'm not here to see Elijah," I say. "I'm here to see you."

She stops brushing at her pants, straightens her hems, and sits up.

"You are wearing a very pretty outfit," I say, trying to remember old lessons in making conversation.

She looks down at her dull-green, wolf-fur-covered pants and shirt with VILLALOBOS printed across the tape. "Hmm-hmm. How far did you get in Human Behaviors?"

"About halfway through the first year."

"That's what I thought. There's something unnerving about Homeland wolves trying to play human. Why don't you just tell me why you wanted to see me?"

I lean against the post support, angled so I can see if anyone starts up the hill.

"After you came that first time, you left for a long time. For six weeks."

"How did you know how long I was gone?" she asks.

"Everyone knew. Elijah spent the whole time…" I mime Elijah's screen swiping and despair. "So what made you decide to come back?"

A half smile plays at one corner of her mouth as she brushes at the fur on her sleeve with the rubber-bristled brush.

"Elijah made me go," she says, moving on to the other arm. "As soon as I left, I knew he was right. It's easy to be swept up in this place when you're here. In the feeling of being part of something special and something that needs saving. But it was important to be sure that I would feel the same way even without Elijah and the pups and wolves"— she looks pointedly at me—"who knock on posts and compliment a uniform that in no way is pretty."

"I guess I'm not entirely sure what pretty is."

"Clearly."

She starts to clean the brush, dropping balls of Elijah's fur to the ground.

"Julia never had any choice," I say. "Cassius brought her here against her will, we imprisoned her, and now she's about to sign over her life outside to be here."

"I know. Elijah looked over the papers."

I watch the fur blow across the porch. Eventually the tufts will catch in a bush and be plucked up by some bird to use for its nest.

"What do you want, Arthur?"

"I want Julia to have the same chance to reconsider that you did. I want you to drive her to Montreal."

"Hmm?"

"And I want you to leave her there."

———————————

I run my fingers across the little purple bottle etched with lilacs and the word Guilt.

"What were the red berries?" Julia calls from the bathroom where she is scrubbing the mud from her feet and hands.

"The ones on the bushes or on the ground?" I call back, loud enough to be heard over the water.

"Both, I guess."

I swirl up the bright-red column in the green tube that smells like wax.

"The ones on the ground are partridgeberry. The bushes are winterberry."

"And the yellow flowers?"

"Witch hazel. Not really flowers. They're bracts. What's left when flowers die." I open the red-gold disk with a curlicue J on it. She calls it a "compact" though it is neither a car nor a covenant.

"Whatever they were, they were beautiful."

We went on a run this morning. Homelands is in that moment where the showiness of fall is giving way to the gilded pallor of winter. I took her past the winterberry and partridgeberry and witch hazel. Near the bright apricot-gold and persimmon-orange beads of bittersweet.

Past birches glowing white against fir green. Past frozen puddles etched with crystalline needles and stars and bubbles that, rising up from the decay below, were trapped in ice like a handful of the iridescent pearls she wore when I first saw her.

I settle everything back on the table—the lipstick, the perfume, the compact—and pick up her phone.

"Did my mother call?" she asks, standing behind me. Dampness rises from her skin like mist from warm ground on the first truly cold day.

"No. I was just looking at the pictures." I turn the phone toward her with the image of Julia leaning over the First Shoes. Leofric peers up at her while she draws on a pumpkin.

She yawns and props her head on my shoulder. Reaching around, she swipes the screen and brings up other pictures of other wolflings.

"We were making jack-o'-lanterns."

I look at it again.

"What are jackal antlers?"

"Jack. *O*. Lanterns," she says with a chuckle. "To add 'narrative plausibility,' as Leonora puts it. In case they end up Offland."

With a disappointed *tchk* of tongue against teeth, she flips past pictures of Leofric, Rainy, Edmund, Aella, sometimes together, sometimes individually, all of them setting about their task with a look of grim determination.

"They were *supposed* to be having fun."

Fun.

"Fun" is jumping out of leaves higher than your chest and alarming a packmate. "Fun" is racing down a muddy hillside, a prized raccoon tail held tight in your jaws. "Fun" is following a scent to a burrow and digging until you can't dig anymore. "Fun" is pulling a fallen branch that is bigger than you are and smells like rain and moss and fighting with everything you have to keep it from your fellow pups.

"Fun" does not come from marking odd geometries in squash.

"They're cooking now. The pumpkins, I mean."

Holding the phone high, she turns her head to mine, her lips against my cheek, and the phone clicks.

"See?" she says, showing it to me. Water drips from her hair onto the screen; I wipe it and the picture away.

"Since the papers are ready for you to sign," I tell her, "the Alpha decided it's best for you to go to Montreal now."

"Now?" she says, her head moving under my lips. "What happened to waiting until after the Iron Moon?"

"The Alpha didn't say and I didn't ask."

She collapses against me. "I wish I'd known before we went for a run. I'm so tired."

"You can sleep in the car. Thea will drive you."

"Thea? Why Thea?"

"Because I don't know how to drive and Thea won't turn into a wolf if you take longer than expected."

This lie feels like a solid thing clinging dry on my tongue and hard against my throat and painful behind my eyes because Thea won't wait for her.

As soon as Julia is safely ensconced in her building, Thea

will turn around and head back to the trailhead and the drunk men who gather there on weekends, hoping to get a shot at the #ADKWolf.

Chapter 35

Julia

By the time Thea shakes me awake, we are on the outskirts of Montreal.

"Sorry," I say, bleary-eyed. "I wasn't expecting to make this trip. We went out for a run this morning, and I—"

"Do you know where we are?" she asks abruptly.

I stare at the flat, nearly treeless landscape lashed down with tangled strands of roads and bridges and parking lots. "You want the right-hand lane. Follow signs to Île des Soeurs."

It starts to rain and Thea turns on the wipers; a leaf from a tree I wasn't awake to see is dislodged and flies away.

The cement silos and gantry cranes give way to low, wide office complexes of glass and concrete. At Rue Saint-Jacques, the buildings shoot up thin and impossibly tall, until a little farther on, they crowd cheek by jowl with the ornate brick and marble of my territory, the Golden Square Mile. The Mille carré doré. Then I'm there, in front of my building on the Rue de la Montagne, staring at the black and brass door surrounded by enormous concrete planters, each with a waxy shrub trimmed into a perfect cube.

I unbuckle my seat belt and open the door.

Thea reaches over to the back seat, retrieving a pink bag. "What is this?"

"Arthur says Leonora packed some things for you to change into when you meet with the lawyer."

"For what Charlus is charging," I say, hopping down to the curb, "I can damn well wear jeans."

"I promised him I would give it to you, Julia."

When I hesitate, Thea pushes it closer. I take the bag, looping the pink straps over my shoulder. "I won't be long."

Closing the door behind me, I lope across the street toward the familiar brass and glass doors, then I turn once more to look at Thea. She raises her hand but her eyes are straight ahead. For some reason, unease circles my spine.

The massive doors of my building are meant to open majestically when the doorman pushes a button at his desk. Having noticed me, the doorman moves toward his desk, slowed by his conversation with a birdlike woman.

I want to get this over with and get home and I don't have time for his slow walking or button pushing or majestic opening and I shove my shoulder into the enormous thing until it groans and creaks open.

"The sign," the doorman says sharply, "says to wait for the door to be opened for you."

Wilson doesn't recognize me. Even though he's been here as long as I have and I've tipped him generously every holiday, he doesn't recognize me. Doesn't recognize the big woman in a flannel-lined oilcloth jacket, a wolf-fur dusted sweater, jeans, and worn work boots a size too large that I see reflected in the mirrored walls and columns.

This apartment may belong to me but I no longer belong here.

"Hello, Wilson. I need my spare key, please."

After a long pause, he asks. "Ms. Martel? Is that you?" When I nod, he tells me that my mother has the key. "She's in your apartment now."

"Can you buzz her?"

"Excuse me," says the querulous woman in black, though she is not really excusing herself. "I'm not done here." She turns back to Wilson. "So is someone going to pick up the towels on the floor of pool area?"

Are you not "someone," Shifter?

Apparently, she's not "someone" and Wilson promises that he will send a message to the porter as soon as he has a minute.

"They're damp and will start to smell," the woman says. "I hope they're gone by the time I get back from my class."

I pick up the phone from the cradle behind the doorman's desk and key in my apartment code. No one answers.

"Ms. Martel, that is the lobby phone," Wilson says. "It's not for visitors."

He hesitates, caught between stopping me and helping the querulous woman who has started to complain that if she doesn't get a taxi now, she'll be late for her class.

I stare at her yoga mat and her parka. She wears a hat even though her hood is trimmed with wolf fur. I lean close, my lips pulled back in a snarl. "Then go outside and Raise. Your. Hand."

She stumbles back with an accusatory look at Wilson.

"Ms. Reiss…" he starts. When he races after her, I slip

behind the desk and look at the panel filled with screens and buttons.

Among the selling points of my apartment are the elevators that will not move without a key or being called by a tenant or being sent up by the doorman. A layer of mistrust parading as security in one of the safest neighborhoods in the city.

One of the things I've learned in Homelands is that the difference between a wolf who eats and a wolf who starves is decisiveness.

I find the button labeled "East Elevator" and push it because I am a wolf who eats.

With a whispered metallic slice, the elevator door opens, and a second later, I am in it.

"Ms. Martel," Wilson calls through the tinny elevator speaker. "You must return to the lobby."

At my floor, the doors open on a mirrored wall behind a low bank of rough stone drilled with holes holding tall sprays of dead branches. They are sharp and narrow, so that no one will make the mistake of trying to sit and tie their shoes while waiting for the elevator.

I pound on the door of my apartment until with a flicker of light, my mother slides back the brass covering of the peephole.

"Julia," she whispers, poking her towel-covered head out and peering down either end of the hall. "I was just finishing up with my hair. What are you doing, coming in here dressed like that?" I push my way in. "And you know better than to wear shoes inside the house."

I keep my boots on.

My mother has made the apartment her own. Filled it with her uncomfortable furniture. With the overstuffed settee that is too small for two and too uncomfortable for one. That chair made of pale-green columns stacked on top of one another that makes you sit with your head pushed forward. That marble coffee table with her prize bowl on top of it.

It's not a bowl. It's art.

Something smells odd. I lean toward her, sniffing her head.

"*Stop that*," she says, carefully unwrapping the towel. "Yes, I've been doing my own hair. But at least *I*"—she runs an appraising look over my clothes—"am *trying*."

"When is Charlus coming?"

"He's coming as soon as he can, but it was so last minute. Ulysse will be coming as a witness."

Which explains why she is coloring her hair at this hour.

"Did I tell you Aurelian left me?" she asks.

"Yes, Maman."

Her hair is oddly orange, and when she touches the strands beside her cheek, she does it gently as though they are made of spun glass and might shatter. "You know, she said we should form a club, the three of us. Call it Les Femmes Désaffectées."

The Women Left Behind.

"Who said that?" I ask, the vague sense of unease I'd attributed to réturning home now solidifying into something harder and more sharp-edged.

"Drusilla. When I told her Cassius had left you too."

"Maman! *You promised not to talk to her.*"

"No, I *didn't*. I promised I wouldn't ask her for *money*."

"What did you tell her?" I snap.

"I don't remember. We talked about all sorts of things. Men. Handbags. Whatever." My mother runs her fingers through her hair.

"No, what did you tell her about *me*?"

"I don't understand why you're so upset. Drusilla is your aunt. She cares for you." I laugh at that. "It's true," my mother continues. "Besides, it's not as though you tell me anything." She sucks in a low, pained gasp. "I left it in too long," she wails and shows me a few broken strands on her palm.

My jaws grind together with a pop in my ears.

"What. Did. You. Tell. Her?"

"*That you were distraught and were taking some time for yourself*. That you'd gone someplace far away. So far away that there were wolves howling in the background. Thought she would appreciate the irony. I need a comb."

The unease I'd been feeling builds to panic. It fills the cavity of my chest and squeezes my heart. I push past my mother, who continues moaning about her hair. At the window overlooking Rue de la Montagne, there is an empty spot where the gray-green Defender had been.

Wheeling away from the window, I dump the pink bag on the table.

"What are you doing?" my mother asks.

There is something wrapped in a tuxedo jacket, a bright-green pleather skirt, a cable-knit sweater, and long johns packed by someone who knew nothing about what I might wear to meet with lawyers.

"What is that?" My mother points an accusing finger toward the hard white skull with the deep sockets and sharp teeth that is precious in Homelands. I pull away the sweater and something else falls out, dinging against bone.

Three diamond rings that are worthless in Homelands and precious here.

And a scrawled letter on the back of a page penciled over with vines.

My hand shakes as I swipe at the wallpaper on my phone, the one with the tiny seed pearls individually sewn on white silk as heavy as chain mail. I head into the bathroom.

Among my hundreds of contacts is one August had given me if I had any trouble and couldn't reach him.

"What kind of trouble?" I had asked.

"Anything: Financial, legal, personal. Anything."

"Julia?" Constantine answers. His voice is bleary and barely audible over the roar of wind blowing through windows and the dull rumble of wheels on macadam.

"Where are you?"

He doesn't say anything.

"I know you're not home. Where are you?"

"Where are we?"

"Just passed Lapeer," Tiberius says, adding, "Michigan."

"Did you find Drusilla?" I ask, looking at the squeezed-out tube of hair color on the sink.

There is a moment of hesitation.

"*Did you find Drusilla?*"

"No. Her compound was empty."

"I need to get home, Constantine."

"To Montreal?"

"I'm *in* Montreal now. Thea drove me here but then she left. I think Arthur… Arthur *lied* to me."

"Thea took her to Montreal," Constantine repeats to Tiberius.

"How. Do. I. Get. To. *Homelands*," I snap. "I fell asleep on the way up here so I don't know where it is or how to get back."

Tiberius must have rolled up the windows, because the sound outside dies down.

"Julia," says Tiberius, his voice tinny on the speaker-phone. "This is not your fight."

"And it's yours?"

"This is exactly what Constantine and I were trained for. The only difference is now we are fighting for something we believe in. Something we love. Arthur was trying to protect you because this *isn't* who you are. You—"

"You want to know who I am, Tiberius? I am a woman *who is sick to death* of men telling her who she is. So why don't you just give me the coordinates and let me take care of the rest."

There's a silence followed by what sounds like the pop of a soda can.

"This is not your fight," Tiberius repeats and hangs up.

In the living room, my mother stares at the pile on her sofa, equally repulsed by the pleather and the groundhog.

"I'm leaving." I pick up my skull and the letter.

"Charlus will be here within the hour," she wails. "You have to wait."

"The only thing I *have* to do is go home."

"*This* is your home."

I spare hardly a glance for the apartment August bought for me, filled with furniture suggested by a designer approved by Cassius before I paid for it with money from my father.

I slide my phone in my pocket and pluck the rings from the pile.

"The maintenance is on auto draft on an account that has enough in it to pay for the apartment for five years. These are worth nearly a million and a half, US. Do whatever you want with them."

I hold my hand out to her. Maybe it's her pride. Maybe it's resentment at being presented with a five-year deadline. She crosses her arms in front of her.

"They're coming. You need to *wait*!"

I toss the rings into the bowl on the coffee table.

"*That's not a bowl. It's art.*"

━━━━━━

I don't bother to hide it. Any taxi driver flummoxed by a groundhog skull isn't going to like driving me to the forests near the cutline between Canada and the United States.

What I needed was this man, a driver who smelled like fried onions and asked only, "*Combien vous me donnez?*"

Jamming my thumbnail between the telephone and its case, I pull out one of the pink bills with the pine grosbeak on it.

"Don't go spending this," August said when he peeled

three from a roll. "The mint doesn't make thousand-dollar bills anymore, but keep it on you. In case of emergency."

The driver takes off his knit cap and scrapes his fingers through his thinning hair, looking at it suspiciously.

"Check it out." I tilt the note so the metallic patch changes from gold to green, but when he reaches for the bill, I snatch it back. "When we get to the border."

He pulls his cap on again and opens the passenger door, bowing with the kind of exaggerated professional courtesy of one criminal for another.

"*Alors, on va où?*"

I look despairingly at my phone.

"*Pour le moment, vers le Pont Champlain.*"

Then I stare at the map, scrolling up and down, waiting for something to seem familiar, for whatever word it was that got buried in my brain to worm its way out.

"*Hinchinbrooke,*" I yell excitedly. The driver frowns in the rearview mirror, the disdain in his eyes making it very clear that nothing about Hinchinbrooke was worthy of my enthusiasm or anyone else's.

When I repeat "Hinchinbrooke," my voice is cold and hard, and he shuffles his ass more firmly into the seat, holds the steering wheel tighter, and does not dare to look at me again.

I unfold Arthur's hastily scrawled letter.

Julia,

I hope some day you'll have a chance to tell me—and I'll have a chance to hear—just how angry you are.

You were brought to Homelands against your will. Kept against your will. We cannot survive without this place and each other, but you can and the idea that you would be hunted here because I could not let you go is more than I can bear.

If I don't see you again…

I drop the page to my lap and stare out the window.

If I don't see you again, know that my last thoughts will be of you, dancing like a samara away from the shadows.

—*A*

Folded inside are two pages thick with notes about what to expect when you're expecting a werewolf. I fold it back, putting the skull on top to weight it down.

Then I look at my phone. I wish I'd paid more attention to that last image. I'd taken it thoughtlessly, like the thousands I'd shot in which Cassius smiled smugly while I tried to keep my neck looking smooth and my expression biddable and lips full without making my cheeks look fat.

If I'd been paying attention, I would have noticed that while my smile is real and unrehearsed, Arthur's beautiful eyes watch me, dark and worried, his jaw tight, his lips compressed.

I flip back through the pictures I'd taken of the First Shoes, noticing how severe and intent the young wolves were as I tried to make them see the fun of carving a scary squash.

I should have understood that their world was already scary enough without make-believe.

Turning the phone over, I rub it against my jeans.

August did an excellent job of convincing me that I was inconsequential and harmless. Now with any luck, Drusilla will believe it too.

When the city disappears and the suburbs and the flat fields give way to forests, I open both windows, letting the cold, clear air in.

"*Eh, il fait froid,*" the driver says and starts to move his hand toward the button to close them until he catches my eyes in the rearview mirror and wraps his scarf around his neck instead.

Absently stroking the smooth bone of my First Kill, I pay attention to the angle of the light and the taste of the wind, looking for any hints, even here surrounded by corn, for the way home.

I lean forward, watching as we get closer and closer until at a dirt road across a little creek marked with nothing but a hand-painted sign that advertises INTERNET and DEAD END.

"*Ici. Tourne ici,*" I say.

"*Mais…c'est sans issue.*"

"*Oui, je sais.*"

With a jerk, he turns into the single lane that bounces a few yards later to a bent red and white sign that says

STOP.
UNITED STATES BOUNDARY

**VEHICLES-PEDESTRIANS
ARRIVAL-ENTRY PROHIBITED**

**ARRÊTEZ
FRONTIÈRE DES ETATS UNIS
AUTOS-PIÉTONS
ARRIVÉE-ENTRÉE INTERDITE**

Beneath are images—a car and a striding figure—with red lines slashed through them. It doesn't matter: I will not enter in either a car or on two feet.

Unbuckling my seat belt, I pass the pink bill up to the driver, tuck my skull under my arm, and head as quickly as I can for the trees. The taxi driver hesitates, but when he finally leaves, I am already surrounded by trees, by their cool amber smell and the soft questioning brush of their dry leaves asking

Why?

Why are you like this?

Why are you so tame?

I don't believe the taxi driver will report me to the authorities but it doesn't really matter, because by the time he does, this "me" will be long gone.

Chapter 36

Arthur

I FOLLOWED THEM AS FAR AS I COULD, FROSTED LEAVES crunching under my feet while every breath dissipated into mist behind me. As the access road met with tarmac, I hid among the bare trees and stiff dry grasses, watching Julia rest her head against the window, her eyes closed, trusting that I would not lead her astray.

When I can no longer hear the sound of tires on asphalt, I start back to the Great Hall, taking the long way past what had been the Junkyard. It's healing now, though the low grasses and young bushes are dry and drained as they wait for winter.

There's even a tiny sapling, probably planted by a forgetful squirrel, though not the one Julia and I watched.

As I get closer, I pass pack putting finishing touches to the preparations for the Iron Moon—closing up windows, checking the emergency generators—as though this was an Iron Moon like any other.

Sigeburg runs toward me as soon as I open the inner door, screeching to a stop, her tiny paws on my knees, waiting for me to lift her, but I pull my leg away, unable to bear the loneliness that weighs on me like a physical thing. She nicks her head to the side, questioning, but forgets as soon as Nils joins her, biting at her tail.

Laughter erupts from the kitchen. The oven door opens. The 8th is sitting in front of a huge pile of apples, coring and slicing and putting the fruit on racks to dry over the Iron Moon so they will be added to our winter stores.

They are not the enormous, round, brightly colored ones we get from Offland. They are small and oddly shaped, but they are ours, from our trees, and they taste like heaven.

Rieka checks on the sourdough mother nesting in the oven, resting her hand on the metal floor to make sure the pilot light is on.

Turning to the Alpha's office, I put my hand on the lever and steel myself.

For one second, I catch her, forehead in her hand, before she straightens her spine. She slumps back as soon as she sees me and nods toward the door.

"Close it."

It snaps to behind me with a click. In two steps, I stand in front of her.

"You haven't told the Pack."

"I have told the Alphas. More than that serves no purpose." She fans the corner of a notebook with her thumb. "Where is Julia?"

"Thea is taking her home, Alpha. It is not Thea's fault. It is mine and I will accept whatever—"

"Thea was not raised pack, but you were," the Alpha snaps angrily. "Let's see if there's a future first, before we go about devising punishments for it." She shakes her head and looks wearily out the window. "Constantine and Tiberius are coming as fast as they can, but I don't know if they'll..."

She looks at a compass on her desk, turning around while the red half of the needle swings north.

"Have you ever thought of moving the Pack somewhere else?" I ask.

"Where? I've looked, but there are so few wild places left. Back when August was trying to convince me to give up the Pack, he said as much. 'The world as it was in the beginning is now at an end,' he said. 'Get used to it.' Now I wonder... Did I make a mistake?"

As I head to the door, I remind her that there was a Thing. That we cast our stones and made the decision together in the way Packs have made such decisions for centuries.

"By one stone," she says. "The decision was made by one stone."

"If Victor had let me vote, there would have been two."

———

The sun has almost set. It's the Hunter's Moon, when deer are fat, nothing is hibernating yet. Enough leaves have fallen for good sight lines.

Eadig waþ, the Alpha says, in the Old Tongue like she always does because "Happy hunting" doesn't begin to capture the full sense of *waþ*, of wandering and journeying.

"And be yourself not hunted," comes the inevitable reply.

Usually I would spend the change with the 12th. Especially

now when the close proximity of my echelon's bodies pro-
vides some comfort against the damp earth and cold air until
the change is over and we rise up blanketed in thick fur.

It was beyond me to play at normalcy with my echelon. I
dreaded the spoken questions they would have asked when
we were in skin: Where is Julia?

I dreaded the unspoken questions they would ask when
wild even more. The feel of noses pressed against my fur
asking, *Where is she?*

Do we need to fear you, werewolf?

It's a fair enough question. I've always been keenly aware
of the need to tamp down anger and despair, the fuel and
oxygen that can turn the ember inside into something I
cannot control. Now there is too much of both.

I head back down the access road toward the entrance to
Homelands, as far from the Pack as I can.

The air has gotten colder. Homelands is changing. There
are so many things I didn't have time to show Julia: The lacy
reindeer lichen. The deep red of the dewberry leaves creeping over granite rocks. The ornate blond and scarlet seed
pods of the great St. John's wort. The frostweed giving up the
last of its summer moisture into tiny, elaborate ice sculptures
like the one melting to my nose.

The veiled clouds of winter that halo sun and moon
melding into the thin, gray ice.

Something turns into the rough entrance. Four big black cars
ease into Homelands from the lands beyond. They start their
way up the pitted and rocky access road, thumping and grinding.

A door opens with a plastic blast of hot air, and a man

carrying a huge bolt cutter heads toward the slatted gate. He shakes at it, testing the depth and hold of the posts and struts, before feeling the locks that are tucked safely in so they cannot be cut.

"We'll have to go around," says a man adjusting a holster to his calf. The other man drops the bolt cutter and fires at the lock with his gun.

The kneeling man jumps up and grabs the shooter's arm. "*Idiot*. She said no shooting until she gives the word."

"Grow some balls, Titus. How's she going to know? She's miles away on the other side."

Titus raises his eyebrows, unsnaps his pocket, pulls out a radio, and hands it to the man with the bolt cutters. "I believe," he says coolly, "it's for you."

"Yes, ma'am, we're here. The door is… I mean, the gate is locked. We can't get it open." He goes quiet, then turns his head, whispering, "It was Titus."

Titus pulls the radio away. "Mrs. Leveraux." He speaks stiffly between moments of silence. "No. Yes. Yes. I'll be sure they know. Yes, thank you."

Turning the radio off, he slides it back into his pocket and pulls the flap over the top, securing it with a snap.

Then Titus pirouettes and with one slice nearly severs the bolt cutter's head from his throat.

"Now," he says, bending down to wipe his knife clean on the dead man's shirt, "for those of you who are new…I don't know how things were with August, but when Mrs. Leveraux speaks, she expects you to listen. Fuck up and you die. Witness—what was his name?"

"Domitian," calls an unseen man in the crowd.

"Witness Domitian here. Don't fuck up and she pays you. Well. You have three days to kill every last one. Oh, one more thing. Mrs. Leveraux does not believe in the honor system. She's not going to give you $50,000 based on your word alone. No tail, no cash."

None of them have any questions. They simply fiddle with guns and flashlights, tie loose laces, complain about the cold.

A man in suede boots teams up with another man who holds his high-powered flashlight upright, so when he fumbles with the on button, he blinds himself. This is where I will begin to cull the herd.

They are preoccupied mostly with elementary calculations—ten wolves equals a Lamborghini Roadster. Twenty wolves equals a house with a heated swimming pool—but when they are sure they are out of earshot of the others, Suede Boots drops his voice.

"Cyrus said Mrs. Leveraux's niece is up here somewhere," he whispers.

Her name is Julia.

"Otho's daughter?"

Her name is Julia.

"Yeah."

"Wasn't she Cassius's girl?"

Her. Name. Is. Julia.

"Fiancée."

"Are we supposed to rescue her or something?" says Man Blinded by Flashlight.

"Not according to Cyrus. He says we treat her just the same as any of them."

"I saw her once. She was fucking hot."

They are silent for a few moments, then Suede Boots yells out, "Wait up. I've got something in my shoe."

Of course you do.

Man Blinded by Flashlight moves on, swatting at the brittle branches while Suede Boots leans against a tree and bends over his foot, his head down, his neck at teeth level, and with no sound but a gentle gurgle, he dies, blood pouring into my mouth. I ease him to the ground.

"Felix?"

"*Felix?*"

"*Hey, asshole!*"

It's the last word Man Blinded by Flashlight will speak into that long silence.

A blast. A crack. A slap. A snap. A pop. A sigh.

Some of the gunshots are near and some are far, and all of them make me run faster. There were shots fired near the Great Hall, and someone with fingers has turned on the lights. My paws on the window ledge, I watch a man inside sing to himself as he tears through the Alpha's office.

He rifles through boxes and drawers, dumping out papers, scissors, ruler, highlighter, pushpins, and gnawed pencils. He sweeps the First Kill skulls to the side, not because there is anything hidden behind them but because in his frustration at not finding anything he considers worthwhile, he wants to destroy everything we do. As he heads out, I run around to the kitchen window, watching as he up-ends the racks of drying apples. The bowl containing the sourdough mother that was brought from Mercia and has fed the Pack for centuries is already on the floor.

He slings a backpack over his shoulders as he comes out. I creep into a grove of balsam firs that are young and full and impossible to squeeze through on two feet but good for wolves crouched low on four.

Inna and Soli must be hunting him too, though I don't understand why they are upwind and why Inna, a dominant from the 12th, would rely on Soli, a CPA from the 8th.

Creeping close through the heavy branches, I see why. There are no wolves, only tails tied with cord, swinging from the backpack of a man singing about taking lives under a bad moon.

In the deepest night, under the shading branches of the young balsam, the world becomes pale silver and the Shifter's voice disappears in the white noise of wind and leaves and the skittering of small feet. His movements are subsumed by the pounding of my heart in my chest.

Still I know where he is, and the taste of his blood is metallic against my tongue and magnetic against my soul.

Chapter 37

Julia

"ALL THE WAY UP TO CHATEAUGAY?"

I hadn't seen the map in the Alpha's office. I hadn't registered what the Alpha had said, only the satisfaction with which she'd said it. I spent thirty minutes searching through the map of upstate New York, waiting for something to ping in my memory.

"All the way up to Chateaugay?"

That's when I told the driver let me off at Hinchinbrooke, the closest point on the Canadian border I could find.

Standing near a hollow tree in a secluded spot, I slid Arthur's letter and my phone in my boots, wrapped my First Kill skull inside my clothes, then hid them all in the big gap.

I lay down, and when I got up again, I ran.

I kept running, sticking to the tree line of a nearly deserted country road. I moved deeper into the woods when the occasional car drove by, its occupants insulated by glass and metal and plastic and cocooned in a fug of hot air and Nicki Minaj.

At Chateaugay, I catch my breath and check the moon, heading east, because of the one other hint I remember.

As far east as Champlain.

I run southeast through pine and duff-scented trees, skirting farms lying fallow, until I catch the smell of wounded land and burned wood and motor oil. Then I keep running toward the eerie echo of a place emptied of trees or the life that lives in them. Finally, my eyes catch the moonlight streaming unimpeded on the mangled earth and the shrubs and grasses just starting to sprout before the cold weather put an end to it.

Without tree cover, the black earth absorbs the sun's warmth and gives it back up at night in a river of mist that I follow, ignoring my lungs pummeling my rib cage, my heart tearing at my sternum.

I am coming home.

————————

A blast.

A crack.

A slap.

A snap.

A pop.

A sigh.

There is a menace of empty black cars parked low on the rough road leading up to the Gin—the Gap—the meeting place between two mountains that forms the glacier-scrubbed passage from this bleak place to Homelands. Hiding among what's left of the forest, I lie down in the cold and change.

A blast.

A crack.

A slap.

A snap.

A pop.

A sigh.

Silence.

My muscles are still trembling by the time I blink away the million floaters and pull myself up on two feet. The last time I was here, this place had been filled with bright lights and generators and silver servers and crystal and meaty Bandol and the presumption of men.

The last time I was here, that kind of thing mattered to me.

When I pop my ears, I hear a woman's voice. I can't make out the words, but I recognize that tone of command. Not like the Alpha, who speaks from a habit of sacrifice, but like August, who spoke from a promise of retribution.

Clinging to the cars, I stumble forward, my legs shivering as I try to relearn how to walk on two legs and how to talk with my short, thick tongue.

"Doosidda," I whisper.

The cars are cold and have been here for a while. I follow footsteps in the mud toward a low wall of stones.

"Doosilla."

On the other side of the stone wall, the Gin is filled with inhospitable soil and loose rocks and emptied of trees and wolves. In the muted moonlight, it is gray and lifeless.

Drusilla's back is toward me, and even though I couldn't

have said what she looked like three hours ago, I recognize her immediately. Something about the steely posture and the way the four men surrounding her hang on every word while looking like they'd rather be anywhere else.

One sees me. Then another, then all of them stare, before Drusilla gradually turns.

One slow step at a time, I descend the stone wall, naked, mud-spattered, and alone, a mantle of mist clinging damp to my shoulders.

It is, I think, quite the entrance.

Keeping my voice low, because, well, *tongue*, I say her name. "Drusilla."

Seeing her conjures up memories from my childhood. Drusilla isn't so much well-preserved as shellacked—every pore sealed off, every strand of hair in stiff blond curls, motionless despite the wind across the empty Gin. She wears dusty knee-high boots, beige breeches, a high-buttoned hunting jacket of charcoal-gray plaid, and a perfectly tied silk ascot. She looks like a character from a costume drama about life among the fox-hunting classes.

Drusilla examines me without any change in expression.

"My love," says the handsome man who was once my stepfather, "may I introduce your niece, Julia Martel?"

She presses her hand to her hair as though some furtive tendril might have the arrogance to escape. She is not, I think, the kind of woman who likes surprises.

Then she laughs a dry laugh with a crack in it where anything resembling amusement must have leaked out a long time ago.

"Water," she says, her arm whipping out toward one of the two men dressed in black parkas with wolf-fur-trimmed hoods.

"So, Julia Martel, my *niece*. What happened to your clothes?"

A man swings a backpack around and pulls out a bottle of water, setting it in her imperious hand.

"I left them under a groundhog skull. In a squirrel's nest. Near Hinchinbrooke."

Extracting a handkerchief from her pocket, she dampens it.

"And you walked naked from the border?" she asks, wiping her hands.

"Ran," I say, holding up my own filthy hands, bloody from running so far so fast, so she will know that I ran on all fours.

A gunshot. More of a pop echoing from somewhere near the Spruce Flats. It sounds weirdly benign, less dangerous than the explosion created by curious pups with an over-blown condom, but I feel the bullet drill into the heart of a wolf like a blow to my own.

Drusilla hands the rust-colored handkerchief back to one of the men in parkas, not seeming to notice at all.

"The last time I saw you, Julia, you were"—she holds her hand near her knee—"so tall and dressed in satin and velvet. Do you remember? It was Christmas, I think. One of your mother's interminable parties. You had a tiara of cultured pearls and peridot. My late brother called you his little princess." She points to a hillock on the ground. "Give her Hadrian's coat."

"I'm not cold."

"I didn't ask if you were. Give it to her."

A huge man slings his rifle across his shoulder and bends toward the hillock. Peeling the coat from a limp body, he throws it to me.

My nakedness makes her uncomfortable. Good. I let Hadrian's coat fall.

Drusilla's eyes narrow.

"I am not a princess, Drusilla."

"No, no. Clearly not. A princess, at least, can be bartered off. Used to increase holdings. Seal a treaty. Get some fucking sheep. Instead you take, take, take until you are eventually fobbed off on Cassius, a man who liked to think he was dangerous but was only armed."

Not by the time we were finished with him, he wasn't.

"Cyrus, did you know my brother?"

It's a simple enough question but the big man clearly feels there is a trap. He shakes his head and blows on his stiff fingers, then bends them, trying to keep them warm and flexible.

Another pop. This one is louder, like a holiday cracker.

Drusilla takes a sip of water, careful not to touch her lips to the rim.

"Why are you here, Julia Martel? If you had made it as far as Hinchinbrooke, you could have made it home. Rejoined your safe and comfortable world of gallery openings and ballroom dancing and Instagram influencing, far from this and far from me. You see, I do know what you are."

"Exquisitely inconsequential?"

Drusilla laughs again. "I like that, 'exquisitely inconsequential.' Did you make that up?"

"No."

"No, of course not. That would have required a degree of self-awareness."

"You think you know who I am but you don't. That is not my world. Not anymore. *This* is where I belong. This is *home*."

This time when she opens her mouth, she doesn't laugh, she snarls.

"What is it with you people? Do you have any idea, my parvenu princess, of what we went through so that you could have that safe and comfortable life that you so thoughtlessly reject?"

She holds out the plastic bottle, but the men seem to have forgotten whose duty it is to fetch it until Drusilla lets go and water drains onto a nest of tumbled granite left from some bygone stream. Then one of the men in parkas leaps forward to pick it up.

"What you have is a case of *nostalgie de la boue*. Need to roll around in the mud, to—"

"I know what it means."

"It's not just you. It's Constantine. It's Atticus here—"

"Me?" says one of the men in the black parka. "Not me, Mrs. Leveraux, I—"

"Don't interrupt me," she snaps. "You've been sniffing the air and scratching at your neck ever since we got here." With a single finger, she slowly brushes one eyebrow, then the other. "Security is a luxury that we bought for you. That we paid for. Now you can't imagine what it's like to live a life where any drunk, bored, weak human can shoot you so that for one second, they can pretend they are not drunk, bored, and weak.

"Even August, who should have known better, had that same itch." She stares at one hand glowing pale in the moonlight and curls her fingers—her nails tipped in sour-cherry red—into stiff claws, putting them to her chest. "I ripped out my heart for him, then that bitch came with her wild heart intact and he loved her for it. Worshipped her for it."

The men around her glance at each other nervously, shifting their weight back and forth. Two of them put their hands to their guns. I look at her pale, blood-tipped hands and wonder what she has done to make four men with guns so afraid.

Suddenly she throws her head back, lips curled away from her teeth, and she howls into the sky. Every man takes a worried step back as terrified of her primal cry as humans are of wolves. They should know but they don't. They have become too tame and no longer recognize the long, drawn-out cadences of a song of sadness. They are too civilized to feel the pain that comes with singing it alone.

Then comes the answering cry of a man screaming.

"There's another," Aurelian says, nervously opening and closing the Velcro closure of his holster. "It's getting closer." He moves toward Drusilla and the other three men.

Drusilla adjusts her white shirt cuffs stained by rootlets of blood and takes a deep breath. "Titus?" she asks.

"I don't know. I can't raise him."

"How many is that?" asks the man who had retrieved her water bottle and still holds it stiffly in front of him.

"Four," Aurelian says. "I think someone should find out what's going on—"

"Then *be* someone," Drusilla says, raising her chin toward me. "Shoot her and go find out."

To give him credit, Aurelian—whose paternal care was restricted to waving to the car as I was taken off to another year at St. Ailbhe's—balks.

"Why not Cyrus?" he says. "He's your bodygu—"

"Because Cyrus has proved himself more useful than a semisolid dick and a pretty face and you haven't."

"I was the one who helped you find them."

"You only told me that you didn't know where Julia was. I was the one who spent hours listening to Sabina's self-indulgent drivel before getting the interesting bit about Cassius and Julia trip from Montreal to New York. Cédric was the one who told me how the lawyers for TransCanNA salivated over a crappy five-acre plot with serious contamination—"

A scream from the High Pines is close enough for even Drusilla to pay attention. She points to the two men in black parkas and gestures toward the High Pines. Drawing guns and flashlights, they start nervously toward the tree line. Drusilla watches until even the hesitant flickers of light are gone.

There are three now. I don't know if I will have another opportunity, but I clearly won't have a better one. Using Aurelian's inattention, I jerk his wrist up against his back, holding him like a shield while I pull the gun from its opened holster and point the muzzle at his temple.

Drusilla watches me, her head cocked to the side, her eyes bright and amused.

"Pick up the radio."

Without a glance at me, she crouches down to pick up Aurelian's dropped radio. The soles of her boots are made of smooth leather.

"Call them off or I will kill him."

"I don't believe you know how to use it," she says. She scratches her fingernail against the pad of her thumb.

I jam the muzzle deeper into Aurelian's temple. "You forget that I am Otho Martel's daughter."

"My love?" Aurelian says nervously.

Drusilla's answer comes in a blinding flash, a deafening explosion, and an acrid eggy smell as Aurelian's head snaps back against my cheek.

I stumble into his collapsing body.

"'I am Otho Martel's daughter,'" she mimics shrilly. "That's exactly why. I knew my brother better than you ever could." Now I see the holster hidden beneath her jacket. "He loved playing the protector. Loved seeing the helpless adoration in his wife's eyes. His little sister's eyes. Why would he treat his princess differently?

"You've never had to face a consequence in your life. I don't think for a minute you are capable of making a decision when death is the outcome. Go ahead and drop him," she says, nodding toward Aurelian's body. "And never imagine you have leverage over me."

I point the gun and squeeze the trigger. It doesn't budge and Drusilla laughs and laughs and fury settles like a warm blanket over my naked body. Furious at my father and August and Cassius for never considering that I might have a life worth living that didn't include them. Furious at Drusilla for being right.

There is a weapon I've taught myself how to use. Dropping the gun, I coil my hunter's legs and leap. Drusilla staggers back, clearly surprised that I was able to cover the impossible distance between us so easily. Shocked as everything I'd paid attention to with my hunter's mind falls into place: the smooth leather-soled boots slipping on the river stones slicked with water, while Cyrus tries to fit his cold-stiffened finger through the small collar around the trigger.

We land with a rib-cracking thud.

Drusilla screams in frustration as her gun skitters out of reach and she finds herself fighting against the iron grasp of Julia Martel: Ballroom dancer. Instagram influencer. Princess and wolf.

I don't let go when she kicks with the hard, sharp heels of her boots that cut into my shins, but when I blink the tears away, I realize I've lost track of her bodyguard.

"*Why don't you fucking shoot?*" she screams to the shadows at the westernmost edge of the High Pines.

He drops something, Cyrus does. It falls to the ground with a thump, and when he looks at his hands, what he's holding is not hard and matte and gun-shaped, it's formless and glistens in the moonlight.

Then he lifts his uncomprehending stare from his intestines and starts to scream.

Drusilla stops struggling and shrinks back as a wolf steps out of the dark.

His fur is black, his eyes are black, and the only color is the white of fangs painted with the bright sour-cherry red.

He moves toward us like smoke on ice.

Drusilla starts to scrabble away. "If you run," I whisper to her, "he will hunt you."

His fur is stiff and bristled and smells of blood, but more terrifying than the blood is the stillness. Pack are always alert—noses twitching, ears turning, eyes roaming. Sealed within his mind, Arthur sees nothing, hears nothing, smells nothing.

Men treasured them and called them Berserkers. Ulfheðnir. Packs feared them and called them Werewulfas—Manwolves—because like men they would kill their own.

He said that I could trust him. That he would always know me and never hurt me, but confronted by his bleakness and blankness, all I can think of is running away to my safe and comfortable life.

I don't.

Instead, I get up on my knees on that sharp rocky ground and spread my fingers across my thighs.

"*Arthur*," I whisper, the sound breaking, barely audible even within my own skull. "*You know me.*"

Then I lift my chin and stretch my neck out impossibly long and exposed. I stare up to the Unwild, hoping that I'm not wrong and that if I am, it is possible for a Shifter to follow the Watcher's Path to the Last Lands, where it is always autumn and the trees are gold and the prey is fat and wolves' fur is thick and the pups have survived denning.

I hear the sounds of claws on stone, I smell the copper of blood, I feel his breath hot against my skin and swallow.

Nothing happens.

Finally, I lower my head. Slowly, I raise my hands to either side of his head. He snarls a warning but there is a whined fillip at the end.

Who?

Who are you?

I tangle my fingers in the blood-sticky fur on either side of his muzzle.

See me.

Please, please, please,

Hear me.

Please, please, please,

Feel me.

He freezes in front of me, caught between straining forward and holding back.

He chuffs out a breath, then runs, dragging me across the rocky landscape toward the border with Westdæl where Thea stands with her gun aimed at Drusilla.

"Don't touch it," Thea says, looking pointedly at Aurelian's gun and Drusilla's hand reaching toward it.

Arthur snarls and snaps and lurches, trying for both Drusilla and Thea equally, urged forward by some raw need for devastation. I lose my grip with one hand, coming away with a large bloody clump of fur in my fingers, but he still surges forward.

I scrabble across the rocks and hold him closer, my cheek rubbing his muzzle, his sharp teeth near my vulnerable throat. I rock against him, repeating the promise he made. That he would always know me.

It's such a small thing when it starts. The flicker of fur against my temple. The movement of his ear. When I pull back, his eye follows me, a black dome save for the thinnest jagged rim of silver floating up from the depths.

In my periphery, I watch Thea pick up Aurelian's gun.

"There are two more. Somewhere over there," I say, waving toward Cyrus, who finally stopped groaning. "Take them," I say, keeping my eyes on Arthur. "I don't know how to use them."

"Is it safe?" she whispers.

"No. But is it ever?"

I had "safe." I had convenience and comfort and the Mille Carré, and I have thrown it away for a vulnerable life in a harsh land with a dangerous love.

Arthur's nose twitches cool against my cheek.

"He wanted to protect you," Thea says. "At the time I thought—"

"I know but I'm done with people—or wolves—deciding what is best for me. It will not happen again."

Thea hesitates, looking across the blue-gray moonlit barrenness of the Gin. "I have to get back to the trailhead. There are a lot of itchy trigger fingers down there."

She turns toward Drusilla, watching her. I see her fingering one of the guns in her pocket.

Drusilla stares at Thea, a ghoulish, inviting smile on her lips.

"She cannot leave," Thea says.

"I know that too."

She's human, an officer of the law, but I can't help feel that if Drusilla gave her an excuse—any excuse—Thea would take it. Drusilla seems to understand that too and does nothing.

Finally, Thea heads back toward the path that leads toward the trailhead and the bored, drunk, weak hunters, lying in wait to kill the #ADKWolf.

"Now that one," Drusilla says carefully, dusting the dry dirt and duff from her pants. "*She* would have killed me."

She doesn't say it and she doesn't have to.

Not like you.

Whatever combination of fear and adrenaline that sped my run from Hinchinbrooke is leaking away. Thea's right though. Before it completely fails me, I have to deal with Drusilla.

"So, Princess, we seem to have reached an impasse. Neither of us has the wherewithal to kill the other. You don't have the will and I don't have the weaponry."

"You don't understand. I don't want to kill you."

"Then what do you want? Is this where I have a sudden epiphany as though there is any alternative you have considered in your short life of exquisite inconsequence that I haven't?"

"I can't let you go, Drusilla," I continue. "I heard your sadness—"

"Oh please."

"I heard your sadness," I continue. "It wasn't just about August. It was about something much bigger. Something that I found here. I think…I think that you and I are more alike than you imagine."

Please, please, please.

She slides two fingers between her silk scarf and her throat, considering me. I can read the calculations in her eyes.

Just do it. Please, please, please.

I am naked, shaking, unarmed, except for a mad wolf she could not outrun on two legs.

Please, please, please.

On four legs, though...

She pulls her hand away, looking at her fingers as though she is trying to remember what they look like with claws.

"Are you going to kill me during my change?"

"Are you going to try to escape?"

She shrugs her shoulders and lies. "No."

"And we won't try to kill you."

A dark cloud scuttles across the moon's full face.

Boots, breeches, jacket, vest, shirt: she removes each piece slowly and deliberately, smoothing them out and folding them in a neat pile until finally she shudders in the cold and stretches out her arms, not ashamed like my mother had been, but scornful.

She lies down, her eyes daring me to look away as she curls her back, the knobs of her spine jutting outward like they are trying to escape the confines of her skin. Daring me to look away while her hips warp and her calves shorten. While her thumb moves up along her forearm. Even when her eyes turn milky like two small moons, they are still disconcertingly intent and steady, though they no longer follow me if I move.

There is no magic about it, August told me. It's simply a long and tedious process during which you are both completely helpless and grotesquely ugly.

But there is magic about it. Even now as her blond curls merge into long gray fur, still yellowed in parts, and a whisker pushes at her skin, finally piercing through.

The thin rim of silver has spread across the black of Arthur's eyes like hoarfrost and his eyes move, focused on a shadow emerging from the foot of Westdæl.

I'd always known she was there. The Watcher, the Alpha. I could smell the whole of the Great North carried on her fur.

Arthur wobbles against me. Whatever fuels the violence is burning itself out, leaving him drained. He shivers as the Alpha nears him and whimpers.

Please, please, please.

The Alpha stills, her head parallel to his, and I feel Arthur's growing fear. Not the fear of what she may do to him. The fear of what he might have done and doesn't remember.

Please, please, please.

Then Evie presses her muzzle against his. One side first, then the other. Arthur stumbles with relief because the Alpha would not have marked him if he had killed her wolves.

I suppose I shouldn't be surprised that wolves knew enough to run.

The Alpha noses his shoulder, then licks him there, and when she does, fresh blood glimmers. I thought he was covered with the blood of others but she knew that some of it was his own.

Without warning, the Alpha leaps, a flash of black in the moonlight fringe studded with long, white teeth, tearing toward Drusilla, who is just getting to her paws.

Once upon a time, my aunt really must have been a fearsome wolf. The kind of wolf from fairy tales: huge, long-limbed, and broad-shouldered. Gray. Not as dark gray as Varya, but close enough. Wolves would know the difference. My hope is that humans with the itchy trigger fingers won't.

The Alpha crashes into Drusilla's chest, fangs laying open her face, before I run across the Gin, the sharp stones tearing into my feet as I throw myself between them, my arms tight around my Alpha's head. She slashes at me as I yell for my aunt to run.

"Run, Drusilla, Run!"

The Alpha whips around and sinks her fangs into my shoulder, shaking her head from side to side. Sharp pain turns to dull cold and my right hand loses feeling; it's useless except as a thing to cling to with my left hand.

I would tell her. I would tell the Alpha, if I could, but the pain and cold have knit my jaw shut.

When Arthur attacks the Alpha, I kick at him with my heels, trying to get him away. I am nothing but a chew toy in the fight between my Alpha and my werewolf, but dammit I am a chew toy with *agency*.

Finally it comes, the sound I've been waiting for. The repeated crack of guns from the direction of the trailhead and the parking lot.

The Alpha raises her head, her blood-covered teeth scraping against bone as she drops me to the ground. She moves quickly and carefully toward the slope that descends to Offland and listens to the whoops and cheers of the drunk and bored and weak men who couldn't tell the difference between the Gray and the Bitch of Vancouver.

Soon they are arguing over who gets credit for killing the #ADKWolf and who will have the right to post the picture on Instagram.

Arthur noses my bloody arm.

With my one good arm, I push myself up, stumbling toward Aurelian's body and the radio under it. I grab it with my left hand and then return to sink against Arthur, staring at it blankly.

"Push the button on the side," says a voice.

I try to focus on Tiberius. When did he get here?

Taking a deep breath, I summon what little fierceness I have left to tell whoever is on the other end who I am. I am Julia Martel and that is enough. Drusilla is dead. Cyrus is dead. Aurelian is dead. Titus is dead. There will be no bounty paid on wolves. But if they are not gone in an hour, the hunters will be hunted.

I lift my thumb from the button and hold the radio to Tiberius, because if I am now the Bitch of Vancouver, he is August's heir.

Who knows what he said. I only know that the small weight that anchored me to my last responsibility is lifted and I slip my moorings, collapsing cold and bleeding to the hard ground under the gray, colorless light of the last Iron Moon of autumn.

In my dreams, the place is white, featureless with no mountains in the background, no trees overhead, no leaves or grasses cushioning my paws. There is nothing to guide me, nothing to aim for. There is no outcropping to block winds, but there are no winds either.

Then I see it. A paw print. I place my forepaw on top of it. It fits perfectly.

Something digs into my thigh. When I turn to dislodge it, a belch rumbles near my calf.

My shoulder throbs, my nose itches, and my lids scrape over my eyes like sandpaper, opening onto a sky that isn't white but steely overcast. Leaves and samaras dance about, buffeted by winds high in the mountains of Homelands.

How is it possible that I am not cold?

I stretch out my fingers and touch fur. I wiggle my toes and touch fur. I move my head and nuzzle fur. Every part of me is swathed in wolves. Wrapped around my feet, lying across my legs, curled around my head, crouched across my chest, flanking my arms are wolves, a warm, moving, burping, loving blanket of life. The wolves of the 12th Echelon keeping me warm even under a gray and windy sky in the exposed Gin.

Arthur raises his head from my shoulder. His fur is no longer stiff but soft with a little remaining dampness from whatever pond or stream washed him clean. He nuzzles my cheek with a worried whine.

Please, please, please.
Please, please, please.

"You are in such trouble."

He sneezes and drops his paw over his eyes, looking sheepish.

It's not fair to yell at him when he can't yell back, so for now I burrow into my wolf, breathing him in until Gwenn's stomach rumbles against my hip. I don't know how long I've been like this but my echelon clearly needs to hunt.

When I sit up, the quilt falls apart, standing to shake out fur and stiffened muscles. One by one, they offer their muzzles, rubbing first my right cheek, then my left, claiming me before they dissolve silently into the protection of the woods.

Arthur noses my arm. My last memory of it had been of a bloody pulp. Someone cleaned it while I slept because now it is scored with bruises and deep worried punctures, but no blood.

"It's a flesh wound," I say and he chuffs because my clawed wolf knows just how searing a flesh wound can be.

It's much worse when I give in to the change. The pain is knife-sharp in my arm, but I know the soft warmth of his fur surrounds me and the sharp bite of his fangs protects me.

My nose is only just clearing when something plops in front of me, smelling irresistibly of fresh blood.

The deer heart is not an apology. The Alpha did what she had to, just like I did. It's more like chicken soup or a casserole for an unwell neighbor and I gulp it down, bite after succulent bite filled with liquid warmth. The Alpha cleans the blood of the gifted heart from her face and fore leg, then sits still and upright, looking occasionally over her shoulder, waiting for me to be done.

I try to head toward her, but lowering my right front paw to the ground is more than the torn muscles at my shoulder can manage. I hold my right front leg curled against my torso and hop forward, awkward on three legs.

The Alpha moves into the land beyond the Gin, the place the wolves with their inimitable knack for naming have dubbed Norþdæl, the North Place.

We keep to the wooded edges, then head west down a steep hill. I do a kind of crab shuffle on the two healthy legs of my left side. Arthur stays in front of me so if I stumble, he will break my fall.

The Alpha stops near the tangled roots of a huge old tree that was brought down by a combination of wind and weight and its precarious position.

At first, I don't understand why we've stopped; when I do know, I turn away, trying to escape the crack of bone between jaws, the snick and tear of a severed joint, the growl warning newcomers away, the smell of blood.

Arthur looks briefly over his shoulder and then turns back, silently keeping watch with the Alpha.

You've never had to face a consequence in your life.

But I am not that girl anymore, the girl who wanted lobster but didn't want to see it fished out of the tank. I join them because I am the woman who made a decision to sacrifice Drusilla to protect the Gray. If I didn't want the wolf to die, I shouldn't have sent her toward the hunters. Now I watch the coyotes eat what is left of my aunt.

We were more alike than either of us wanted to believe. We both remade ourselves to become what we'd been told we needed to be. The difference was I still had all the original pieces left. I'm not sure Drusilla did.

She was a broken person, but in a different world, a more accommodating world, I believe she might have been a good wolf.

I throw back my head. My voice is cracked and breathless like a leaky bellows and the Alpha looks at me confused, unable to understand my stuttered cry. Arthur hears my song of sadness, though, and translates it with a low and mournful howl until the whole pack sings along with me, not because they understand but because one of their own is sad and cannot be allowed to sing alone.

Chapter 38

Arthur

WE STAYED LONG AFTER THE ALPHA WAS GONE. WE stayed after the coyotes have eaten their fill and the crows had moved on. For whatever reason, Julia felt a need to see this to its end, so we did.

There wasn't much left of the Iron Moon and we couldn't afford to find ourselves naked and in skin so far from the Great Hall. We climbed the steep, forested slope into Norþdæl and looped around the plateau that used to be a river, fed by the runoff from our mountains, but even before August's machines came, the deer had eaten everything—trees and bushes and sedges and grasses, anything with roots that could glue the land together—and slowly the river died and with it the waterfall that leapt from the edge of this plateau to the rocky ground below.

The new plants that managed to fight their way through the muddy, desecrated plain are icy and they crunch under our paws.

There are two wolves—one gray, one white—who aren't in any danger of finding themselves naked in this cold landscape. They sit at the very edge of that plateau, staring out over what will be their land.

The Gray looks over her shoulder and, catching sight of us, slips away with her mate into the trees.

Through the months to come, we would often see the forever wolves sitting right at the edge of the plateau, looking over the river of snow in the winter, a river of mud in the early spring.

We didn't return again until summer, after Julia recovered from an endless lying-in when she was calm and strong and I was little better than roadkill.

This time, we are not alone.

The Alpha and I settled into a spot upwind, so the Gray would be able to recognize us. We were close enough to swoop down and pick up our pups, far enough to make it clear that we meant no threat to the Gray's own.

Julia sat a little farther off watching carefully, her hind paws dug into the green earth so she could leap without slipping.

Before long, the Gray came out and sniffed the air. She made a circuit around the Alpha and me and our pups— Varya Juliasdottir and Inna Juliasdottir—who were fighting for the latest in a long succession of squirrels' tails. The Gray came closer, sniffing the ground around them, pretending not to notice that the boldest of her three had nosed his way out of the den, eyeing the squirrel's tail with avid interest.

Soon he was joined by the little white female who inherited her father's fur but not his eyes and an orphan brindle male who the wolf conservation people had brought to Westdæl with a crate and the anxious hope that the Gray would take him into her tiny pack.

Which she did.

I remember how nervous we were and how unconcerned

the pups were when the Gray's boldest grabbed the squirrel tail. We all leaned forward, unbreathing, legs shivering until the five pups devolved into a snarling, snapping, grabbing, playing ball of fur. The white wolf with the blue and green eyes, the Bone Wolf whose presence presages the end of the world, plopped down beside them and was immediately covered by pups playing chase the tail and bite the ear.

Lorcan tossed a newly killed groundhog just beyond the unspoken but understood boundary that every wolf constructs around their pups.

Ours raced for it immediately, pulling and growling at the fur, and when the Bone Wolf stood, the three little forever wolves tumbled off his back and joined them. The Gray finally nudged away one little pup, not knowing she was named Varya Juliasdottir, for her.

She tore through the fur and hide, releasing a wisp of warm damp into the still cool mountain air, and the pups growled and pulled and argued and ate.

Over the years that followed, the Pack took in more forever wolves. Shifters too, who had been tormented by the aching loss and the need to be part of something greater.

Each addition made the Pack stronger.

The land too.

On a recent run through the woods above the green plateau, we saw the Gray and the Bone Wolf sitting once more at the edge, looking out over the land below.

That's when we heard it, the tiny trickle of water falling onto the rocks below.

The wolves are back.

Acknowledgments

For the fifth time, I give my extravagant thanks to Deb Werksman, my editor at Sourcebooks. She has been nothing but patient during this trying year. And of course, my agent, Heather Jackson, who took a chance and has stood fiercely by my side ever since.

I am so grateful for the other women of Sourcebooks like Susie Benton, Heather Hall, and Diane Dannenfeldt, who read the words and made them better. Dawn Adams has made every cover beautiful.

A special shout-out to Laurence Boischot both for her sensitive translations of Sauvages, as the Legend of All Wolves is known in French, and for helping me with the translations here though, of course, every muck-up is mine alone.

One of the best parts of writing is meeting authors I have loved as a reader—Amanda Bouchet, Jeaniene Frost, Terry Spear, Adriana Anders, Diana Muñoz Stewart, Olivia Dade, Jeffe Kennedy, and many others—who turn out to be wonderful human beings as well. I have been so grateful for their support when things go right and for their advice when things go sideways.

Finally to the readers who have reached out: You are my pack. You made the world seem a little less quiet.

My door is always open.

Maria
mariavale.com

About the Author

Maria Vale is a journalist who has worked for *Publishers Weekly*, *Glamour*, *Redbook*, and the *Philadelphia Inquirer*. She's a double RITA finalist whose Legend of All Wolves series has been listed by Amazon, *Library Journal*, *Publishers Weekly*, *Booklist*, and *Kirkus Reviews* among their Best Books of the Year. Trained as a medievalist, she persists in trying to shoehorn the language of Beowulf into things that don't really need it. She lives in New York with her husband, two sons, and a long line of dead plants. No one will let her have a pet. Visit her online at mariavale.com.

WHILE THE WOLF'S AWAY

David Davis and his fellow Arctic wolves are seeking a new life in the wilds of Minnesota, away from the controlling pack leader who exploited them. Elizabeth Simpson helped David escape, but the pack leader won't let her go. It'll take everything David and Elizabeth have to get out and make a new home…together.

"Spear takes readers on a pulse-pounding ride."

—*Publishers Weekly* for *SEAL Wolf Christmas*

THE LEGEND OF
ALL WOLVES

For three days out of thirty, when the moon is full and her law is iron, the Great North Pack must be wild…

Don't miss this extraordinary series from Maria Vale

The Last Wolf

Silver Nilsdottir is at the bottom of her Pack's social order, with little chance for a decent mate and a better life. Until the day a stranger stumbles into their territory and Silver decides to risk everything on Tiberius Leveraux…

A Wolf Apart

Thea Villalobos has long since given up trying to be what others expect of her. So she can see that Elijah Sorensson is Alpha of his generation of the Great North Pack, and the wolf inside him will no longer be restrained…

Forever Wolf

With old and new enemies threatening the Great North, Varya knows that she must keep Eyulf hidden away from the superstitious wolves who would doom them both. Until the day they must fight to the death for the Pack's survival, side by side and heart to heart…

Season of the Wolf

Evie Kitwanasdottir leads the Great North Pack into new challenges, like taming the four hazardous Shifters they've taken into custody. Constantine, the most dangerous, is assigned to Evie's own 7th echelon, but if anyone can show what true love, leadership, and sacrifice looks like, it's Evie—the Alpha.

Wolf in the Shadows

Once a spoiled young Shifter surrounded by powerful males who shielded her from reality, Julia Martel is now a prisoner of the Great North Pack, trusted by no one and relegated to the care of the pack's Omega, Arthur Graysson. But being the least wolf has its advantages...

"Wonderfully unique and imaginative. I was enthralled!"

—Jeaniene Frost, *New York Times* bestselling author

"Prepare to be rendered speechless."

—*Kirkus Reviews*, Starred Review, for *Forever Wolf*

For more info about Sourcebooks's books and authors, visit:
sourcebooks.com

Also by Maria Vale